VENGEANCE

AT MIDWAY AND GUADALCANAL

a novel by

LIEUTENANT COMMANDER LELAND C. SHANLE, JR. USN (RET.)

p7A Aviation
Saint Louis, Missouri

Published in the United States by p7A Aviation
in conjunction with Treehouse Publishing Group LLC.

Cover design by Kristina Blank Makansi
Cover art courtesy of Ron Cole, Coles Aircraft, www.colesaircraft.com

Library of Congress Control Number: 2013920653
ISBN: 978-0-9837107-2-1

www.project7alpha.com
www.treehousepublishinggroup.com

To Laura Lynn

VENGEANCE

AT MIDWAY AND GUADALCANAL

CHAPTER 1

1942
05:30 Local, 04JUN (11:30 GMT, 04JUN)
Fort Worth, Texas

David awoke mesmerized by the steady rotation of the ceiling fan. Dreams of his father and brother had come again. He let them swirl away in the artificial breeze. As he lay contemplating the similarity of the fan to an aircraft's propeller, there was a soft knock at the door.

"David, are you awake?"

"Yeah, Mom, I'm awake. Come on in."

His mother stepped into the room wearing a white silk kimono. She gracefully crossed the room and sat on the edge of his bed. David rose to one elbow, painfully aware that he was now the man of the house.

"Is something wrong?"

"No, honey," she said." Irish is here."

"Irish? What's he here for?"

Laura smiled gently, watching him rub the sleep out of his eyes like a little boy.

"Davey, you asked him to teach you to fly. I suspect today is lesson number one."

He lay back and stared at the ceiling. Laura brushed back his brown hair and spoke quietly.

"You don't have to do this just because your father and brother—"

He didn't let her finish. He couldn't stand to hear it verbalized.

"It's not that," he responded in the same quiet tone as his mother's." I want to fly."

"Then, what is it?"

"I don't know if... I mean, Trey and Dad were great pilots, and—"

"David," Laura stopped him, "you will do fine. You are going to be taught by the best pilots in the world. Don't overthink it; just let it happen."

She stood and pulled his leg.

"Hurry up, before Irish drinks all my coffee."

David jumped out of bed and pulled on a plain white T-shirt and a pair of old blue jeans. He laced up his black Converse high tops and rushed out of his room.

In the middle of the well-lit kitchen, Irish stood in full glory. Center stage and impossible to be ignored, he exuded the self-confidence, bordering on arrogance, of a professional aviator. A hardened ace from the recently renamed Great War, the current American Airlines captain was now a wounded combat veteran of a second world war.

He stood before his fledgling squire of a student like a knight in full regalia. A rich, brown leather flight jacket immediately identified him as a pilot. Under his jacket was a starched khaki shirt, open at the collar. A brown leather belt (matching, of course) held heavy, forest green wool trousers in place. They hung perfectly until abruptly tucked into laceless, knee-high leather boots; the boots—as expected—also matched precisely. This aviation fashion masterpiece was topped off with the required white silk scarf, which offset Irish's dark red hair nicely.

Accentuating his quintessential pilot ensemble, medically retired Major James Myer, Army Air Corps, formerly of the British Royal Air Force, airline captain extraordinaire, stood with one hand on his hip, holding the right side of his jacket aft. He glared down upon his unworthy charge, clearly annoyed that the boy had the temerity to stare back. Finally, he spoke.

"It's going to get a tad chilly in the spring morning air at 10,000 feet, Junior."

Laura had eased out of the room during the show. She had seen it before. Returning to the kitchen, she handed David a well-worn Army Air Corps jacket. He looked at it: the silver pilot wings and "C.H. Brennan" were still clearly stamped in the leather of his father's jacket.

Before David could get lost in his thoughts, Irish quipped, "Lesson One: we don't dress like this simply because it looks smashing!"

He waved at the back door.

"Into the car with you, Junior."

David quickly followed directions, not really sure what had just happened.

Irish and Laura were well acquainted with the show that had just taken place on center stage. It was the establishment of primacy, superiority—one step removed from deity—that the instructor pilot/student pilot relationship was based on.

Flying was not inherently intuitive; a student must react without question to an instructor's direction. More importantly, the instructor had something that the student craved. It wasn't tangible like leathers or money; it was much more esoteric: knowledge—specifically, the knowledge man had sought since watching a bird float on warm currents of air from the mouth of a cave.

God had indeed played a cruel hoax on mankind by letting him dream and imagine the ecstasy of flight, even to be cognizant of the mechanics. Ancient lore and myth was alive with legends of man reaching for the heavens, but it would be many millennia before he actually achieved it. Irish, a deeply philosophical man under his crass veneer, was ever aware of the greatest achievement of mankind. He dutifully treated it with the piety it deserved.

Laura was less impressed with the great achievement in her presence.

"Hey, El Guapo," she snapped as Irish followed David out the back door, "bring him back in the same condition he just left in."

Irish was a fearless man, but he had not survived two wars by being careless or foolhardy. He performed an about-face and snapped off a precise RAF salute.

"Yes, ma'am! There will be no discernable physical change except the slight hint of a smile on the lad's face."

"That would be nice," Laura retorted as the screen door slammed. "It has been a while."

Then she added one last warning: "Not a scratch, Irish."

01:30 Local, 04JUN (11:30 GMT, 04JUN)
Pacific Ocean

Half a world away, the most powerful invasion force on the face of the Earth steamed toward the US base on Midway Island. Aircraft carriers Akagi, Hiryu, Kaga, and Soryu, with two battleships, three cruisers, and countless destroyers, silently skimmed across the dark water. Escorting a transport group with 5,000 amphibious assault troops onboard, their presence was menacing.

VENGEANCE

As the full moon cast their shadows across the smooth Pacific, phosphorus trails extended from each ship's wake, generated by plankton electrified from the turning of the ships' screws.

CHAPTER 2

19:30 Local, 04JUN (11:30 GMT, 04JUN)
Luzon, The Philippines

In the waning twilight, a lone Imperial Japanese Army patrol snaked its way up a mountain path in central Luzon. The silence of the jungle creatures announced the patrol's progress. Twenty men moved methodically toward a small clearing in the dense rain forest.

Concealed in the foliage around the clearing were ten other men, patiently lying in wait. They did not look much like soldiers. Their uniforms were mere rags. Most of them were stripped to the waist, their hot skin against the cool, damp jungle floor. In the bush for two months, three Americans had transformed from intruder to accomplice. With them lay four Filipinos and three Negrito aboriginals.

The Americans were newcomers. The Filipinos had an innate ability to slide in and out of the jungle, easily transitioning into civilization, welcome in both. The Negrito had been a part of the jungle for thousands of generations. Negrito aboriginals had always been intertwined with the jungle; they did not fit in this millennium or the last ten. They were a people frozen in time, forgotten, left alone in their primeval paradise only to be touched by modernity in times of war.

Captain Dave Butler, United States Army Infantry, formerly of Hot Springs, Arkansas, was in command of this ragtag outfit. He and two of his men had been cut off when the US Army's main force retreated to the Bataan Peninsula. Escaping to the mountains, they had decided to carry on the fight from behind enemy lines.

Overhead, the birds went silent. The vagabond warriors remained motionless as their quarry closed in. The Japanese patrol appeared slowly around a corner of the jungle trail, moving without purpose or discipline, led by a young lieutenant. As he reached the clearing, he looked around and motioned his men to rest. They dropped their packs and rifles as they sank to the ground. Most drank from canteens or rummaged through their rucksacks, searching for food. None seemed aware of the jungle or any outward concern, preoccupied only with personal, immediate needs.

Butler and his men remained motionless.

Lieutenant Zakowa intently studied his map. He looked up to see his fat, lazy sergeant sitting cross-legged on the ground, eating sardines from a tin. Before Zakowa could bark an order to his platoon leader to properly deploy the patrol, Butler's .45 caliber Thompson sub-machine gun shattered the silence. Lieutenant Zakowa took three rounds to the chest.

The other nine bush fighters opened fire. It was over in less than five seconds. The undisciplined patrol members fell where they sat, not a single shot fired in defense. The Japanese platoon sergeant writhed on the ground among spilled sardines and blood, his eyes wide with shock. Sergeant Paul Donnelly, US Army, stepped stealthily from the jungle's edge and popped two quick rounds into his incompetent counterpart. In fluid motion, he moved from man to man. Any sign of life was quickly terminated by a single round to the head. The rainforest fell silent.

Donnelly directed his men to drag the bodies of the Japanese patrol around the next corner of the trail, where they were pushed over the side into a deep ravine while he and Butler rifled through the backpacks. Next, they policed the entire area, using large fronds to dissipate the blood, knowing the daily evening rain shower would take care of the rest.

With the ambush site properly sanitized, Butler and his men melted back into the heartless jungle, welcomed with shrieks of approval from the animals within.

CHAPTER 3

06:00 Local, 04JUN (12:00 GMT, 04JUN)
Weis Airfield, Texas

The ride to the airfield was a quiet one. David had again sought refuge in his thoughts, and Irish, realizing the magnitude of this first step, left him to himself. Irish pulled his 1941 black-on-black Cadillac Deluxe convertible coupe right onto the field and sped toward an airplane parked just off the side of the runway in the lush, green grass of a Texas spring.

David looked up and couldn't believe his eyes: a brilliant yellow bi-plane, the Boeing N2S-2 Stearman, sat on the green background. It was beautiful, majestic, painted in US Navy colors: yellow with a red stripe on the fuselage and a blue tail, known to instructors and students alike as the Yellow Peril. The primary flight trainer of both the US Navy and Army Air Corps, to David it was a war bird.

"Holy cow, Irish. Did you steal this?" he yammered nervously.

Irish laughed. "No, kid, I own enough Boeing stock that if I want to borrow a couple of aircraft they will give them."

"Wow," was all David could manage to say. "Wait a minute—a couple?"

Irish nodded over to a hangar. Inside was an Army version, a PT-17 Kaydet. While it had the same yellow wings, the fuselage was blue. J.T. Dobbs and Jon Gaus, fellow American Airline pilots and friends of David's father, were leaning on the Stearman.

David didn't say another word. He slid out of the Cadillac and went straight to the nose of the Stearman, letting his hand glide over the surface of the spruce propeller and looking closely at each of the seven exposed silver cylinders of the Continental R-670-5 engine. He felt the fabric surface beneath his fingers; it was firm and supple, not even a crack in the brand new paint.

Moving to the trailing edge of the wing, David inspected the right aileron and pushed it up, then down. Up, he knew, would push the wing down, causing the aircraft to turn right. Down would cause the wing to rise, turning the aircraft left. He tried to watch the left aileron move in opposition but couldn't see it until he looked under the belly. Turning aft, he followed the length of the fuselage with his eye until it almost touched the ground. At its end was the empennage, or tail section. It sat on a small tail wheel with the rudder assembly at the end.

David knew he would have to combine rudder with aileron to make a balanced turn. However, it was one thing to read about and quite another to actually do. Moving down the length of the fuselage, he couldn't take his hand off it, inspecting every nuance in the structure until he reached the horizontal stabilizer and elevator. Grasping the back edge, he moved it up.

That will make me climb, he thought. Then he moved it down. And that will make me descend.

David ran through the aerodynamics in his mind as he continued along the left side of the airplane. He consumed the aircraft with his eyes, off again in his own world. When he arrived back at the propeller, the three veteran pilots were waiting for him.

"First rate pre-flight, David."

J.T.'s smile was big and warm. Even so, David could see that his eyes betrayed a deep melancholy.

J.T. Dobbs had been his father's best and oldest friend. David knew that he had flown on the same mission on which Charles Henry and David's brother, Trey, had been shot down and killed at the beginning of the war, but that was all he knew.

At the behest of President Roosevelt and the head of American Airlines, J.T. had put together a volunteer group of AA pilots that included Irish and Jon as well as Charles Henry and Trey. The hush-hush mission across the Pacific was called Project 7Alpha, and J.T. was its commanding officer.

Now, it was clear that he felt responsible for the death of his best friend and his best friend's son. David knew that others had died, too, one in J.T.'s own cockpit. But the deaths of Charles Henry and Trey visibly haunted him; he clearly could not get past the gnawing guilt.

Jon had changed too. He had left on the mission cock-sure and immature; he returned a humble professional. Still in his early twenties, he had the eyes of an old man. Something was eating at him, too, and like J.T., he kept it to himself.

Irish was, as always, Irish. What swirled inside no one knew for sure; only a select few would ever see a hint. To the world, he was the consummate aviator, unflappable and impenetrable. He stood with arms crossed, staring down upon his squire.

"Listen up, knucklehead! Many forces act upon an aircraft, not just aerodynamic; basic physics in the form of gyroscopic precession and p-factor, to name just a few. However, we are not going to overanalyze this. Simply put: to get this machine into the air, we need to overcome its weight and drag by creating adequate wind over the wing, thus generating enough lift to elevate it into the sky. To do that, we need the thrust provided by this engine and propeller combination. We use the flight controls to maintain the attitude necessary for sustained and balanced flight and to counter the forces I have already mentioned."

Irish glared down at David for effect and continued.

"The key to coordinating all of these forces is being smooth. By being smooth we can minimize the various factors of flight and their adverse effects."

Pausing for emphasis, he pointed toward the engine and propeller.

"Power," he said, shifting his point to the wing, then the tail, "plus attitude, equals performance. Got it?"

David couldn't suppress a smile. He was not intimidated by Irish's cadence.

"Sounds easy," he said in a matter-of-fact tone.

"Well, it's not!" barked Irish. "If you jam on the power for takeoff, the p-factor and prop wash will push your nose left. If you then raise the tail abruptly, you will compound that motion by adding the gyroscopic effect as you come up on the main wheels only, and will not be able to counter it with rudder. The result will be a ground loop, inflicting damage on the aircraft—and your body."

David was introspective for a few seconds.

"Why do you raise the tail?" he asked.

Irish looked up, amused.

"To get the elevator and vertical stabilizer out of ground effect so it can fly, and thus influence the wing into the air."

David responded with another question.

"Why does pushing the stick forward make the nose move left?"

Irish moved his hands to his hips, pleased with the caliber of questions he was getting.

"Gyroscopic precession effect from the spinning propeller."

David looked at the prop intently.

"Explain that."

Irish walked to the prop.

"Have you ever played with a spinning top?"

David gave a hesitant nod, not knowing where the conversation was headed.

"What happens when you nudge it forward or aft?" Irish asked.

Pausing to think David responded,

"It moves left or right."

"Exactly!" said Irish, excited. "A gyroscope will move ninety degrees to the direction in which it is disturbed."

David rubbed his hand over the wooden propeller, lost in deep contemplation.

"So," he said at last, "a spinning prop is a gyroscope, and if I disturb it by pushing forward on the stick, the nose of the aircraft will move to the left. Correct?"

"Correct!"

"And if I disturb it by pulling, will it go to the right?"

Irish was now smiling.

"Yes, it will."

"Is there a correlation to how hard I push and the reactive effect?"

"A direct correlation."

David thought in depth about what he just learned.

"Why?"

Irish shook off the question.

"Laws of physics, who cares? As an aviator you need to know the answer, not the equation; the what, not the why. We are piloting aircraft, not designing them."

Satisfied with that answer;, David met Irish's eyes with a newfound confidence generated by knowledge.

"Let's go fly," he said.

"Now you're talking." Irish slapped him on the back. "Get in."

CHAPTER 4

06:16 Local, 04JUN (12:16 GMT, 04JUN)
Weis Field, Texas

David tried awkwardly to climb into the cockpit. Irish stopped him before he fell off the airplane, showing him where to put his feet on the wing and where to step in the cockpit. David was already learning that it was attention to the little details that made flying easier.

Irish instructed him on how to strap on the parachute and hook up the aircraft restraint harness. The double set of shoulder and seat belts was uncomfortable and took some getting used to. After tightening all the straps, Irish handed David a leather flight helmet and heavy glass goggles. They were what he expected, except for long rubber tubes coming from the center of the ear cups and disappearing toward the aft cockpit.

"What are these for?" asked David.

"Listening tubes," Irish replied, "so I can talk to you above the engine noise."

David turned the contraption over in his hands inspecting it closely.

"How do I talk to you?"

"You don't," Irish added with a wink. "Perfect system, don't you think?"

David chose not to answer, pulling on the leather helmet instead.

Irish manned up the cockpit and snapped on all the straps in an instant. After pulling on his helmet, he held what looked like an oxygen mask to his face. Inside, a stethoscope-type device amplified his voice, carrying it down the tubes to David's earpieces.

"Comm check," Irish spoke into the mouthpiece.

David sat motionless.

"Comm check!"

Again, nothing in response from the front cockpit.

"David, if you can hear me, give me a thumbs-up."

David complied.

"That is a comm check, comm as in communication. Got it?"

David held out another thumbs-up.

Watching from the sidelines, J.T. and Jon could tell exactly what was going on. They held their hands over their mouths to hide the smiles, more from Irish than David. As Irish grew visibly aggravated, they had to turn and walk toward the hangar to let out a laugh.

Jon looked at J.T., a man he had always respected as an airline captain, but now after 7Alpha, his respect was much more profound, not just as a pilot, but as a man. All the 7Alpha men had come back changed. The horrors of war are amplified when watching lifelong friends go through the grinder, especially when coming home to face the families of those who wouldn't return. J.T., Jon, and Irish were doing that right now. Jon thanked God they had the distraction of flight.

The seven cylinders of the Continental R-670-5 engine popped to life. Irish steadied the idle and taxied immediately to the downwind end of the field. After visually checking that the pattern and final were clear, he pulled the Stearman onto the grass runway, pointed into the wind and stopped.

"Okay, David," he said into the mouthpiece, "you have the aircraft. The brakes are on the top of the pedals; hold them. Take your left hand and grip the tallest black knob on the throttle quadrant; it is the engine throttle. When I clear you, slowly ease the throttle forward until it stops. As the engine comes to full power, it will take an increasing amount of right rudder to track the center of the runway. Hold the stick aft into your lap until the airspeed indicator comes alive. When it does, ease the stick forward to the neutral position, and the tail will fly. By the time that happens, we will have sixty knots indicated, so then ease the stick aft and rotate the nose into the air. Got it?"

David answered, his excited voice lost in the throaty idle of the Continental engine.

"I can't hear you," Irish snapped at him, irritated. "Shake or nod your head."

David dutifully nodded his head in the affirmative.

"One more thing," said Irish. "If I say I got it, put your hands in the air and your feet flat on the floor. Acknowledge."

David nodded his head again.

"Okay, knucklehead, let's go flying."

David could feel the sweat roll down his back between his shoulder blades as he pushed the throttle forward. He stepped on the right rudder, and to his surprise, the nose followed his input. Distracted, he subconsciously jammed the throttle to the stop and at the same time pushed the left rudder pedal to counter the drift.

As the left rudder input took effect, the engine raced to full power. A combination of torque, prop wash, and incorrect rudder swerved the nose sharply left. Desperate, David stabbed in right rudder with his foot. He almost had the nose movement stopped when he remembered to raise the tail, but in the excitement of the moment his input was very abrupt. That re-established the left drift due to the gyroscopic effect of the propeller.

Now headed off the side of the runway toward the hangars and out of options, a single conscious thought formed in David's mind: Pull! The aircraft obediently left the ground—pointed directly at J.T., Jon, and the looming hangar. Both observers rose to the balls of their feet, muscles instantly taut, ready to flee for their lives.

Meanwhile, David wrestled with the laws of physics, determined to bring them to heel through aerodynamics. With acceleration, the controls became more effective as the air rushed over them at a higher velocity. Instinctively, David banked away from the hangar, passing it—and the tensed spectators— barely ten feet off the ground. Capitalizing on his temporary advantage, he willed the aircraft back over the runway and began an unbalanced climb.

Jon let out a Texas-sized, "Yee Haw!" as the Stearman rose into the still morning air, rotating around every axis. Through it all, Irish sat calmly in the back cockpit, elbows out, clearly having anticipated the entire event.

J.T. looked at Jon with a spark in his eyes that Jon had not seen for a while.

"Did you notice?"

"I've got to admit," Jon replied, "I was contemplating my exit strategy, J.T. I didn't notice anything except that Stearman getting bigger."

"He was smiling when he went by."

"Who?" asked Jon, surprised.

"David!" responded J.T. with registered pride.

Jon laughed out loud. "Do you think Irish was having as much fun?"

"Doubtful, Jonny-boy, very doubtful."

02:30 Local, 04JUN (12:30 GMT, 04JUN)
Pacific Ocean

The Imperial Japanese naval flotilla cut through the moonlit water on a collision course with the United States Marine Corps on the island of Midway. Its crew expected an easy victory; Wake, a similar base, had fallen in a single day. Abandoned by the Pacific fleet, the garrison on Wake Island had had no chance.

Below decks on the four aircraft carriers, men scurried around, moving bomb carts, loading and fueling aircraft for a ground attack. The first wave of attackers was already on deck and ready for launch.

Unknown to the flotilla's command, a large United States naval force with its own aircraft carriers steamed toward Midway, hell-bent on defending it. A historic showdown was now set, one that would change the course of the war in the Pacific by the end of this day.

06:31 Local, 04JUN (12:31 GMT, 04JUN)
Overhead Weis Field, Texas

The Stearman continued to hurl uncontrollably toward the heavens. David felt as though he were trying to balance on top of a bowling ball while trying hard not to spill a cup of water. He was beginning to wonder if he had given Irish a heart attack when Irish finally spoke.

"I got it."

David put his hands up in surrender with relief. The aircraft instantly smoothed out. Irish's calm, curt voice came through the tubes again.

"Look in your mirror."

David looked up at the mirror attached to a strut near the top wing. It was pointed to enable the pilots to see the empennage, or tail section. It also gave a good view of the aft cockpit. In it sat Irish, his face smug, his hands over his head.

David quickly scanned the horizon and instruments—the Stearman was climbing out, perfectly content, with no one at the controls. He looked back in the mirror; Irish pulled the mouthpiece to his face.

"Okay, David," he said. "You got it."

David put his hands and feet on the controls, gingerly.

"This isn't a wrestling match, boy. It's a dance. Be firm and directive with your partner, but treat her with respect. And be smooth. Always be smooth."

When David took positive control of the Stearman, it transformed from a bucking bronco to an attentive dance partner, one that responded to the most subtle input. The Stearman seemed to come alive in his hands. David had never felt exhilaration like this. He felt one with the machine and morning.

On his own, he started shallow, clearing turns as Irish barked encouragement from the back.

"Coordinate that turn. Use the balance ball; it works like the bubble in a carpenter's level."

A turn slip indicator was located in the center of the instrument panel, consisting of a replica control stick and a balance ball. The control stick showed direction of turn and measured the rate; a full stick length was a standard rate turn. Below that was a banana-shaped glass with a ball floating in a clear liquid. This was the slip indicator. If the tail was not following the nose, the ball would deflect in the opposite direction. By stepping on the rudder in the same direction the ball was out, the pilot could center the ball and bring the aircraft back into balance.

To the right, and slightly above the turn and slip indicator, was the airspeed indicator, directly below that the altimeter. Two hands measured the number of feet: hundreds, long hand; thousands, short hand. Barometric pressure changes caused the altimeter to move, so to get an accurate reading the reference pressure was constantly updated by twisting a small knob that changed the barometric pressure shown in a small window. The number 29.92 meant 29 point 92 inches of barometric pressure was set in the window and would cause the altimeter to indicate the proper altitude, if 29.92 was also the current barometric pressure of the area. The fastest way was to merely enter the elevation above sea level of the airfield while you were sitting on the ground. Field elevation was always posted at an airfield just for that reason; it was a backward way to work the problem. And it was easier than calling the weather office on the phone and getting a long boring brief. Pilots normally preferred easy, especially for local hops on a beautiful day. Above the turn and slip indicator was a standard wet compass for directional navigation.

Engine instruments were on the left side; they consisted of RPM (revolutions per minute); next down was the MAP (manifold air pressure).

Smaller gauges showed the oil pressure and cylinder head temperature. RPM indicated how fast the prop was spinning, MAP, how hard the engine was working, and the pressure and temperature indicated the engine's health.

With David taking it all in, Irish explained the function of each instrument between flight instructions. It was a nonstop monolog.

"David, center the ball," he instructed. "It's out to the left—step on it! Center it up—no, too much. Do you see that strut near the horizon? Use that to hold your angle of bank and altitude by keeping it on the horizon. Stay smooth.... Hold that stick with your fingertips. Don't make a fist. Center that damn ball!"

David continued to nod and try to comply. He was sweating profusely in the cool morning air, even as it rushed by at a hundred miles an hour. It was a good sweat; he was smitten, his destiny now clear and mated to machines of the air.

CHAPTER 5

Battle of Midway
04:30 Local, 04JUN (15:30 GMT, 04JUN)
Pacific Ocean, Northwest of the Island of Midway

The Kido Butai (carrier strike force) turned into the wind, while on the flight deck of the Hiryu, Ensign Ishiro Rabato stood with the wind at his back. In front of him, twenty-seven propellers spun in the pre-dawn darkness, reflecting glints of light from the dim takeoff centerline lights that were built into the deck. He knew that within the dark cockpits, the pilots all had their eyes on his shadow as he flipped on his red, coned flashlight.

Checking his watch at exactly 04:30, Rabato waved the light in a tight circle as the strike leader, Lieutenant Joichi Tomonaga, ran his Aichi D3A Val's engine to full power, and the Kinsei 54 pumped out 1,070 horsepower. Rabato leaned into the wind, extending the flashlight and touching it to the deck. Tomonaga released his brakes and raced down the deck, coaxing the heavy Val dive bomber into the black air.

09:30 Local, 04JUN (15:30 GMT, 04JUN)
Weis Field, Texas

David and J.T. taxied the blue and yellow PT-17 Kaydet into takeoff position on the grass strip. J.T.'s style was much more relaxed than Irish's. After bringing the aircraft to a halt, he brought the voice piece to his mouth.

"Okay, Davy-boy, put your hands and feet on the controls and follow me through the takeoff."

J.T. started the takeoff roll with David lightly touching all the controls and feeling their movement. As the RPM of the engine increased, he felt the gradual increase of right rudder. Then the airspeed flickered and the control stick centered to the neutral position, raising the tail. Very quickly, sixty knots showed on the airspeed indicator and the stick moved slightly aft, rotating the aircraft smoothly into the mid-morning sky.

04:30 Local, 04JUN (15:30 GMT, 04JUN)
Midway Field, Midway Atoll

Captain Paul Lady of VMF-221 kissed off his wingman and pushed the throttle forward on his Twin Wasp R-1830-86 engine. The F4F-3 Wildcat accelerated quickly and leaped into the air. It was a vast improvement over the lumbering F2A-3 Buffalo his wingman was wrestling with behind him. Even though the Buffalo's Wright Cyclone R-1820-40 engine produced the same 1200 horsepower as his Wildcat, the design was so poor, aerodynamically, that its performance was terrible. Pilots simply called it the pig.

Captain Lady pulled the power back so his wingman could catch him while he manually cranked up the gear. The single advantage the Buff had over the Wildcat was hydraulically actuated gear. With his wingman now aboard, he started a slow climb to altitude to take his CAP (combat air patrol) station.

Pigs can fly, he thought, even if it's not very pretty.

04:45 Local, 04JUN (15:45 GMT, 04JUN)
Overhead Hiryu, Japanese Aircraft Carrier, Pacific Ocean

Each squadron rendezvoused overhead Hiryu at its own altitude, and the squadron commanders joined the strike leads squadron at 14,000 feet. Overhead Akagi, Kaga, and Soryu, the same meetings were taking place. After each air wing was formulated, the strike came together over Hiryu and sortied toward Midway at 05:24. One-hundred-eight war birds turned toward what they believed was an under-equipped garrison abandoned on Midway. The Japanese aviators were intent on crushing its defenses in a single, decisive blow.

05:34 Local, 04JUN (16:34 GMT, 04JUN)
US Navy Catalina PBY, Patrol Plane Number 3V58
150 nautical miles northwest of Midway

Petty Officer Third Class Elmer A. Kiel, Jr. scanned the water from a blister window protruding from the fuselage of the PBY. The design of the window allowed him great visibility as he searched the waves 20,000 feet below, looking for the Kido Butai. Only nineteen years old, he had already survived the Pearl Harbor raids, having arrived on board Kaneohe Naval Air Station a few weeks before December 7, 1941. The grandson of the mayor of St. Louis, he knew he could have missed the show altogether, but he had left the comfort of a privileged life behind to seek adventure in the US Navy. He had found it.

Kiel put down the binoculars, rubbed his eyes, and reached for a sip of cold coffee. As he raised the cup to his mouth, his tired eyes detected movement. They widened as he focused on 108 aircraft passing 6,000 feet below, just barely visible in the early dawn sky. Looking at the reciprocal of the air armada's course, he could see in the distance the Kido Butai with at least two aircraft carriers.

After passing the information to the aircraft commander, Kiel quickly tapped out in Morse code: Many planes heading Midway, 320 at 150 nautical miles.

05:45 Local, 04JUN (16:45 GMT, 04JUN)
CAP Station Whiskey, 50 nautical miles northwest of Midway

Captain Lady received a hot vector toward known Bandits over his radio receiver, steering him toward the enemy. (A vector is a compass heading, hot means suspected bad guys or declared Bandits—known bad guys—are on that compass bearing, i.e., turning the CAP to face the enemy.) The message was chilling.

Snap vector 320 for 100, one group, multiple Bandits, angels 14, declared hostile weapons free.

The hair stood up on the back of Captain Lady's neck as he turned to a heading of 320 degrees and pushed his power up as high as he could and still keep the Buff on his wing. At their combined speed, he figured he was fourteen minutes from combat, fourteen minutes away from a life-and-death struggle with a far superior and experienced foe.

What the hell, he thought, *no balls, no glory.*

VMF-221 scrambled all twenty-eight of its fighters, nineteen Buffs and nine Wildcats, to meet the enemy. Ordered to escort their own strikers, instead they flew straight toward the fight. Every other aircraft on Midway took to the air: six TBF-1s, four Army Air Corps B-26s loaded with torpedoes, and fourteen B-17 Flying Fortresses. The last aircraft into the air were VMSB-241s sixteen SBD and eleven SB2U-3 dive bombers, at 06:10.

Kiel transmitted the Kido Butai position, course, and speed to Midway, Task Force 16 and Task Force 17. Positions were plotted. Rear Admiral Fletcher planned for a 07:00 launch of strike packages from Enterprise, Hornet, and Yorktown.

06:01 Local, 04JUN (17:01 GMT, 04JUN)
78 Nautical Miles Northwest of Midway, Pacific Ocean

Captain Lady rolled in on the biggest flight of aircraft he had ever seen from 20,000 feet. With the sun at his back, he and his wingman were undetected. He was surprised to see the Zero fighter escort below the bombers; they obviously didn't expect an airborne threat. Using his 6,000-foot advantage to gain speed, he was quickly at redline. Picking a Val dive bomber, the outside wingman of the last division, Captain Lady desperately tried to concentrate; he had never seen so many planes in the sky at once. Before him stretched 108 aircraft from four carrier air wings, all headed for his home base on Midway.

Focus, focus, one at a time, he told himself. *Gun sight to target, master arm on, charge the guns, piper to target, piper to wing root. Three thousand feet, 2,500 feet, steady, trigger down!*

The words resonated through his conscious as the six .50-caliber machine guns erupted. A fusillade of destruction rained on the Val. It succumbed immediately, disappearing in a black-and-orange blur as Captain Lady streaked past the debris.

Flashing overtop of two divisions of Zeros on his attack run, he knew he would not be allowed to attack with impunity for long. Still at combat-rated power on his R-1830-86 Twin Wasp engine, his speed advantage would give him a shot at one more Val before he had to sweat the Zeros' counterattack. Suddenly, the morning sky lit up with tracer fire from all the other Val's tail gunners as his quarry's explosion dramatically announced his arrival.

His next target was a target of opportunity, literally centering itself in his gun sight after he had pulled off his first kill. Estimating the distance at 2,000 feet, Captain Lady admired the Japanese air crew's formation discipline as he centered the piper on the Val. Tracers from the collective fire of the tail gunners began to converge on his Wildcat as he squeezed the trigger; again, the aircraft immediately exploded. He flinched as he saw tracers pass off of his right side, until he realized they were from his own wingman; he too had drawn blood, plunging a third Val to the calm sea below.

Captain Lady felt exposed now. He immediately pulled five Gs, straight up. With his Wildcat's nose pointed in the pure vertical, he unloaded the induced drag by pushing to zero G. Having started at his redline speed of 275 knots, he was now temporarily a rocket ship, ascending out of the fight and, he hoped, out of danger. He knew the Zeros were behind him and his wingman; he also knew they could not shoot at zero G, because their guns would jam. He prayed they had not reached top speed in the chase. If they had not, he could out zoom-climb them by converting excess airspeed, his potential energy, into kinetic energy to gain altitude. If they had—he was toast.

Captain Lady climbed as high as he dared. His airspeed was being rapidly tugged away by the Earth's gravitational force. At 50 knots indicated, he used that force and sacrificed all his remaining energy in the form of airspeed to get the nose coming down by yanking the control stick into his lap.

As it was approaching the horizon, with airspeed dropping to zero, he pulled the throttle to idle and neutralized the ailerons and rudder so he wouldn't induce a spin but kept the stick all the way in his lap to keep the nose coming down.

Once the heavy nose began to seek the center of the Earth, Lady was able to turn his attention back to the fight. Scanning below for the enemy, the Marine fighter pilot instantly knew his gamble had paid off: 500 feet below him, a Mitsubishi A6M2 Zero-Sen fighter was falling toward the ocean with him. As gravity pulled at the heavy nose of the Wildcat, it began to regain airspeed. With the first twitch on the airspeed indicators needle, he began to feed in throttle and right rudder to keep the Wildcat in balanced flight.

It was then, to his horror, that he saw his own wingman spinning out of control. Captain Lady forced himself to let it go. He was still in a fight for his life. With smooth precision, he continued to accelerate his Wildcat until he had enough airspeed to pull the nose onto the Zero for the kill.

The Japanese Zero pilot was attempting the same delicate dance so he could escape; he didn't make it. Captain Lady got the piper on the Zero's exposed belly and blew him out of the sky.

Continuing to fly aggressively, he pulled aft of the debris field and finished the bottom half of a loop. Now nose-low and accelerating dramatically, he rolled right to make a head-on pass at two Zeros that were climbing toward him. They closed at over 500 mph as he made every attempt to shoot them both in the face. Tracers filled the morning sky again.

He didn't stick around to see what happened as they flashed by, guns blazing. Finding himself in the middle of the largest enemy formation in the Pacific, he decided to scoot out their six o'clock by extending in the opposite direction at full speed and live to fight another day. He still had some ammo and figured he could re-attack them on their way out, if he played his cards right.

06:15 Local, 04JUN (17:15 GMT, 04JUN)
Hiryu Japanese Aircraft Carrier, Pacific Ocean

To Ensign Ishiro Rabato, the eastern sunrise seemed remarkably similar to the Imperial Japanese Naval Fleet flag that flapped wildly from the yardarm of the Hiryu. Viewed through the flickering propeller of a turning Mitsubishi A6M2 Zero-Sen fighter, the kaleidoscope effect made the rising sun look like the Japanese battle flag: red rays emanating from a circle of the same color in the center.

Surely the sight before him was a good omen. No doubt, Midway would fall like Wake before it. Hawaii would be next, and then the Imperial Fleet would rule the Pacific from its new base at Pearl. America would certainly sue for peace, the war would be won and the *gi jinge* driven from the Pacific forever.

A launch signal of a black square with two black balls going up the yard arm refocused Rabato's attention on the task at hand. He quickly wound up his flag in a tight circle. The Nakajima Sakae 21 engine ran up to full power. Glancing at the flags to ensure the ship was turned into the wind, he touched the deck and launched the Zero. Its 1,130 horsepower strained against the wind as it rumbled off the deck, settling slightly due to its weight before it began a climb overhead. In quick succession, he launched the other seven CAP aircraft. With each, the flight deck crews bowed and waved jubilantly in unison as the fighters took to flight. They were sure that the end of this day would bring endless glory to the Emperor's navy.

06:20 Local, 04JUN (17:20 GMT, 04JUN)
3 miles Northwest Midway, Pacific Ocean

VMF-221's remaining twenty-six fighters slashed through the Japanese Strikers, taking Lieutenant Tomonaga by surprise. The intelligence reports claiming a defense force similar in size to what had been on Wake were egregiously in error, and he was furious. He knew even before the attack runs began that another strike would be required before putting the amphibious force on the beach.

All around him, a furious dogfight raged. Its progress could be tracked by the smoking aircraft plunging into the Pacific. This was certainly not to plan, but what Tomonaga did not realize was that most of the flaming aircraft were American F2A-3 Buffalos. After bombing and strafing Midway, Tomonaga had his radio man raise the fleet and signal the need for a second raid. As the signal was being sent to the Japanese command, a lone Wildcat attacked from the northwest, flaming his wingman and riddling his Val with .50-caliber rounds.

11:20 Local, 04JUN (17:20 GMT, 04JUN)
Weis Field, Texas

After an hour-and-a-half of basic air work, J.T. took the airplane and entered the landing pattern at Weis. Flying up the runway, he made a sharp, 180-degree turn to the downwind portion of the pattern. Abeam the end of the runway, he set 1700 RPM and 23 inches of MAP. He flew the descending half-circle of a military-style pattern, talking to David throughout the entire approach. Rolling wings level for what seemed to David to be a very short groove length, J.T. eased off the power and flared, smoothly rolling onto the grass strip.

David was surprised how much the throttle moved aft in the flare, and J.T. seemed to read his mind as they rolled to a stop.

"Military aircraft are heavy and produce a lot of drag in the landing configuration," he said, "especially these bi-planes. So we have to hold some power to keep from falling out of the sky. Bottom line: maintain a constant airspeed and rate of descent."

David nodded and tried to absorb the control inputs he felt as he followed J.T. on the controls. They had come to a stop only a third of the way down the runway.

"Okay, David, your turn. Take off, climb to pattern altitude, then turn downwind and land."

His first approach was rough. However, because he was preoccupied worrying about that, the takeoff went much better. J.T. had a knack of saying the right thing at the right time.

"Don't overthink it. Just keep the airplane pointed straight, and be smooth," was all he said as they rolled down the runway.

David's newfound skill at keeping control during takeoff did not transfer to the landing phase, however. His biggest problem on approach was being rough on the power. He would alternate between not enough and way too much, going from falling like a rock to climbing instead of descending. He got fast, then slow, then fast again.

It all culminated in three bounces before J.T. took control and powered them back into the air. He kept the control of the aircraft for the next approach. At the abeam, he set landing power and smoothly rolled into an approach turn.

David was looking at the touchdown zone over his left shoulder when J.T. brought him back into the cockpit.

"David, the first ninety degrees of turn should be mostly on instruments: power, turn needle, airspeed, and rate of descent. Scan them all, check your progress over the ground to see what the wind is doing to you, adjust, and back into the cockpit," he said.

"Look at me in the mirror."

David looked back and saw J.T. with his left hand, the throttle hand, held over his head. Quickly scanning the instruments, David was surprised to see that they remained stable. His gaze alternated between the mirror and instruments, waiting for a massive fluctuation, but it never happened.

In the flare just before touchdown, J.T. called over the mouthpiece, "Ease the throttle to idle."

David complied, and the Stearman settled nicely onto the runway.

They did a touch-and-go, and on climb-out, J.T. turned it back over to David.

"Less is more," he said.

David shook his head; he didn't understand.

"The less you move the flight controls, the more control of the aircraft you keep."

David nodded, finally understanding. Power plus attitude equals performance. A stable platform is easier to control; correct with small, conscious movements.

07:15 Local, 04JUN (18:15 GMT, 04JUN)
Midway Atoll

Midway radio transmitted the all clear and called all fighters to land and re-service. Of the twenty-eight fighters that had launched, only ten returned. Of that ten, only two would ever fly again. Captain Paul Lady's Wildcat was one of the two.

He flew low over the field to get a look at the runway, staying fast in case he got jumped by a Zero. Satisfied that the runway was intact, he pitched up steeply to the abeam, extending the gear and flaps. Flying a very steep and tight approach, he landed in seconds, then hustled over to a revetment.

07:15 Local, 04JUN (18:15 GMT, 04JUN)
Hiryu Aircraft Carrier, Pacific Ocean

Admiral Nagumo, convinced by Tomonaga's transmission and the attack on his fleet by the B-26's, had already directed the reserve strike group to be reloaded with fragmentation bombs for a second raid on Midway.

The American fleet had not been found. He must act on the information he knew to be fact, not endless possibilities. Nagumo was the product of the absolute structure of Japanese society. He had a cultural inability to act on a hunch. American naval officers were the exact opposite: risk takers, even gamblers. And more important, they were used to making decisions on their own, far away from micro-managing command staffs. Rear Admiral Fletcher had launched air strikes without knowing exactly where the Kido Butai was located.

Admiral Nagumo ordered all air wings to download the War at Sea weapons packages and upload fragmentation bombs for another attack on Midway. This meant unloading torpedoes and armor-piercing bombs, then reloading strike aircraft with anti-personnel fragmentation bombs.

Nagumo's staff still worried about US carriers in the area. A scout had reported a task force consisting of five cruisers and five destroyers at 08:10. Satisfied, they continued to load for the Midway strike.

A mere ten minutes later, at 08:20, the same scout reported a carrier in the task force. Members of his staff called for an immediate strike, but Nagumo rejected it because the strikers were now loaded with fragmentation bombs and his fighters were not yet refueled. He directed that the load be changed again, back to War at Sea packages, and set a launch time for 10:30.

On deck, the Japanese ordnance men reversed the load for a second time. Space on a ship was always an issue. Since constant indecision on weapons loads was never foreseen, there were only enough weapons carts for a single load. They had to violate standard operating procedure by laying the fragmentation bombs on the flight deck as they uploaded the War at Sea package. Then they could load the frags onto the carts and take them below to the armored weapons magazines.

During the change in weapons loads at 08:37, the Kido Butai had to turn into the wind to recover the first Midway strike and the CAP. Tomonaga flew his Val at full speed over the Hiryu. Performing an aggressive carrier break turn at the bow, he jerked the throttle to idle and pulled four Gs to slow his aircraft. After 180 degrees of turn, he dropped the landing gear and extended the flaps, keeping a 45-degree angle of bank turn in as he pulled to centerline and slowed to his approach speed, leveling his wings in the groove of the Hiryu. Five seconds later, the LSO, Landing Signal Officer, gave him a cut signal and he trapped on board. Taxiing clear immediately, he shut down and ran to Flag Plot, the admiral's planning room, where they "plot" all ship's movements. Confusion reigned on deck after the recovery finished at 09:18. Fuel line hoses were stretched everywhere among the bombs and aircraft.

Two minutes later, the first American strikers started their torpedo attack runs against the Akagi and Kaga. Lieutenant Commander Waldron led the fifteen TBD Devastators of VT-8 against the Kido Butai. Only Yorktown had managed a coordinated launch, so Waldron led his squadron against the heart of the Japanese fleet with no fighter escort. Zeros pounced on the torpedo bombers, and the slow-moving aircraft were savaged by the fighters and the anti-aircraft artillery, or AAA. One by one, they fell into the sea. Ensign George Gay was the only pilot to get his aircraft to a launch point before he was shot down. Gay was also the only squadron member to survive the attack.

VT-6 followed Torpedo Eight. The squadron lost ten of fourteen aircraft. VT-3 was the next squadron in the grinder. As they began a run, they shifted to the Hiryu. This move dragged the Japanese CAP along; over thirty Zeros descended on them. The commanding officer, Lem Massey, had tried to coordinate a high/low attack with McClusky's Bombing Three, but he could not see them through the clouds. When Massey was flamed, the squadron formation fell apart, and they met the same fate as Torpedo Eight and Six.

Not a single torpedo struck a targeted ship; three squadrons obliterated in what seemed a futile attempt. However, the torpedo squadrons had brought the Zero CAP virtually to the surface to engage them. The few Zeros at altitude were engaged with Thatch and his Wildcats. Using his new tactic, dubbed the Thatch Weave, they were holding their own against superior odds but could not help VT-3.

When VT-3 turned to attack the Hiryu at 10:20, the Akagi began its launch as the Zeros pursued the torpedo bombers. Overhead, VB-6 and VS-6 SBD Dauntless dive bombers, twenty-four in total, rolled in on Kaga with vengeance in mind.

Simultaneously, Lieutenant Commander Dick Best led six SBD Dauntless aircraft in a plunging dive toward Akagi, pointed almost straight down. With the Zeros out of position, they were all able to drop their bombs unmolested. Two thousand-pound bombs landed amid the Akagi's air wing as the first aircraft were taking off. Four more fell on Kaga. Both ships were instant infernos as the bombs on deck and fuel lines fed the conflagration.

Less then two minutes later, Lieutenant Commander Leslie led Bombing Three's seventeen Dauntless SBDs in an attack on Soryu. Three thousand-pounders ignited the same kind of inferno that was burning on Akagi and Kaga as the Zeros chased the few surviving torpedo bombers down on the deck (low altitude).

At 10:50, Rear Admiral Yamaguchi ignored Admiral Nagumo and launched eighteen Vals and six Zeros from the Hiryu against the American task force. He would follow an hour later with his Nakajima B5N Kate bombers. With the rest of the carrier force in flames, he had no intention of getting his air wing caught on deck. Yamaguchi wanted to strike the Americans quickly and put them on the defensive.

The Hiryu strike, led by Lieutenant Kobayashi, flew east to engage the Americans. Rear Admiral Fletcher put a fresh CAP up over Task Forces 16 and 17. At 12:00, the forces met, a mere twenty miles from Yorktown. US Navy Wildcats dropped seven Vals in rapid order, and more CAPs joined the melee. Their Zero escort finally caught up after chasing another flight, and the Wildcats were forced to fight for their lives. Seven surviving Vals attacked the Yorktown. Three bombs found their mark, one doing severe damage.

Task Force 17, having only one carrier, the Yorktown, sent its CAP to recover on the Hornet and Enterprise with Task Force 16. They, in turn, put up a CAP over Yorktown as her crew fought to get her speed back up.

At 13:00, the Hiryu finally got confirmation that it was up against three

US Navy aircraft carriers. Ten Kates and six Zeros were readied and launched at 13:31, led by Lieutenant Tomonaga. Task Force 17 was only eighty-seven nautical miles away.

By 14:30, Yorktown's crew had her speed up to 19 knots when Tomonaga found her. Formed in a battle formation called a chutai, he had the Kates formed up in a ten-plane V with two Zeros in the middle and two on each end. TF-17 radar picked up the attackers and vectored Yorktown's CAP toward them. They missed. The FDO (fighter direction officer) quickly reversed them, and the F4F-3 Wildcats gave chase.

Catching the Kates, two Wildcats shot down two of the bombers before being engaged by the Zero escort. Yorktown began to launch fighters in an attempt to fend off Tomonaga. Thatch had just cranked up his gear when he saw Tomonaga pierce the screen of cruisers and destroyers. Turning toward the Kates, he got off a string of fifty just as Tomonaga dropped his torpedo. The Kate's right wing collapsed and Tomonaga impacted the water. His torpedo missed.

Two more Wildcats came off the deck of Yorktown, each downing a Kate immediately. The fourth to come off was jumped by two Zeros as he turned toward the second flight of Kates. Lieutenant Barnes, engaged in a two-to-one fight, held them off long enough for McClusky's division of Wildcats to come to his rescue, downing both Zeros in a single slashing run. Two more Zeros jumped Barnes, and the seven fighters got into a swirling dogfight over Yorktown.

Yorktown launched more fighters as the last Kates closed on her. Wildcats made a firing pass but missed; four torpedoes went into the water and two hit. Yorktown slowed and went dead in the water.

As the USS Yorktown began to list to starboard, the new flight leader, Lieutenant Hashimoto, sent a message to Yamaguchi: carrier engaged two certain hits. Yamaguchi misinterpreted the message to mean two carriers hit.

Fletcher received new coordinates for the Hiryu from one of Yorktown's scouts. After passing the information to Task Force 16, he gave the order to abandon ship on the Yorktown. At 15:25, as the Yorktown was sinking, the Enterprise launched another strike of twenty-five dive bombers and eight Wildcats.

Lieutenant Gallaher was in the lead SBD Dauntless dive bomber. Thirty-four aircraft and crews were depending on him to find the Hiryu. Glancing west, he saw that the sun was low and he had no time to waste. Plotting the last known latitude and longitude on his movement board, he also plotted the last known course and speed. Gallaher projected the rendezvous point and wagged it a bit to the south. He sweetened up his course and checked his time again.

At 16:20, he saw the Kido Butai and it sent a chill down his spin. He was very aware of how many men had already died today and he didn't much want to join them, but his duty was clear. After maneuvering his strike to a position overhead the Hiryu at 19,000 feet, Gallaher rolled, inverted, and pulled toward the Hiryu below at 16:58. Thirty-three aircraft followed.

Ensign Rabato was at his station waiting to launch another scout plane. His confidence was rattled by the day's events. He had seen the Akagi and Kaga destroyed and he yearned for retribution. He was waiting with anticipation to launch the strike group being readied below in the hangar deck.

Anti-aircraft artillery guns came alive, announcing yet another attack. Rabato looked up and saw the first SBDs dropping their bombs. Mesmerized, he watched as the tiny dots grew; he knew two of them would hit. The first bomb hit aft, knocking him to the deck with its concussion. Without thinking, he stood as the second one hit amid ship. Again, he was knocked to the deck. The scout plane was ablaze—he couldn't believe his eyes. Rabato tried to get up and noticed his legs were gone.

Strangely, incomprehensibly, a calming silence filled his ears as the destruction and chaos raged around him. Reduced to a mere spectator of his own existence, he watched as another bomb fell close by and blew him overboard. The cool Pacific water revived him just long enough to get a glimpse of the Hiryu in flames, bow to stern.

Rabato slipped below the surface while half a world away, David drifted asleep, unaware of the titanic struggle that had taken place as he was floating on the gentle spring air of Texas.

CHAPTER 6

Day two of David's enlightenment found him in the cockpit with Jon, sitting on the runway, engine run-ups complete. Jon ordered him to take off and climb straight ahead to 5,000 feet. Not a word of instruction or encouragement was offered. David glanced in the mirror and saw Jon sitting, elbows out, looking uninterested, not seeming to pay a bit of attention to David's pending takeoff.

He began the takeoff roll, not sure if the nonchalance was a show of confidence, resignation, or even a death wish. Jon had come back from India much changed, David knew, and he had not known Jon well. The happy-go-lucky attitude, full of bravado, was gone, replaced by a quiet confidence and a fatalistic outlook.

Surprisingly, the takeoff was smooth and controlled. As they climbed out, Jon closed his eyes, basking in the morning sun. David caught a glance of a slight smile in the mirror. He genuinely seemed happy to be alive this morning, definitely out of character. At 5,000 feet, Jon pulled the mouthpiece to his face.

"Okay, David, every idiot is a savant at something, and mine is aerobatics. J.T. and Irish think you need to get upside-down ASAP. I agree, so here we are. I'll demo a squirrel cage. In sequence that's a loop, to a half Cuban eight, into an Immelman, and finish up with a split S."

David sat motionless in the front cockpit. The only thought he could formulate was, *Huh?*

"Don't worry," said Jon. "You will love it. Okay, I got it."

David put his hands over his head as Jon pushed the Stearman into a full power dive. At 140 knots, he started a four-G pull. David's ten-pound head now weighed forty, and he struggled to keep it upright. His vision began to close off at the edges, as if he were looking down a tunnel. Jon spoke effortlessly as David became more and more disoriented.

"Bear down with your gut muscles like you are taking a dump," he said. "It will force the blood back into your brain; it's all headed to your feet right now from the G-force."

David grunted, tensed his muscles, and his vision returned to normal. Jon continued his narrative.

"We get to looping speed, begin a coordinated pull, wings level and four Gs toward the vertical."

At the mention of vertical, David looked out of the cockpit and noticed they were pointed straight up. He flinched involuntarily, grabbing the windscreen frame. The calm narrative continued in his ears in total contrast to the turmoil bubbling in his brain.

"We continue to program in back stick pressure," Jon said, "to maintain the constant G as our airspeed bleeds off. Next, we'll pull onto our back and ease the pull to three Gs. We need to hold three over the top so we arch in a perfect circle, not an egg shape, because we have Mother Earth's gravity working with us."

David heard but did not comprehend as they continued to pull until they were upside down. His overriding concern was to not fall out of the open cockpit to the cotton fields below, but even if he had not been securely strapped in, the G force alone would have held him snugly in place. Realizing this, a strange euphoria swept over him as they continued to pull through the back side of the loop.

"Now that we're nose low," continued Jon, "Mother Earth will pull us toward her. Our G will increase as we speed up so we need to hold the pull until hitting four on the meter, and then begin to ease the pull to maintain it. We finish up by playing the G to arrive at our starting altitude and airspeed. And go right back up to do it again."

Jon pulled through the beginning of another loop. As they came down the back side, inverted at forty-five degrees nose low, he bunted the stick forward, unloading the G, and rolled upright using aileron and rudder. Now going in the opposite direction, they continued to dive to their starting altitude and airspeed and pulled up into the beginning of another loop, again rolling out of it on the back side, leveling at the starting altitude and airspeed. The shape made through the air was a figure eight turned on its side.

Before David could catch his breath, the four-G pull came back on. This time, Jon stopped the pull when they were flat on their back, pushed forward, and then rolled upright using mostly rudder. They lumbered along at a low airspeed that made the aircraft feel very mushy.

"What we just did," explained Jon, "was trade airspeed for altitude. During the Great War, a fighter pilot named Immelman developed the maneuver as a counter to an opponent attacking from above and behind. The obvious disadvantage is that we are now slow. Feel how sluggish the controls are."

Jon turned control over to David; they were indeed sluggish and heavy. Big deflections were required to get even small movements from the aircraft.

"It would be damn hard to get out of the way of bullets at this speed, wouldn't it?"

David nodded, confused by the comment.

"Okay, I got it," said Jon, taking back control of the aircraft. "When we are slow and cocked up, rudder is king. To roll, we need to use rudder as the primary flight control. We can use the gyroscopic effect to help influence the roll. So if we snap on a pull and kick in a boot of right rudder, we will execute what is appropriately called a snap roll."

Jon jerked the stick into his lap as he stomped the right rudder pedal to the floor. His inputs resulted in a rapid, almost violent 360-degree roll around the longitudinal axis of the Stearman. Passing through the inverted portion of the roll, Jon slowly released the inputs and stabbed in momentary inputs in the opposite direction to stop the Stearman where it had started: wings level, nose slightly above the horizon, cruising along as if nothing had happened.

He could see David smiling in the mirror. Jon smiled big as well, for the first time since he had left the Assam Valley. He went back to work.

"We can also use the torque of the engine to roll," he said.

Jon slowed the Stearman further, and it began to buffet. J.T. and Irish had already taught David that this was bad, a warning of impending breakup of the flow of air over the wing: a stall.

"Here we go!" said Jon. "I'll jam on the power; you try to stop the roll rate with the rudder and aileron."

The Continental R-670-5 howled, and the Stearman started to roll off to the left. David countered with opposite rudder and aileron to no effect. The airplane rolled over to the left.

"Good, David. Now recover from the stall."

David eased the stick forward, reducing the buffet, and instinctively pulled the power to stop the torque roll. He regained control and then fed the power back in as he stopped the rate of descent.

"Very good, very good," Jon said. "Most guys would have continued to rotate around the propeller because pulling power is not a natural act when stalled. It is the opposite of what J.T. and Irish taught you during stall recovery practice, isn't it?"

David nodded. This was an unexpected complication.

"You'd be screwed if you did that down low or in the landing pattern, wouldn't you?"

He nodded again. Talk about being between a rock and a hard place, he thought. Unable to speak, he shrugged his shoulder in a question.

"Only high-powered aircraft will flip you on your back like that," Jon explained. "Don't get slow on final is the moral of the story. And if you do, it will be quite a balancing act to recover from a stall without hitting the ground—or flipping over, then hitting the ground. Either way, you buy the farm."

Buy the farm. David's father had explained to him what the pilot slang meant. When military aircraft crashed, it was usually in a farmer's field. Invariably the farmer would demand huge payment for damages done and then pay off the farm's mortgage with the government proceeds. Thus, the pilot literally bought the farm. Jon returned to his narrative.

"We are slow," he said. "We couldn't get out of our own way. An aircraft needs wind over the wing to turn. No airspeed, no turn. So if we find ourselves wallowing around slow like this, and we have some altitude, we can trade it for airspeed. I got it, David."

Jon eased the stick forward to neutral as he used left rudder to roll the Stearman inverted; the nose fell through the horizon on its own. As they gained speed he began a pull and ended up completing the back side of a loop at their original altitude of 5,000 feet and speed of 140 knots. Jon turned the aircraft back over to David.

"Feel how alive the controls are now?"

VENGEANCE

21:55 Local, 05JUN (12:55 GMT, 05JUN)
Imperial Japanese Fleet Headquarters, Tokyo, Japan

Fleet Admiral Yamamoto, Commander of the Imperial Japanese Navy, stared at the after-action report in total disbelief: Akagi, Hiryu, Kaga, and Soryu, all sunk. Four of his six aircraft carriers were gone forever. Very aware of his country's industrial capabilities, he knew they would not be replaced—not now, not ever. This was a true turning point in the war; they had failed. They would now have to assume a defensive posture, the initiative gone. More than that, he knew this was the end.

Imperial Japan's only chance had been to quickly seize the Pacific and force the Americans to sue for peace. The Midway plan was an absolute requirement. Half of the plan had succeeded: his forces had captured Kiska in Alaska's Aleutian chain of islands unopposed. Now he knew why. It was not Midway that would be sacrificed; it was the Aleutians west of Dutch Harbor. With his aircraft carrier fleet cut by two thirds, the Americans would now go for the kill and hunt down the last two.

Yamamoto's staff stood motionless, silent in the austere room; all eyes were on him. Everyone had heard the rumors, and they knew the Kido Butai and Midway invasion force had been recalled.

"Recall the Ryujo and Junyo from the Aleutians at once," Yamamoto ordered. "Bring them inside the inner defensive ring north west of Hokkaido."

Yamamoto's chief of staff, Captain Yoji, looked at him in shock.

"Admiral, we need the aircraft to support the invasion of Attu tomorrow."

"The Attu invasion will be unopposed."

"But sir, how can we know this?" Yoji protested.

"Captain Yoji, we need them to defend the mainland."

"Admiral-San, certainly we can sortie a carrier from the Midway group—"

"They are all gone, all of them."

"Gone, Admiral-San?"

Yamamoto started toward the door.

"Sunk. The Americans met us at Midway with three carriers. Two now roam unopposed."

A teacup crashed to the floor, dropped by one of his staff. This was their worst naval defeat since losing to the Koreans centuries before. Yamamoto stopped and turned to his staff, ordering no one in particular, "Draw up a short term plan for the withdrawal of our forces from the Aleutians. Long term, prepare a plan to defend a perimeter consisting of the Solomon Islands to the south, Tarawa, Iwo Jima to the east, Kurils in the north, and Indonesia, Burma in the west."

All hands present realized the defensive nature of the perimeter; they were no longer on the offensive. The grand plan to rule the Pacific had been sunk at Midway; this was now a fight of survival.

07:05 Local, 05JUN (13:05 GMT, 05JUN)
In the Sky Over Texas

David moved the stick and rudder pedals slightly and the aircraft reacted instantly. The controls were firm and responsive in his hands. He was contemplating the significance when Jon's voice came over the tubes again.

"When we are fast, the wing is flat and thus the airflow smooth over it. That makes the ailerons king. To initiate the roll, first, we pull the nose up a bit, stop it in place, and then push the stick in the direction we want to roll."

He rolled the aircraft 360 degrees to the left as he talked.

"The torque of the engine and gyroscopic effect of the prop are insignificant at high airspeed. Okay, David. You try it," Jon said as he rolled upright.

David took the controls and pushed the stick to the left. As the aircraft rolled left, the nose sliced toward the ground. Once inverted, all David could see was farmland. Confused, he stopped rolling and the nose buried toward the Earth. Slightly panicked and not knowing what else to do, he pulled for his life. Jon pulled the power to idle from the back seat to prevent over-speeding the aircraft. David continued to pull until he realized they were wings level again, going the opposite direction, a thousand feet closer to the ground.

David was sweating so profusely that his leather gloves were soaked through and slimy.

"Well, wasn't that nifty?" Jon's voice, dripping with sarcasm, reverberated through the voice tubes. "A perfect split-S. Unfortunately, we were attempting to do a simple aileron roll! Let's try it again, shall we? And maybe, just maybe, if we do both parts of the two-part maneuver, we won't lose control and plummet helplessly toward the Earth. Lift the damn nose ten degrees up before you roll. I say again, *before* we roll the aircraft."

David nodded sheepishly, a little less sure of himself. He had indeed lost control of the Stearman and had been merely along for the ride.

Below, Irish and J.T. sat watching the show from the prime position of the right fender of Irish's Cadillac. Irish looked at J.T., a smug smile on his tan face.

"Told you, mate. Which will cost you one sawbuck."

J.T. grumbled incomprehensibly and slapped a ten-dollar bill into Irish's outstretched palm. Above them, the Continental engine howled, racing its RPM, revolutions per minute, up and down as David executed his own rolls and went into a squirrel cage.

The schedule remained constant for a week: three flights a day, one each with J.T. and Irish working on basic airmanship and landings. Tired and sweaty, David would then man up with Jon and get flogged by aerobatics. Even exhausted, he had gotten quite good at the maneuvers. Right on schedule, just as he got comfortable, Jon introduced new ones.

"Today," he began, "we will combine the two types of maneuvers we have learned, overheads and rolls, to perform wingovers and barrel rolls. Most instructors start with these maneuvers, because to a mind trained to function in the three-dimensional world of aviation, they are simple. To the novice, however, they are not."

David slumped slightly, not looking forward to starting from scratch again. Tugging his lap belts tight seemed to pull his mind back to task as Jon continued.

"The first maneuver will be the wingover. It is simply a U-turn in the sky, except we will use altitude to help us. We will gradually pull and roll simultaneously to arrive on our wing halfway through the turn. We'll go into a ninety-degree angle of bank as we hit ninety degrees of heading change. Then we will reverse the roll and pull, letting the nose ease down as we simultaneously roll, wings level, heading the opposite direction from where we started. Two in a row completes the exercise, and we arrive at the same altitude, speed, and heading we started at. Got it?"

David shook his head no.

"Have you ever ridden your bicycle in one of those giant drainage pipes under a bridge?"

David nodded his head yes, thinking about how he and his brother Trey challenged each other to see who could ride the farthest up the side.

"Did you try to go way up the side, as far as you could go?" asked Jon.

He laughed at himself. Trey had always won because David would try to go too far, crashing to the bottom. He was, however, still convinced that if he got fast enough he could have ridden right over the top. Again, he nodded yes.

"So up the side you'd go," said Jon, "and then glide down to the bottom and up the other side as you moved through the pipe. Those were wingovers."

They practiced them, gracefully floating up, then down, just like David and his brother had done on their bikes so many years before. Once he'd mastered them, they moved on.

"Next," said Jon, "is the barrel roll. It starts out like a wingover, except we will step up the G and roll rate. By pulling harder and rolling faster, we will arrive at the halfway point inverted and ninety degrees off heading. The biggest difference is we will continue to roll in the same direction and keep the pull on. It will result in us arriving back at the same altitude, direction and air speed we started at. However, we will be offset in whichever direction we rolled."

For two more days they perfected the maneuvers, always ending every flight with at least ten circuits of the landing pattern.

The following morning, Irish picked up David as he had every day for two weeks. Sundays were the exception; Laura insisted he go to Catholic Mass first. Today was a Sunday, so they had attended Mass together and were now headed for the field.

"So how do you like it, David?"

"Flying?"

"No, Latin Mass—even though you don't speak Latin," snapped Irish. "Of course I mean flying."

"I haven't had much time to think about it; everything has come so fast. I guess ... I guess I love it!"

Irish nodded his approval. "Well, you will have a little more time to be contemplative today."

"How's that?" asked David.

"You'll see," Irish responded brusquely, his demeanor demanding the subject be dropped.

The big black Cadillac rolled to a stop on the carpet of green grass where J.T. and Jon stood waiting. David moved wearily toward the Stearman. These last two-plus weeks had taken a lot out of him. He had put his all into his flights, mentally and physically.

Throughout morning Mass, emergency procedures and limitations had run through his head, going over his assigned maneuvers one by one. Irish had noticed his coordinated hand and foot movements during the sermon. They were slight, but even so, he could identify each one as David did his pew flying. Irish couldn't help smiling to himself.

David reached the Stearman still lost in his thoughts. He turned looking for Irish, who was standing with J.T. and Jon as their eyes met.

"Don't wreck it," Irish said. "Be back in an hour."

Turning back to the aircraft to conceal his nervousness, David noticed the front cockpit had been configured for solo flight. All the belts were fastened and pulled tight. The Stearman was soloed from the rear cockpit due to center-of-gravity limitations. He began his preflight but could not concentrate, his mind racing in a thousand directions. Internally he was panicked, convinced he had forgotten everything he had been taught in the past few weeks. To the world, and most importantly his three instructors, he presented a cool methodical persona as he climbed into the cockpit as a first-time aircraft commander. The three instructor pilots were not fooled.

"Do you think he peed himself yet?" asked Jon to no one in particular.

They all laughed.

"He will be fine once he gets the engine started," J.T. responded.

"How long until he applies to the Air Corps, do you figure?" deadpanned Irish.

J.T. shook his head.

"He won't. He will apply to the Navy. David wants vengeance, very specific vengeance. He won't chance a European assignment in the Air Corps; he wants to go to the Pacific and kill Japanese."

J.T. suddenly, audibly, choked back a sob. He was shocked at how it had convulsed so unexpectedly, so rapidly, from within. Irish and Jon said nothing; there was no point. Each had and would continue to deal with his own demons. The three men stood silently, bonded, comforted by their shared experience, their shared trauma. They consoled J.T. in their silence, embracing him with their mutual melancholy as the Continental barked to life.

David goosed the engine and taxied toward the runway. He glanced left and right as he turned onto the runway and ran the power all the way up, charging headlong into the midmorning air. His fingers tingled as the Stearman came to life and alighted from the Earth. Passing 500 feet, he executed a perfect victory roll; he was free.

CHAPTER 7

05:30 Local, 19JUN (21:30 GMT, 19JUN)
The Jungle, The Philippines

The putrid smell of the jungle filled his senses as he awoke. Sergeant Donnelly stood over him.

"Captain Butler, we kicked a hornet's nest," Donnelly whispered in a thick, south Boston accent.

"What's up, Sarge?" asked Butler, irritated.

"I doubt they found that Jap patrol we whacked, but there is a lot of activity. Could be just lookin' for them."

"Doesn't much matter which, does it?"

Donnelly shook his head in agreement. Butler sat up wiping the jungle from his eyes.

"Okay," he sighed. "Let's get deep into the jungle. Tell our scouts to get us so deep the Japs won't follow."

"Roger that, Captain. I'll get them on the move."

For eight hours, the jungle fighters had moved into the heart of the dense, tropical foliage. The heart of darkness, thought Butler, as he brought his men to a halt by merely clenching his raised fist. Silently, they stopped, tactically dispersing without an order uttered, sitting among the overgrown roots of the immense trees of the Philippine rain forest. Donnelly moved from man to man, saying nothing, receiving no words in return. A collective consciousness enveloped them; eye contact was all he needed to assess each man.

Butler watched, reclining between two huge ribbons, exotic roots of a tree that seemed alive, not as a plant but a creature. He was unfamiliar with its botany; regardless, he knew it—he felt it. That comprehension sent a twinge of fear down his spine. He was afraid he was becoming a part of it, the jungle, along with all of his men.

They moved with relaxed ease in the jungle; even so, he felt as though they were being swept along by an unseen force. It was as if the jungle itself had turned liquid and he and his men were mere flotsam, trapped in the slow steady current of the languid stream, unable to break free, losing free will and civility, flowing along in the primordial ooze, their destiny pre-ordained. Fleeting thoughts of his home and family were swept away in its power. Could he ever go home if he survived this? Could he save his soul?

Slowly, they got to their feet and moved out, the jungle pulling them deeper.

CHAPTER 8

15:36 Local, 19JUN (21:36 GMT, 19JUN)
Dallas, Love Field

Captain Mark Hass, American Airlines, stood on the ramp just outside the aircraft door. Irish stepped hard out of the DC-3, stiff from flight, old wounds, and age. Glancing at Hass-man, Irish could see he had a bug up his ass: his chin was set and jutting with a slight tilt of his head. Irish straightened up.

"What's up, Doc?" he asked with a wry smile and a Bugs Bunny accent.

Hass-man, unflappable as always, didn't crack under the pressure of humor. He got right to the point.

"I heard you are training Charles Henry's kid to fly."

Irish nodded.

"I hear also that you have two Stearman."

Again Irish nodded, slower this time.

"I want you and J.T. to teach me how to fight."

Irish raised an eye brow. "And what, pray tell," he asked, "do you have swirling around in that little Prussian head of yours?"

"Payback!" said Hass-man.

"Oh, Jesus, Joseph, and Mary," Irish replied in a thick Dublin lilt, then shifting seamlessly to Latin added, "Et tu, Brute?"

10:00 Local, 20JUN (16:00 GMT, 20JUN)
Weis Field, Texas

Two Stearmans sat on the runway, waxed and polished wings glistening in the morning sun. Their R-670 engines ran up in unison, and the aircraft began a takeoff roll together.

Irish sat behind Hass-man in the lead aircraft, filling his ear tubes with orders.

"When in the lead," he instructed, "you have to be smooth as silk, especially in a fighter. Fly it like you are on instruments with Greta Garbo in the back."

Hass-man nodded and eased the tail off the grass runway. In the wing aircraft, J.T. sat behind David, also dictating orders.

"You have to maintain your position," he said, "by getting ahead of the lead. Go to full power and tap the brakes to maintain the proper bearing line. All power corrections come in three movements, just like the landing pattern."

Sweat ran down David's back, *I was just getting used to flying and now this,* he thought as the lead aircraft left the runway.

"Match his attitude!" J.T. shouted into the mouthpiece.

Hass-man held a stable platform while David flailed nearly out of control on his right wing. As he snuck a peek, his earphones filled with sage advice.

"It's best not to watch," said Irish.

Hass-man nodded, returning his focus to flying the absolute smoothest lead possible while trying to remain confident that J.T. would not let them collide.

"David," J.T. ordered, "stop squeezing the life out of the control stick! Hold it lightly ... fingertips ... the hands of a surgeon."

Realizing he did have a full-force death squeeze on the stick, David willed himself to relax his grip and the violent pumping of the Stearman's nose stopped. When it was clear that he was semi-comfortable being next to another aircraft in flight, the pre-briefed maneuver signals started. Hass-man held up a clenched fist, signaling for the wing aircraft to cross under to the other side. David's voice tubes again came alive.

"Pull a little power," urged J.T., "and ease the nose down. Too much! Power back on! That's it, now stop us ten by ten, ten feet down and ten aft. Give it a little wing wag toward the lead and we'll slide right under to the other side."

David's Stearman slid majestically to the other side. The relative movement exhilarated him.

"Stop the movement with an opposite wag of the wings," said J.T. "That's it, now add power and pull us back into position on the left side."

David squeezed; the Stearman bucked.

"Easy with it!" rang through his earphones.

They continued to practice until David thought his brain had turned to mush. Right to left, left to right, over and over again. Easy with it, stabilize into position, stop squeezing the damn stick!

Finally, Hass-man waved him forward and passed him the lead. Going back to just flying the aircraft was a relief, relaxing actually, especially when he watched an experienced pilot like Hass-man flail a bit. J.T. read David's mind.

"Flying fighters is a different kind of flying," he said. "It's not always easy to teach old dogs new tricks."

Next came break-up and rendezvous. *It sounded simple in the brief,* David thought. The lead aircraft will break away from the wing aircraft with a hard pull, for 180 degrees of turn. The wingman will wait until the lead has turned forty-five degrees and follow him. Once the airborne U-turn is complete and the wingman is in trail of the lead, the lead will initiate an easy, ten-degree angle of bank turn. Again, the wingman will wait for forty-five degrees of turn, then aggressively turn inside the lead's radius of turn, doubling the angle of bank to drive out to the lead's forty-five-degree bearing line and close on the lead, using a five-knot advantage in airspeed. We will complete the maneuver by crossing under, then closing up into a tight parade position.

David, his confidence freshly restored, started in the wingman's position. His confidence was short-lived. Hass-man broke away; waiting for the proper separation, David followed. With his attention focused on the lead, David let the Stearman's nose fall below the horizon, beginning a descent. His airmanship initiated a nonstop stream of orders from the back seat.

"Watch your nose," warned J.T. "Don't let it fall below the horizon. Keep the pull on!"

Again, the Stearman was recalcitrant, fighting David's harsh inputs as the turn was completed. J.T.'s voice pierced his confusion.

"David, look at your altitude."

He shook his head vigorously; the thought of looking inside the cockpit was absurd.

"Look at your damn altimeter."

David snuck a peek: 260 feet high.

"Look at him."

He was!

"You're looking down on him. It means you are high. No more than twenty feet of step up."

David laughed out load, his sarcasm lost in the rush of air. Twenty feet, ridiculous! I'll be lucky to keep it within a thousand, he mused, fighting to maintain his composure.

"Fingertips, fingertips, stop squeezing that stick! You are going low now."

Too low, the Stearman flew into the turbulence created by the wing of the lead aircraft. Powerful vortices swirled off the wing tips of Hass-man's Stearman, capturing his wingman in the circular motion. David, sensing he was losing control, yanked hard on the stick to escape the tortured air. It leapt up so quickly they lost sight of the lead under the big nose of the Stearman—the ultimate taboo for a wingman.

J.T.'s calm voice floated through the tubes.

"I got it, Davy."

David's hands immediately went over his head, and J.T.'s instantly calmed the beast as it raced for the heavens. He slowly rolled inverted, regaining sight of the lead while continuing to roll and bringing the nose back down, ending up in the perfect trail position.

Sorcery, thought David. Not only had J.T. rescued them from an extreme situation, he gracefully put them back into position. Incredible. It humbled him, even deflated him. How could I ever get that good?

J.T.'s voice refocused him.

"David, look at your instrument panel: altitude, airspeed, heading. Now look at the lead. Inside, outside—never stop scanning both. You have to fly your airplane and put it where it needs to be in relation to the lead. But never forget to fly your airplane first."

David nodded apprehensively, thinking his head would explode just sitting there.

"You got it, David."

Retaking control, he concentrated less on the lead and more on flying his own aircraft, working hard to maintain the trail position without losing control. At last, he smoothed out.

Irish had been watching the circus in his mirrors. After David had finally stabilized in position, he saw J.T.'s arm raise in the back cockpit with two fingers up, making a circular motion.

"Okay Hass-man," he said. "Start a turn."

06:48 Local, 20JUN (16:48 GMT, 20JUN)
Naval Hospital, Pearl Harbor

Gunnery Sergeant Michael L. Paillou jerked awake, grasping for a weapon that wasn't there. The antiseptic smell of the hyper-clean hospital filled his nostrils, snatching away his confusion like smelling salts. Its artificiality sickened him.

Shit, I'm still in the damn hospital, he thought, feeling a tug on the arm he had used to grasp at the imaginary Colt .45. Glancing down at his wrist, he saw the tubes running to an IV that hung from a chrome pole next to his bed. *Screw this,* he thought, and yanked the fat needles out of his arms.

He winced as he swung his legs over the side of the bed and put his feet flat on the floor. Testing his right leg, which had a rather large hole in it, he stood, deciding it was sound.

A rotund nurse watched from the door of his room, arms crossed under her ample bosom.

"What exactly do you think you are doing, Sergeant?"

"Getting the hell out of here, sweetheart," he grunted.

"That is Lieutenant Commander to you, Marine."

Paillou smiled a devilish smile.

"Roger that," he replied. "Getting the hell out of here, Lieutenant Commander Sweetheart. Now, where are my clothes, ma'am?"

"We had to burn them," she laughed and left the room, convinced that she had prevented his escape.

"Great," Paillou mumbled as he took a cigarette from the bedside table and lit it with his only possession, a Zippo. "Just great!"

11:22 Local, 20JUN (17:22 GMT, 20JUN)
In the Sky Over Texas

The boldly painted blue-and-yellow aircraft contrasted sharply with the soft blue of the sky and muted green and brown of the fields below. Also in sharp contrast was its movement compared to the aircraft that was chasing it. All yellow, the wing aircraft moved up and down, fore and aft, earning its nickname of Yellow Peril. In the rear cockpit, J.T. raised his mouthpiece.

"Keep his aircraft right on the horizon," he instructed, "and your altitude will be exactly the same as his. Imagine a forty-five-degree line coming out of his wing root, and go right up it—piece of cake."

David shrieked in vain, a response lost to the slipstream. J.T.'s calm voice in the presence of certain death was beginning to aggravate him.

"Fly your airplane, not his," he continued. "Set your power. He's at ten degrees angle of bank. Match it and keep him on the horizon. If you get ahead of the bearing line, ease the angle of bank behind the bearing line, and wrap it up in a tighter turn."

The running commentary continued as they closed on the lead Stearman. As they got in close, J.T. added another parameter.

"Kick a little rudder to align the fuselages."

He must have sensed the question mark over David's head. Certainly, he could not hear the *Huh?* muttered up front.

"If we aren't aligned," he explained, "we will not match his heading."

They closed to a parade position and stabilized.

"Okay, cross under."

Finally, David thought, something I've done before. He was wrong. Having never crossed under with the lead in a turn, he was spit out the other side. After a big wing waggle and a short exploration of positive and negative G envelope, he wrestled the Stearman into position. Hass-man rolled out, and they repeated the entire process over and over.

After too many rendezvous to count, it was Hass-man's turn. The ease in which David transitioned to flight lead was subconscious and lost on him. But it did not go unnoticed by J.T. in the back. He watched closely as David trimmed the aircraft and tweaked the power to maintain the exact pre-briefed speed. Not just precise, the aircraft was being handled with a natural smoothness some aviators would not achieve in a lifetime of flight. With rolls switched, the rendezvous continued. J.T.'s voice broke the repetition of the multiple rendezvous.

"I've got it."

David dutifully relinquished control by raising his hands so J.T. could see them. For the first time during the flight, he looked out and scanned the Texas countryside. He was surprised to see that they were abeam the airfield. J.T. let the nose of the Stearman fall through the horizon as he eased the power back and began a turn toward the field. The nose fell to thirty degrees below the horizon as the turn increased to sixty degrees angle of bank. *Holy cow*, David thought, *he is going to try and enter the pattern from here.*

As the bank increased, so did the G-load. Wondering what had happened to Irish, David looked to his right and was amazed to see him hanging over them in a tight parade position. J.T. continued to pull for the runway, lining up perfectly 500 feet overhead the approach end. He rolled, wings level for a brief moment, and broke aggressively into a four-G level turn away from Irish. They were tight, real tight. Easing the turn to forty-five degrees angle of bank, he pushed the nose lower. Flying a circular approach, he never leveled the wings until just before touch down. As they taxied clear, David noticed Irish was taxiing in formation. *He must have been right behind us. Wow!*

07:49 Local, 20JUN (17:49 GMT, 20JUN)
Marine Corps Headquarters, Pearl Harbor

A young corporal scurried through the office door of Sergeant Major Thomas Shelby. The unannounced disruption caused a menacing frown to form on Shelby's face.

"Speak!" he demanded.

The corporal looked nervously around the austere office as if seeking an escape route.

"Sir, there is some short guy out here in nothing but a hospital shirt! He claims he's a gunny named Payloo or something like that. If you ask me, I think he escaped from the loony bin. We better call shore patrol."

Sergeant Major Shelby jumped to his feet.

"You have got to be shittin' me," he said, and burst through the door to his outer office. "Paillou, you old China leatherneck, you're supposed to be dead."

"So they keep telling me. How about some utilities? My ass is getting cold."

CHAPTER 9

11:52 Local, 20JUN (17:52 GMT, 20JUN)
Weis Field, Texas

The mid-morning sun had already burned the dew off of the grass airfield. It was going to be a hot day. David sat on a wooden crate listening to the hum of early summer. He was thinking about the maneuvers he had seen J.T. perform so effortlessly today. They just seemed to flow; the controls moved almost imperceptibly and yet the actual result was so magnificent. J.T.'s soft voice joined the hum.

"Had enough for one day?"

David nodded, seemingly detached.

"How did you get so good?"

"David," J.T. laughed, "I'm just an average fighter jock. Now your daddy is another story. He was something special. He didn't fly an airplane; he strapped it on and wore it."

David slipped back into himself and for the first time felt real self-doubt. J.T. instinctively sensed it and put his arm around David's shoulder.

"You have your father's hands."

David's brown eyes probed J.T.'s for an answer.

"What do you mean?"

"During the rendezvous when you were lead, you didn't even think about flying mechanics. You just did them—smoothly, naturally, correctly."

"I was just doing what you told me to do."

"Negative, you were not, because I didn't say a word while you were flying lead. I just sat back and enjoyed the morning. You might as well have been solo. That is how you need to fly as a wingman too. Just let it happen: maximum result for minimum input."

David sat contemplating his words. J.T. let him absorb them for a while, then nudged him.

"Come on, let's go debrief."

Another week of two-a-days went by. As Hass-man and David grew comfortable in flying formation, Irish and J.T. subtly showed their confidence by riding with their elbows out, arms resting on the edge of the cockpit, their hands away from the controls.

Week two of formation brought an entirely new level of flying. This new phase would combine everything they had learned thus far. David and Hass-man's eyes locked for an instant when Irish announced in the brief that they would be performing formation aerobatics. As the crews walked to the aircraft, David looked nervously at J.T.

"Don't sweat it," J.T. reassured him. "All you really need to know is that everything happens to the lead first: gravity, G-force, and acceleration. The key is to jump the lead's move, and as always, be smooth."

With farm fields tumbling in the background, David was pleasantly surprised how easily he maintained position. When the lead Stearman's nose went low, he led it by adding power to stay in position. As it rose above the horizon, he would immediately start pulling the throttle back, then inching it back forward. He hardly noticed the Earth somersaulting as he focused intently on the lead aircraft.

Rolls, loops, and wingovers in close proximity filled their days. It was challenging, it was a workout, and it was fun. By midweek, it was also old hat. Both were good students, so J.T. and Irish decided to throw in one more little twist to the training.

Air combat, or dogfighting, was the most challenging skill in aviation—with the obvious exception of landing on a ship after an engagement. Irish and J.T. conferred in private during a break mid-Wednesday, while their students watched intently. The instructor pilots nodded in agreement and walked over to their students.

"Okay, boys," said J.T., "Irish and I agree we are wasting time now. You guys are sharp; it is time for some graduate level study. You know how to fly a military aircraft. Now you need to learn how to employ it as a weapon. So we are going to have a little fun."

J.T. stood in front of a blackboard, chalk in hand, inside the shade of the wooden hangar. He drew three simple diagrams on the chalkboard. The first was a half-circle with a small "V" on the end with a second line and V just inside the first, stopping right behind it. The second diagram was two lines that started level, then moved together, crossing in the middle, then moving back to opposite starting points in a scissoring move, repeating several times. Third and last was a crude rendering of an aircraft with a dashed line and a small circle at the end. J.T. finished drawing and turned to face David and Hass-man.

"Okay, I'm going to keep this simple," he said. "We are going to reduce things to the basic essentials. A lot of dogfighting is aircraft-specific, so we are going to show you guys just the main building blocks. A dogfight is nothing more than an attempt to rendezvous on your opponent before he rendezvouses on you. The final step of that rendezvous is done with bullets."

David and Hass-man laughed. Neither Irish nor J.T. joined them. J.T. pointed to the diagrams and stepped toward his students.

"This is all you have to know to live," he said. "You will need to learn more to kill."

Both students lost their smiles. This was starting to sound serious.

"Diagram one depicts a two-circle fight. If you find yourself in a two-circle fight, you are in a contest to see who can out-turn whom; it is a rate fight. That means the fighter who turns with the highest rate gets behind the other. Diagram two is a one-circle fight. The objective of the one-circle tactic is to make the smallest circle; it is a radius fight. Got it?"

Hass-man and David looked at each other and confessed in unison: "Ah, no."

Now J.T. and Irish laughed. Irish jumped into the lesson.

"Look, boys," he said, "I'm a simple Celtic warrior, not an educated engineer like J.T. So let me give it to you Irish-style. A two-circle fight is identified by having the same wing down as an opponent. It means you gotta turn, and to turn, you need airspeed, preferably your best turning speed. A one-circle fight is ID'd by opposite wings down, and you want to get behind the bad guy, so you get slow, to float him out in front of you, for a shot. You come at each other in a scissoring movement, pulling to get behind the other guy."

He pointed to the second diagram.

"One circle: get slow; two circle: get fast, and never, ever stop pulling."

Irish demonstrated maneuvers with his hands as the two neophytes looked on, trying to comprehend. J.T. spoke up again.

"Think of it as a rendezvous during loops, barrel rolls, and wingovers."

After briefing some specifics and general flying procedures, they all started out of the hangar.

"Wait a minute," David stopped them. "What's the third diagram?"

"Good question," responded J.T. "That is the control point where you want to go, approximately 200 to 300 feet behind the bad guy. We will show you why in the air."

For the first flight, they did simple tail chases. Each took turns chasing the other and trying to stay behind him in the control point while the other did his best to shake him. David put all of his lessons to work. He floated effortlessly, gracefully behind Hass-man. Their airborne ballet was beautiful. An hour later they were back in the hangar de-briefing, then briefing for the third flight of the day.

In the air, they set up for some canned engagements. David started in the offensive position on a perch 200 feet higher and slightly aft of Hass-man. When Irish wagged the wings of the lead aircraft, David pulled aggressively toward his foe. Hass-man seemed to wait too long to react, so David pulled a big lead for a shot. Suddenly, all he saw was the plan form, the top of the Stearman as Hass-man put a maximum performance break turn on his aircraft: it was growing in size at an alarming rate.

"The geometry of this engagement," J.T. warned, "has exceeded the aircraft's performance capability to comply."

As David pulled and attempted to decipher what J.T. meant, his aircraft blew past Hass-man's six o'clock position, overshooting in close. Immediately, Hass-man reversed his turn, and the hunter became the hunted.

"Get your nose up," said J.T. "You have to get him into a defensive one-circle fight now. Reverse and pull over top and behind him."

Now in a slow, horizontal scissors with their noses extremely high, the two Stearman slashed at each other, both on the edge of stall as they attempted to get behind the other. J.T. continued a calm deliberation behind David.

"Remember, Davy, you've got to control the closure rate just like a normal rendezvous. Unlike a normal rendezvous, you go for the control point, not the other aircraft."

David spent a lot of time looking over his shoulder for the rest of the flight. His maneuvering was smooth and precise, but Hass-man was eating him up in the dogfights. After being bludgeoned for another forty-five minutes, they were back in the pattern and landing at Weis.

Exhausted, David stretched out on a sun-bleached bench as Irish and Hass-man continued to talk with their hands by the Yellow Stearman. He stared blankly at them, not comprehending. J.T. sat down next to him.

"Davy, listen up. A lot of guys fly fighters, but there are damn few fighter pilots."

"What do you mean, J.T.?"

"Look, when you strap on a fighter you are a killer, a madman. The only thing that matters is the fight! You don't have family, you don't have friends; you only have wingmen and bandits. You must be consumed with the fight. It has to become your life, your very being. Nothing else matters or exists. It must be that way if you are to survive."

15:30 Local, 27JUN (21:30 GMT, 27JUN)
Weis Field, Texas

By Saturday morning, David's fangs had grown. Hass-man's style had taken on a methodical, exacting cadence; it was very Prussian. In sharp contrast, David's style was aggressive, almost wild. He had taken J.T.'s talk to heart. His moves flowed in a smooth, fluid manner, always turning and rolling in an aggressive attempt to get a shot, one continuous maneuver. By contrast, Hass-man strung multiple moves together like a chess game.

On their last flight of the day, it all came together for both of them. They fought furiously, slashing, rolling, and twisting. A constant G-load compressed their spines. It was quite different from aerobatics, where the G-load fluctuated up and down. In air combat, it stayed a constant four to six Gs.

Hass-man jammed on a six-G turn as David pulled for a shot. The young pilot responded by unloading, pushing below Hass-man's Stearman, then looping back into firing position. Threatened again, Hass-man yanked the throttle to idle and reversed his turn as he stood the N2-S2 on its tail, virtually stopping it in mid-air. David stood his Stearman on its tail in response and rolled away from Hass-man to control his closure, then dropped in behind him for a shot. Now in extremis, Hass-man had no option but to duck and run. He twisted the N2-S2, inverted and pulled for the Earth below, doing a split-S. David tracked him through the move: fight over. They rejoined and headed back to the field. Once on deck, Irish sauntered over to J.T.

"That was a nice little move there, J.T., but I think the kid would get more out of it if you stayed off the stick."

J.T. grinned wide and responded like a proud papa.

"I didn't touch it or say a word, Irish. That was all him."

"Wow, that little shit is good."

David and Hass-man joined their instructors for the expected debrief. Irish had a better idea: a celebration was in order.

"Gents, let's go to Webber's for the debrief."

J.T. winced. He knew Irish was up to something.

"You think that is a good idea, Irish?"

"No, I think it is an excellent idea. We have not wetted down this lad properly for his first solo, a tragic oversight. Unconscionable, actually!"

Hass-man smiled. J.T. shook his head in surrender, now sure Irish had something up his sleeve.

"Outstanding! We are off to Webber's, then."

All four aviators piled into Irish's Cadillac. He wasted no time getting to the open road, wheeling onto a long, straight gravel road bordered on both sides by cotton fields. He opened the throttle, feeding all eight cylinders of the Caddie's flathead V-8 generously. The 346 cubic inches pulled them through the fields at an impressive rate. David watched as the cotton rows flew by in a blur. After two harrowing turns, they slid to a stop in front of a ramshackle building on the edge of a field.

Its wood exterior was so sunbleached, there was no hint of past color. All the walls leaned in at the top, giving the impression the building would collapse like a house of cards. Topped off with a rusted tin roof, the only indication of an establishment was a brightly painted, green, four-leaf clover sign printed with "Webber's Irish Pub" in gold letters.

Irish banged through the door first, yelling into the darkness.

"Paddy, you scoundrel, stop watering down the whiskey. Me and the boys are here."

"Watered down whiskey is all your Americanized butt can handle," replied a Gaelic voice in the dark. "Who's the bed-wetter?"

"This fine lad is the reason we've come," said Irish. "Charles Henry's boy has soloed and we have yet to celebrate."

"Charles Henry's boy?" the Irish accent again emanated from the dark.

"In the flesh," Irish responded as he pushed David into the sightless void.

"Ah yes, I can see that. Well then, the drinks are on the house."

"Thanks, Paddy, but not today. Today, they are on J.T. and me."

He slapped two crisp, hundred-dollar bills on the bar. Four Lone Star beers emerged from the black, settling onto the edge of the bar.

"Solo, eh?"

"That's right," gasped Irish after a long pull off the Lone Star.

"I'll get my shears," replied Paddy, and they heard him move into a back room.

David didn't like mention of shears but before he could register a complaint, Irish shoved a beer in his hand and dragged him by his collar across the dark room. Irish stopped and announced to the darkness:

"Gents, I give you David Brennan, solo pilot and aviator-under-training extraordinaire."

Hoots, catcalls and clapping erupted from the blackness. Finally, David's eyes began to adjust. His father's friends were standing in front of him. In fact, every pilot he had ever met was there—Jon, Roper, Two Dogs, Thumper, Danny Boy—all of the Project 7Alpha guys. And off to the side, standing among the bar's strange mix of Irish and aviation memorabilia, was the man himself: C.R. Smith, president of American Airlines and the man behind 7Alpha.

"We waited because C.R. wanted to be here, David," said Irish. "Mr. Smith, I give you the latest flying Brennan."

C.R. came forward and shook David's hand.

"Your father would be very proud. Big shoes to fill, young man."

"Yes sir," was all David could muster.

"On with the ceremony!" bellowed Irish.

Irish maneuvered David to the center of the room, pushing tables aside as the crowd came alive again and the beer flowed. David's head swam. He had no idea what he was in store for, but he definitely did not like the look of the big sheep shears Paddy Webber was holding.

Irish raised his hand to speak. He had the aura of a philosopher about to bestow his disciples with pearls of wisdom. As the cacophony of voices calmed, he glanced left, then right.

"Crap, anybody got a tie?"

The crowd roared with laughter. C.R. stepped forward, handed Irish his beer and pulled off his custom red silk tie.

"Geez, Irish, you forgot the most important part?"

"Ah yes, Mr. Smith, I am but a humble line pilot. It is up to our leadership to provide the logistical support."

His status re-established, at least in his own mind, Irish received the tie with a bow. He slipped the tie, still knotted, over David's head and pulled it tight—a fashion statement that could best be described as comical: David was wearing his usual white T-shirt, blue jeans and his father's flight jacket.

Irish's hand rose above the crowd.

"Gentlemen, today we witness a ritual that welcomes a new member to our tribe of flight. This necktie represents a normal human's tie to the Earth. We shall symbolically sever the bondage that holds young Brennan to the ground. He will be transformed and instead be bonded to us forever, men of the air; his charge simple, yet profound."

Irish glared into David's eyes with conviction and spoke the same words his father had said the last time he saw him.

"David Brennan, you must always do the right thing."

Feeling a tingle go up his spine, David's sense of loneliness and seclusion, even in a crowded room, dissipated. He was glad he didn't have to speak; he could not have. The emotion of communal acceptance enveloped him. To be welcomed as a peer, even a junior peer, by these men was tantamount to being taken into his father and brother's world. He felt close to them for the shared experience. This ceremony honored them and all the aviators before them. For a young man, it was like being knighted into the Templars; this dingy bar set in the cotton fields of Texas, the Church of the Holy Sepulcher of Jerusalem. Self-doubt left him. If these men judged him worthy, then he must be.

"J.T., you may have the honors."

Irish reverently passed the old shears. J.T. jerked them away, smirking at Irish.

"Thank you, oh, High Priest of Flight."

Stifling a giggle, J.T. stepped close to David, opening the shears and setting one of the blades on the initiate's chest. He placed the tie into the jaws of the glistening blades and raised them toward David's throat until he became noticeably uncomfortable.

"The knot is the symbol that binds us," he said solemnly, then shrugged and smiled. "Sometimes, it's all we got."

J.T. snapped the shears closed. The tie below the knot fell to the floor as the crowd howled its approval.

CHAPTER 10

Captain Butler squatted in fronds, mosquitoes feasting on his blood. He neither flinched nor swatted them. There was no point; they were a part of the jungle. He was part of the jungle. Sergeant Donnelly crept up next to him and whispered in a voice quickly consumed by the foliage.

"The last village we pass is ahead," he said. "Something is wrong. No sound, people, dogs, nothing."

Butler nodded as the men glided forward in total stealth, every sense alive in anticipation. Their primordial companions, the Negritos, moved with them. They knew something was out of sync.

From their concealment they could see Rubio, their Filipino guide, standing in the middle of the village's clearing, his rifle at his feet. He stood motionless with his hand over his mouth. Slowly, they emerged from the edge of cover into a field of carnage and barbarity. The Japanese Army had visited. Swiftly, the jungle warriors deployed into a skirmish line, moving deliberately in a squat stance toward the village center.

Butler crouched, rounding a stack of woven baskets. He reeled at the sight of a young Filipina's body, crumpled on the ground at his feet. No more than seventeen, her clothes had been torn from her; the rope that had strangled her was still around her neck. In her right, partially open hand lay a crucifix. She had clutched it so firmly it had pierced her hand at the four points of the cross.

Butler swept the tree line with the sight of his Thompson submachine gun as he knelt on one knee. He glanced at the young girl's body again. Her eyes were wide open, not with accusation but fear. He wanted to protect her but could not; he was too late. She seemed to hold the crucifix out to him. He took it from her hand and covered her with a thatch mat. It was all he could do for her.

As he moved toward his scout, a deep feeling of remorse and foreboding swept over him. Could he reject the savagery of the jungle? Could he seek its cover and resist its darkness?

As he pressed forward in a half crouch, his weapon constantly moved, seeking out targets. What is wrong with Rubio? He has seen this before. Finally reaching him, Butler followed his horrified gaze.

My God, they are cannibals!

CHAPTER 11

The party spread throughout the bar as more pilots trickled in. David remained the center of attention. Irish made him keep the tie knot in place so late arrivals knew who got the free beer.

With a Lone Star in each hand, he slipped away from the group, feigning a trip to the lavatory. The aviation memorabilia that covered the walls and hung from the ceiling intrigued him. David moved from wall to wall, looking at the pictures of man-made birds and their pilots. Suddenly, he froze in place. His father and brother smiled back at him, standing in front of a DC-3. They were thinner than he remembered and his brother, not even two years older, had aged ten.

Jon watched David work his way around the perimeter of the room. He knew where the picture was; he had hung it. He eased up behind David, who was transfixed by the black-and-white image.

"It was just a couple of days before it happened."

David turned away from his father and brother to face Jon directly.

"What did happen?"

Jon looked away, staring into space even though the wall was a mere five feet away.

"I don't really know. J.T. won't talk about it. What I do know is that Irish made an emergency landing, Danny-boy was all shot up—shit, so was Irish, for that matter. He told J.T. some troops were jammed up and needed ammo. I was clue minus, pre-flighting a go bird, when your Dad grabbed me to go with him. But your brother was already in the cockpit and refused to get out. So Charles Henry sent me to go with J.T. I ran for his bird but it was already taxiing out; he had Man-Child with him as his co-pilot. Charles Henry and Trey taxied by, waved, and rolled down the runway."

His voice trailed off. "I was the last one to see them. I should have been in your brother's spot, or Man-child's."

Jon's guilt was palpable; it oozed from every pore of his skin, echoed in every corner of his conscious. It was eating him alive. David tried to say something to ease his pain, but Jon turned and walked away. J.T. watched the exchange from across the room, averting his eyes when David turned and scanned the crowd. He cursed himself for cowardice, set down his beer, and moved toward the bar in search of something with more numbing qualities.

08:15 Local, 28JUN (00:15 GMT, 28JUN)
The Jungle, The Philippines

Butler eased the crucifix over his head. He was squatting on his calves next to the young girl's body in the manner of his Filipino hosts. Donnelly crept up next to him.

"Captain? Captain Butler?"

He gave no response to Sergeant Donnelly. He was as far away as his mind could carry him. Donnelly spoke softly again, piercing his refuge by using his given name.

"Dave, what are we going to do?"

Butler stood up slowly. "Bury them, Paul. No trench, no mass grave. Get the men started. Quickly, please."

"Yes, sir," Donnelly responded, but he lingered awkwardly, finally speaking. "They'll know we're in the area, sir."

Butler turned to face Donnelly, emerging from his trance, a cold glare meeting his sergeant's eyes.

"Oh, they will know, all right. They are all going to know! That, I damn sure guarantee."

00:15 Local, 28JUN (06:15 GMT, 28JUN)
Paddy Webber's Bar, Texas

Hours and hundreds of beers later, Irish surveyed the chaos he had wrought. It was good. However, there would be an issue with getting the remaining revelers all home. Tequila had splashed onto the scene an hour earlier. He looked around for who did not have a shot glass in front of him. Yikes, only three including me, he thought. That is seven per car. Oh well, glad I got the Caddie.

"Hey Roper, Danny-Boy," he called. "Over here—we need to talk."

Roper, a tall, thin Oklahoma boy, ambled over with Danny-Boy in trail.

"What's up?" he asked.

"It appears you boys and me are the only ones that stayed out of that Mexican firewater. We have got to get these drunken monkeys home."

"Roger that, Irish. So who gets to take our young soloist back to Laura Lynn?" Roper asked with a raised eyebrow. Irish glanced over at the obviously inebriated eighteen-year-old and winced.

"I see what you're saying," he said. "I better take him."

Roper nodded in enthusiastic agreement. "Good luck with that!"

Irish leaned back against the bar, observing the crowd. Around David, a constant rotation of pilots shared wisdom, technique and sea stories, often gesturing wildly with their hands. As the beer and tequila flowed, the hand flying had become increasingly uncoordinated. Irish nodded a final approval as he moved to the center of the mayhem.

"Okay, gents. Let's let Paddy get some sleep. Roper, Danny-Boy, and I are driving. Leave the rest of the cars here. We'll get them in the morning."

No one argued as they slowly filed out, guzzling the last of their beers. J.T. grabbed a six-pack to go and guided David toward the door. After bidding Paddy adieu, he pushed David into the front seat of the Caddie and slid in next to him. Once on the road, Irish kept everyone conscious by telling jokes. The last thing he wanted was six drunk pilots passed out in his car; he would never get them out. David, however, succumbed to the mesmerizing effect of the cotton fields strobing past, partially lit by the big Caddie's headlights.

An hour later, Irish silently coasted up Laura's driveway and came to a stop, lights off, engine shut down. He had even pre-opened the driver's door to minimize all noise. Carefully, he exited the car and began to pull David out the driver's side, making a vain attempt to stifle the young aviator's giggles.

"That car would work better with the engine running."

Irish jumped a country mile, then turned to face his automotive critic. Laura Lynn Brennan stood on the back porch glaring down at Irish from her three-step advantage, hands on hips.

"Top of the evening to you, Mrs. Brennan," Irish attempted to charm in his best Dublin cant.

"It is morning, actually."

"So it 'tis, so it 'tis."

As Irish squirmed, David's giggling stopped. The silence, however, did not last long, as his body began to reject the tequila and beer combination. Irish used the distraction for an attempted getaway; he didn't make it. He was caught literally by the scruff of his neck.

"Where do you think you are going?" asked Laura.

"I thought I would take my leave, good lady."

"You thought wrong. When he is done, get him in bed. He's too big for me to carry."

"Yes, mum."

"I'm going in to make some coffee."

"Laura, I don't think that's a good idea. He'll just toss it."

"It's not for him, knucklehead."

"Oh, right you are," Irish responded, having slipped completely into his ancestral accent.

"The hose is over there." She pointed to a neatly coiled garden hose. "Clean him and my driveway when he's finished. Damn pilots," she muttered and disappeared into the house.

Irish dutifully complied, not daring to flee, now that orders had been issued. After getting David tucked into bed, Irish joined Laura at the kitchen table. She poured them both a cup of coffee.

"You won't be able to sleep if you drink that, Laura."

She shrugged. "I don't sleep much these days anyway."

Irish nodded. Before the melancholy could seize the room, he reached inside his jacket and slid a thick envelope across the table.

"What's this?" she asked.

Irish sat silently while Laura opened it. Inside was an investment account and deed to her house paid in full, in her name.

"Irish, we are doing fine, we don't need charity. I'm working and David hopes to be hired by C.R. after training."

"Mr. Smith will hire him, but he won't stay, Laura."

"What do you mean by that?" she met his eyes intently.

Irish chose his words carefully.

"He's looking for revenge."

Laura looked shocked. "David, my David—he is so sweet and quiet."

Irish cleared his throat. He felt as though he had betrayed his protégé's trust.

"Never mind," said Irish. "You are probably right."

They sat in silence, Irish sipping his coffee and Laura nervously fingering the papers.

"Why, Irish?" she asked, tapping them.

"Why what?" he answered, more into his coffee than to her.

"Why are you taking this family under your wing?"

Irish felt vulnerable. He did not like letting anyone in, not even old friends.

"Debt to be paid," he mumbled.

"What debt. We didn't have any money to lend, that much I do know. I have always done the bills."

Irish fidgeted, obviously conflicted, not wanting to speak. Finally, he did, without looking up.

"He never told you, did he?"

"Told me what, Irish?"

"Typical Charles Henry, I suppose. He didn't talk much about the Great War?"

"No," said Laura, "and I didn't ask. I got to relive enough of it at night. After the dreams stopped, I didn't see any point in opening old wounds."

Irish nodded and continued to stare into his coffee.

"He saved my life in France," he said slowly. "Damn near lost his because of it."

He returned to his uneasy silence. Laura broke it, looking sideways at Irish, knowing how hard it was for him to voice.

"I'm sure you would have done the same—"

"No, no," he snapped, looking her in the eyes. "I couldn't have. Even if I did have his guts, I didn't have his skill. Your husband was good, Laura, real good! Better than any of us."

A smile crossed his face as he reminisced.

"He could fly that fighter and shoot like no one else. If he had gotten to the war sooner, he would have been an Ace of Aces. He became a Triple-Ace in very short order as it was." He paused, collecting his thoughts. "Anyway, I had put my rump in a very deep crack, six Gerries firmly planted on my six, each taking a turn at shredding my Spad with machinegun fire. I was able to keep them off me by descending and keeping my speed up to maneuver. They were disciplined, beating me down gradually. Finally I was out of altitude, airspeed, and ideas. I was done for, you understand?" His voice strained. "Done! The only question remaining was which of the Kaiser's finest would get credit for the kill. No parachutes back then, chivalry and all, so a kill was truly a kill."

Irish suddenly laughed, shaking his head.

"Into the middle of this, out of nowhere, Charles Henry dives, guns blazing. He flamed two on the first pass, the closest to me. Do you understand the significance of that?" Irish's voice quaked. "He shielded me. He flew himself between me and the other shooters. I turned left with a maximum pull."

Irish grew more animated, his voice alive with the fight.

"Charles Henry looped back onto their six o'clock, scoring another kill as the other three chased me. I reversed hard to pull the Gerries back in front of him, and he got another in the ensuing melee. The last two must have looped back behind us. All of a sudden, Charles Henry took a blast to his engine. It quit and started on fire. I was able to shoot the Gerrie off his tail as he descended for a crash landing in a field.

"The last Gerrie was tenacious. I was able to keep him at bay, allowing Charles Henry to reach the woods. I kept trying to land to pluck him out of there, but the Gerrie kept attacking me."

Tears began to stream down his face.

"I had to leave. I left him."

Behind Laura and Irish, David stood in the kitchen door listening, unsteady but coherent. He turned quietly and returned to bed before he could be noticed.

CHAPTER 12

07:42 Local 28JUN (13:15 GMT, 28JUN)
Dallas, Texas

C.R. Smith slid another cup of coffee across the antique oak table. "You look like shit, J.T."

"Thanks, boss. I appreciate that."

C.R. turned to J.T.'s wife. "Hey, Kate, you better get him some eggs or something."

J.T. held up his hand. "Not unless you want to see them twice."

"Roger that," said C.R. "Scratch the eggs, Kate. How about some toast?"

J.T. nodded painfully in agreement and locked C.R.'s eyes with his own.

"You didn't come here to order me breakfast, boss. What's up?"

C.R. glanced nervously over his shoulder at Kate and back at his cup as he stirred away the swirl of cream. He knew Kate was listening and would not surrender the room.

"I need your help again, J.T.—in Europe."

The glass coffeepot exploded as it hit the floor with a pop. Kate stood motionless. Neither man flinched, staring intently at each other.

A few miles away, Irish stood over his young page. He kicked the bed a second time. Slowly, sand-filled lids revealed bloodshot orbs of gelatinous goo.

"Good morning, sweet prince." Irish smiled.

David couldn't comprehend the inverted view of the man staring down on him. Rather than try, he closed his swollen eyes to stop the pain. Irish promptly flipped the bed, dumping David out.

"Don't put in you what you can't handle the next day, knucklehead. Now get out of that rack."

Slits made a second attempt at opening on David's face.

"Technically, I'm on the floor, Irish."

"So I see, so I see. Now, get off of it and into some clothes! We have Mass and a flight lesson on the calendar. And the good Lord has provided us a beautiful day to do both."

David's eyes rolled into the back of his pounding head.

"Fly?" he groaned.

During Mass, Irish glanced over at David. There was no hand-flying today in church. In fact, he was sure he could actually see the blood vessels throbbing in the young man's temples. He actually felt sorry for the lad.

The drive to Weis Field was even quieter than normal, only interrupted by the occasional sound of David heaving out the open window. As they manned up the N2-S2, Irish pushed David toward the rear cockpit in a move of self preservation and hygiene.

"Okay, okay, Irish," moaned David. "Lesson learned. Can we just go home now?"

"Nope. You have to learn to fly when you are at your worst, physically. Someday your life may depend on it. You will have to man up, sick or fatigued to the bone. You don't always have a choice, so stop whining and get in."

* * * *

The screen door slamming behind him sent a spike of pain across David's brain. Laura looked at her son with ambivalence as he entered.

"Sorry, Mom, I won't do it again. It was stupid."

Laura set down her needlepoint and sat in quiet contemplation.

"No, you go," she said finally. "You'll learn more at the bar than you ever will in a book."

He looked surprised. "What do you mean?"

She stood up and moved to the refrigerator, pulling out a cold soda pop.

"Davy, if I know anything, I know pilots. And pilots hate to admit they made a mistake. Their fragile egos take a dent from any perceived mistake, even a firm landing. But put a few beers in them and they just can't keep it in. They just have to regale you with their near misses and derring-do. It is probably the only time you can count on them to tell the complete truth.

You go and learn from their mistakes and pick up their secrets; watch the overgrown boys talk with their hands and learn how to survive. Just stay away from the tequila."

She handed him the soda.

"Yes ma'am."

For the next few days J.T. and Irish had to fly trips for American Airlines. Jon had disappeared after the night at Paddy's. David assumed he was also on a trip, but on the second of July he saw the N2-S2 doing aerobatics off in the distance. He couldn't be sure but he thought it was Jon flying by himself.

Laura gave a Fourth of July party that was attended by numerous AA guys and neighbors. David enjoyed relaxing with his family. Irish showed up late, coming directly from his trip. He slid over to David, who was trying his best to control the inferno under the dripping hamburgers. Irish dumped his beer on the out-of-control flames.

"Hey, sport. I had to give back the Stearman, but that's okay because I finagled a little trade."

"What do you mean, Irish?"

"Don't worry about it. Just be at the field tomorrow, packed for a week. I already cleared it with your mum."

"Where are we going?"

"On a cross-country extravaganza, young man," Irish answered, a sparkle twinkling in his eye.

CHAPTER 13

16:05 Local, 04JUL (22:05 GMT, 04JUL)
Dallas, Texas

Captain Mark Hass of American Airlines stood in front the Army Air Corps pilot recruiting desk. Five years Junior to his thirty years, the First Lieutenant obviously had a world of experience already. Ribbons on a military uniform told a detailed history of the man wearing them to those who could decipher the code. The young recruiter's uniform boasted the purple-with-white stripes of a purple heart received for wounds in combat, and the blue-and-orange ribbon of an air medal specifically signifying air combat. To the initiated, it was clear that he had already been in the fray. The crutches leaning on the desk verified it. Finally, the recruiter looked up.

"You're a little long in the tooth for flight school," he said. "Supply corps is down the hall."

Hass-man didn't respond. He dropped his license and American Airlines ID on the desk. Before the young lieutenant could reach for them, Hass tossed his own air medal on top of the IDs. The lieutenant picked up the air medal.

"Where did you get this?"

"The Hump: China, Burma, India Theater, flying for Project 7 Alpha."

Still looking at the medal, the recruiter nodded subtly. "Yeah, I heard about that. You guys took some big hits."

Hass-man did not reply, standing expressionless in his Prussian way.

"Sure, we can use you," said the young man. "Lots of C-47 billets, same aircraft as the DC-3."

"No, I've got some payback to give," Hass-man responded curtly.

"All right, I can get you bombers." The recruiter was starting to show some exasperation.

Again, Hass-man's response was short and to the point: "No. Fighters."

The lieutenant had had enough from this arrogant airline pilot.

"Look, pal, the Army isn't in the personal vengeance business. We will put you where we need you. We don't have time to retrain a trash hauler."

Hass-man's Prussian temper flared.

"Sonny Boy, I've forgotten more about flying than you'll ever know—and that includes dogfighting. I've been taught by two of the best WWI Aces, Dobbs and Myers." He dropped his logbook on top of the IDs and nodded toward the crutches for punctuation. "I don't intend to get shot down."

"It was ground fire," the recruiter said, clearing his throat. He was not used to being put on the defensive.

Hass-man shrugged. "Fighters, or I go down the hall to the Navy."

"Okay, okay. There is a huge ramp-up for the 7th in Europe—"

"I'd prefer the Pacific."

Now the young officer's temper showed. "Yeah, and I'd prefer to be on the beach with Marlene Dietrich, but here I am taking crap from you."

Cocking his head, Hass-man analyzed the young man. His nametag read Piffel. Hass detected a slight familiarity in his inflection. Staring directly into the lieutenant's eyes, he snapped off in brusque German: "Ich will es schriftlich." I want it in writing.

Without batting an eye, the recruiter replied, "Sie bekommen sie bei der Vereidigung." You'll get them at the swearing in.

"Sehr got, Herr Leutnent," Hass-man said. Switching seamlessly back to English he added, "A perfect Berlin accent—you didn't pick that up in Germantown, USA."

"I spent my summers in Berlin until the Nuttsies chased my family out in '38."

Hass-man nodded, a knowing scowl on his face.

"I intend to go back, Herr Hass. I will see you in the 7th. My orders are cut, awaiting medical clearance."

"And when will my orders be cut, Lieutenant?"

"Day after tomorrow," the recruiter shot back.

"Roger that. I will see you then."

The stoic Prussian exited without another word spoken.

17:10 Local, 04JUL (05:10 GMT, 05JUL)
Pearl Harbor

Gunnery Sergeant Paillou sat at the bar of the Top Three Club, sipping an ice-cold Budweiser that had been brewed a few blocks from his childhood house in St Louis. After years of roaming the planet, it gave him a strange feeling of linkage to home, even though his parents were long gone. His wife and children were lost to him in China. Still, for some unexplained reason, he felt the simple act gave him just a touch of the bedrock that had been his youth.

The Top Three was a senior enlisted man's club. Its name signified that only the top three enlisted ranks were welcome: Gunnery, First and Sergeant Majors for the Corps, and Chief, Senior Chief, and Master Chief for the Navy.

The bar was done in dark mahogany, cut from the ancient trees of the islands. Their deep texture and tone were accentuated by the dim lighting. The effect was to beckon patrons within, enveloping them in tranquility. A place of refuge for the men who truly ran the Naval Service, here they would not be disturbed by eighteen-year-olds who had too much to drink. Prima donna officers dared not enter either. In this place the senior non-coms were left alone.

Sergeant Major Shelby pulled a bar stool up next to Paillou.

"I got some terrible news for you, Mike."

Paillou rose off his elbows, straightening his back with a stretch as he exhaled a blue cloud from his Lucky Stripes cigarette.

"What's up, Tom?"

Shelby slid a set of orders across the bar.

"Nursemaiding a bunch of future flyboys," he said with a twinge of disgust as Paillou began to read them. "What could be worse?"

Paillou set down the orders.

"Oh, I can think of a few things."

"Yeah, no shit." Shelby slapped him on the back. "Well, at least it's not all bad news today." He tossed the collar rank of a first sergeant into Paillou's glass of beer. "You got promoted this morning."

"Thanks," Paillou said and guzzled down the beer, catching the insignia in his teeth. "How about some pomp and circumstance? Bartender, two Budweisers."

23:01 Local, 05JUL (15:01 GMT, 05JUL)
The Jungle, The Philippines

Sergeant Donnelly eased out of the jungle next to Captain Butler.

"Rubio found them, Captain—company strength, about forty troops. They look to be straight infantry, no heavy weapons, four men on watch—two east, two west."

Butler nodded acknowledgment. "Send the Negritos to slit the throats of the western post."

Donnelly cleared his throat. "Sir, they got us outnumbered four to one, and they can get reinforcements."

"They will move west at daybreak, back toward the village. We will position to the east of their camp. They will leave the lame and lazy to watch the rucksacks and double-time toward the perceived threat. We will then attack the camp."

Butler moved his unit as planned, east of the Japanese encampment. He lay among a fall of rotting trees; the mosquitoes and ants neither bothered nor made him flinch anymore. They seemed to have accepted his presence, and in return, he accepted their need for his blood. In mutual acceptance, they did not swarm and he did not swat.

As the putrid haze began to lift from the jungle floor, the Japanese bivouac erupted in noise and action. The guards had been found at the western post, stretched out peacefully next to each other with their throats slit. Butler had ordered that they be laid out meticulously, hands crossed over their chests in insult.

CHAPTER 14

13:15 Local, 05JUL (19:15 GMT, 05JUL)
Weis Field, Texas

A brand new Navy version of the Beechcraft model 18, a UC-45J, glistened in the sun. Its twin tails and engines made David's stomach tighten. Here we go again, he thought. Just when I was getting comfortable, something completely new.

"Okay, sport," Irish barked, "I'm a little bit out on a limb on this one. We only have it for a week."

David just stared. He didn't know what made him more nervous—the twin engine Beech or the thought of being on the road with Irish for a week.

"All the preparations have been made," Irish said. "No need to thank me, lad."

03:15 Local, 06JUL (19:15 GMT, 05JUL)
The Jungle, The Philippines

Indeed, the insult had found its mark. Butler could hear his Japanese counterpart shrieking orders. He had lost face, he had been taunted, and someone must pay. Just as Butler had predicted, they strapped on ammunition and water only, then double-timed after Captain Nogushi's lost honor. Donnelly crawled up next to Butler.

"You were right. They went west and left five with the rucks—they look none too sharp."

"Do you think we can take them alive?"

Donnelly smiled and shrugged. "Why not?"

It was almost too easy. By the time Butler got into the encampment, five Japanese soldiers were face down with their hands bound behind them. Donnelly stood with a foot on a corporal's back.

"Now what, Captain?"

"We are going to convene a court marshal and hang them as the criminals they are."

"Yes, sir." Donnelly snapped off a rare salute.

13:30 Local, 05JUL (19:30 GMT, 05JUL)
Weis Field, Texas

Twin propellers turned in the afternoon sun, the chrome spinners in the center contrasting against the aircraft's dark blue Navy colors. The propellers were each powered by a Pratt and Whitney R-985 Junior Wasp radial engine. Their nine cylinders popped and snorted, capable of churning out 450 horsepower. Inside the cockpit, David was trying to get used to the plethora of levers and switches, sixteen on the throttle quadrant alone. Slowly, he set the mixtures to rich and props to full pitch. Next, he opened the cowl flaps and oil shutters to keep each engine cool for the impending takeoff and climb out. Irish sat next to him, apparently not concerned at all with the proceedings of ensuing flight.

"Son," he said, smiling, "we are going to have us some serious fun! I have arranged for overnight accommodations at the nicest resort in Hot Springs. And I have secured us proper escort."

David smiled as much with trepidation as anticipation.

"Well," Irish ordered, "roll this thing, boy!"

David pushed the throttles up and taxied onto the grass runway. As he aligned himself with centerline, he slowly advanced the throttles to takeoff power. The twin R-985s dug in, propelling them down the runway at an exciting rate. At sixty knots, he raised the tail. Irish called out V-1 at the speed of ninety knots—it meant there was no stopping if they lost an engine.

Just as David was rotating, to his horror, Irish reached up and pulled the fuel mixture of engine number two to idle cut-off, shutting it down. With only one engine producing thrust, the aircraft yawed wildly. Flying sideways dangerously close to the ground, it stopped climbing.

"You better get this thing flying straight," Irish commented calmly.

David wrestled in opposite rudder, finally getting the tail to follow the nose. He grasped the landing gear handle and yanked it to the up position. Still, the aircraft would not climb!

"You better get that propeller feathered," Irish added, still sounding disconnected from the precarious situation. David immediately complied by pulling the prop lever all the way aft, still fearing for his life. Slowly, the Beechcraft began to climb.

"Put five degrees angle of bank into the good engine," Irish advised. "It will climb better."

David sweated profusely, straining to keep the rudder deflected enough for balanced flight.

"Trim the rudder, knucklehead."

He spun the rudder trim wheel, cursing himself for not thinking about it first. With the rudder trimmed all the way into the good engine, the climb became just short of comfortable. Once they had climbed to 2,000 feet over the city of Dallas, Irish restarted the number two engine. David quickly re-trimmed and powered up number two slowly, then continued a normal climb to an altitude of 8,000 feet. At their cruising altitude, he trimmed the aircraft for 120 knots, set cruise power, closed the cowls and shudders, and got out his map.

He and Irish had spent hours plotting their routes at his mother's dining room table after the barbecue. Irish's plan was to spend the first two days navigating by pilotage, simple reference to the ground. They picked prominent checkpoints: lakes, rivers, bridges, and unusual geologic features. While preparing the charts they drew lines from point to point, with the course and time between each, a basic DR plot. DR stood for dead reckoning, which was only accurate when adjusted for winds. If they lost reference to the ground due to clouds, they could turn to the new course at the appropriate time; it was little more than an educated guess.

A common error for fledgling navigators was looking at a feature on the ground and then to the chart to find it, thus turning early or late, leaving the DR plot. Leaving the DR plot threw the plan out the window and always resulted in the same result, a lost aircraft.

"Chart to ground, David."

"What?"

"Study the chart, know what is coming and when, and never leave the DR plot unless you are absolutely positive you are off course. Normal winds will not blow you that far off from one point to the next. Plus, you can look at the ground and see your drift adjusting for it as best you can. Trust the DR plot!"

David just couldn't—a lake was a lake; a bridge, a bridge. He kept turning early, chasing a similar checkpoint. Exasperated, Irish took control of the twin Beech.

"I got it."

Visibly deflating in his seat, David raised his hands, as much in acknowledgment of the shift in control as in defeat to the combination of geography and trigonometry.

Irish aggressively pushed the nose over and pulled back on course, letting the speed build in the descent to get them back on time. Closing on the navigation checkpoint within ten seconds of their planned timeline, he leveled out barely 500 feet above the trees.

"Okay, David, that train trestle is this checkpoint." Irish pointed to the chart and then the bridge. "We are back on time, so turn and get us back on speed and course, and get your head out."

14:21 Local, 05JUL (20:21 GMT, 05JUL)
Naval Air Station, Pensacola, Florida

First Sergeant M.L. Paillou stood rigidly at attention, precisely three feet in front of the desk of the officer in charge of Aviation Officer Candidates School. His uniform was impeccable; it fit perfectly. The addition of a single pound would have made it too tight, but there was no chance of that. His khaki shirt and tie were highly starched under a green tunic with an over-the-shoulder Sam Brown belt. Topping it off was a drill instructor's campaign cover, commonly referred to as a Smokey the Bear hat.

Paillou willed himself not to sweat in the mid-summer humidity of Pensacola. At the desk sat a Navy lieutenant studying his service record. Obviously distracted, he shoved it aside, instead looking directly at the ribbons over the left pocket of the first sergeant's jacket. It was Paillou's résumé, posted for all to read, and it was an impressive one. In a glance the lieutenant could see that Paillou was a warrior of experience. The top row alone showed a Silver Star, Bronze Star, and Purple Heart, endorsement enough for Lieutenant Stutzman.

Out of his peripheral vision, Paillou read the lieutenant's résumé as well.

He caught sight of enough to know that below the wings of a naval aviator hung the testament of aerial battle. A Navy lieutenant is the equivalent of a captain in other services; the rank of captain in the Navy was reserved for the skippers of capital ships and equal to a full colonel. This lieutenant was obviously a salty dog.

"Well, First Sergeant," Stutzman said, "I suppose you are about as thrilled as I am to be here in the back echelon?"

"It'll give me a chance to heal, sir," Paillou barked, moving only his jaw. "Then I hope to return to the fight in the Pacific."

"Don't we all, First Sergeant? But until then, we are stuck here transforming civilians into naval aviators. I'm giving you Battalion One—BAT I. The knuckleheads will be yours as will the other non-coms, twelve weeks a class. You teach them to be officers, and I'll teach them to fly. I'm an old salt; I've been around long enough to know who really runs the military. You run your BAT as you see fit, in accordance with AOCS regulations. I'm not going to micro-manage you; tell me what you need to do your job and I'll get it. The command sergeant major will be your direct super. I fly a lot over at De' Vale Field, so I'm not around much."

So far so good, thought Paillou.

16:38 Local, 05JUL (20:38 GMT, 05JUL)
Northeast Texas

David took control of the aircraft, turning to the pre-planned heading and slowing to 120 knots indicated. He knew that at this low altitude, his indicated and true airspeed would be the same. He set cruise power and re-trimmed the aircraft for hands-off flight, and scanned his map. At this low altitude, any ground features would have to be almost directly on course for him to see them, thus would limit the distractions.

"What's our next intermediate checkpoint?" queried Irish.

David looked at the chart.

"We cross a railroad track."

"At what time?"

"Ten seconds from now."

"Look for the tracks."

As the railroad tracks came into view, Irish barked more commands.

"Look at the chart. How can we tell if we are on course?"

David studied the chart closely.

"A crossing, there should be a road crossing!"

"Bingo, now find it on the ground."

David looked out the front windscreen, excited that he was starting to understand. He had begun to think he couldn't find his own rump with two hands. Irish smiled. He loved to watch the enthusiasm of a young aviator when the clue light came on.

"There it is," David declared.

"So how are we looking?" Irish asked.

"We will pass to the right of the checkpoint," David responded.

"What is the wind doing to us?

"Pushing us left to right."

Irish nodded his head in agreement, "Exactly. Correct by crossing over the top on course."

David quickly turned the aircraft to fly over the checkpoint and turned to the pre-planned course.

"Hack the time," Irish added as they marked on top.

David noted the time on the aircraft clock and checked it against the planned time on his flight log.

"Still ten seconds fast."

"What's that mean to us?" Irish encouraged a response.

David thought for a moment.

"Quickly," Irish prodded. "We must adjust."

"Quartering tail wind, coming from the left."

"Exactly. Now correct for it."

David eased in a correction for the wind, adjusting five degrees to the left of his planned course and slowing five knots.

"Too much," exclaimed Irish. "We don't want to overcorrect. Try just a couple of knots and a couple of degrees on the heading."

David re-corrected. "How do you figure the right amount?" he asked.

Irish chuckled more to himself than David, the howl of the engines drowning out the sound. Raising his voice above the noise, he added, "Well, Davy-boy, I'd love to feed you some cock and bull equation, but to be honest I've never been able to do math in the airplane. I feel it."

"Feel it?"

"Yeah," Irish responded. "If I'm a little bit off, I make a little correction; a lot, I make a big one. We have no instant check for our progress. If the correction is too big, we can miss our next checkpoint. If that happens, we are playing a guessing game—not good in navigation. It must be an absolute as much as possible. That being said, I have seen guys so caught up in working equations, they wander right over their checkpoint and never see it. You have to keep the big picture."

"Big picture?"

"Yeah, big picture. What direction are we going?"

David scanned his instrument panel and glanced down at his chart.

"Zero-eight-eight degrees."

"Big picture," Irish demanded.

"East?" he replied sheepishly.

Irish nodded. "How fast?"

"A hundred-twenty knots indicated."

"What if your compasses failed? Or let's say, just for argument's sake, you got the entire instrument panel shot out?"

David stared back in disbelief at the question. Irish swept his arm in front of the windscreen toward the Earth beyond.

"Come on, David. Think. You have to think to stay alive. It's morning—how do we maintain an easterly course?"

The hint sparked cognition.

"Fly toward the sun."

"Yes. How do we sweeten it up?"

Again, David stared back, not comprehending the question.

"What did we learn about farm fields?"

He smiled. "They run north-south and east-west."

Irish nodded in agreement. "Big picture."

David sat quietly, digesting this simple yet profound concept. "How do you determine airspeed?" he asked.

Irish smiled. "Power plus attitude equals performance."

He said no more, preferring to let David figure it out for himself. Again, the trainee drew within, then replied, straining his voice against the engines.

"In level flight, 24 inches of MAP, manifold air pressure, and 2200 RPM will give us 120 knots."

"Yes," replied Irish. "And we further know that 120 knots is two nautical miles a minute. Simple, isn't it?"

David laughed over the clamor of the R-985 engines. "If you say so, Irish."

He went back to managing his flight, measuring the progress from intermediate points and utilizing small corrections. A few minutes later they hit the turn point and turned northeast for Hot Springs, Arkansas. David surprised Irish with a question.

"How do you land without instruments?"

Irish reveled in the fact that David had kept thinking while he was flying as well as navigating. He turned in his copilot seat to face David while he thought about his answer. Finally, he spoke with another riddle.

"Well that depends on whether you are a poet or an engineer."

David responded to the comment with a look that made Irish hoot with laughter.

"Here's the deal, laddie: some pilots fly by feel, some by calculus. There is an age-old debate on who is the superior pilot, the poet or the engineer? I'm a poet."

"I still don't get it, Irish."

Irish retreated into contemplation, trying to form proper words for such an esoteric subject. "I sit low in the saddle."

"I noticed," said David. "Why?"

"Two reasons, actually. One, it forces me to scan down the runway when I flare during a landing. If you fixate on your intended landing point, you will lose depth perception and plunk it on. The second reason is the answer to your question: on approach the aircraft has a stable position. If we get slow, what does it do?'

"It comes up," responded David.

Irish nodded again; it was easier than trying to speak over the volume of the engines. "If it comes up too far, then what?" he asked.

"You stall the wing," David replied instantly.

"I sit so if the nose comes way up, I lose sight of the landing area—the poor man's airspeed indicator."

"How does an engineer do it?"

"Precise, memorized power settings to precise altitudes. Same result, more work."

David again slipped into his inner self. Irish had become used to it, still waters he chose not to disturb. After a few moments of silence, the young pilot spoke again.

"J.T. is an engineer, isn't he?"

"Absolutely! You have just identified my nemesis in the great debate."

"And my father?" David asked quietly, his question almost lost to the drone of the radial engines.

"Your father was a poet laureate, a true artist." Irish refused to let melancholy enter the day. He sat forward searching the horizon. "There, the field is twelve o'clock!" he shouted, pointing to Hot Springs Airport. He began to rub his hands together excitedly, like a child about to receive a gift.

"Start us down, leave the power up!" He slapped David on the back. "Hot Springs, hot toddies, and hot ladies. Hot damn, boy, push up the power!"

06:18 Local, 06JUL (22:18 GMT, 05JUL)
The Jungle, The Philippines

Nogushi's bellicose ranting abruptly ceased when he saw the reason none of the guard detail was on watch. There in the still, fetid air hung five of his men. They neither twisted nor swung. Motionless, they dangled from the jungle canopy, their bodies elongated, drawn by the Earth's gravity.

The sight had a chilling effect on his men. They were used to being the hunter, not the hunted. A cold drop of sweat ran down Captain Nogushi's temple. Before fear could fully grip them, a single grenade landed in the middle of the Japanese camp. When the smoke cleared, three more of his men lay lifeless, crumpled, their blood soaking into the jungle floor. His troops returned undisciplined, panicked fire, but the single Negrito tribesman had already been welcomed safely back into the dark arms of the harsh, tropical forest.

18:22 Local, 05JUL (22:22 GMT, 05JUL)
Hot Springs, Arkansas

The Beechcraft bounced not once, but twice, upon arrival at the municipal airport. Irish was so preoccupied looking toward the terminal that he made no comment. In fact, he didn't seem to notice at all.

"There they are! There they are—oh, goddesses of beauty and delight."

David slowed the Beech twin and stole a glance toward the terminal. Even at a distance their beauty was apparent, strikingly so. Momentarily dumbstruck, David let the aircraft drift off centerline.

Irish felt the imbalance and snapped, "Don't kill us just yet, sport."

He returned his attention to the two lovelies and waved to the tallest, with the auburn hair. David regained his composure and straightened out the UC-45J. They taxied up next to the yellow Marathon cab and shut down the engines. Irish was instantly out of the cockpit, leaving David to run the shutdown checklist by himself.

When he joined them next to the cab, he couldn't stop staring at the ladies. Their beauty was breathtaking. Irish opened the back door of the cab for them and helped them in.

He motioned to the front. "David, up front with our chauffer."

As the two women slid into the backseat, Irish tugged at David's collar and whispered into his ear.

"Stop staring, bub, they'll think something is wrong with you."

David looked sideways at Irish, who winked, shoved him into the front seat and moved to the back door, all in one smooth motion.

"Ladies, may I join you?"

The redhead glided to the far door, motioning him to sit in the middle. She nodded toward David, raising a finely tweezed brow in question.

"Ladies," said Irish, "I'd like to introduce my godson, a mere lad of seventeen."

"Eighteen," David piped in from the front seat.

Supple lips formed a feline smile, green eyes dancing in delight.

"It is so like you Catholic boys," said the redhead, "to be the good shepherd."

CHAPTER 15

18:43 Local, 05JUL (22:43 GMT, 05JUL)
Arlington Hotel, Hot Springs, Arkansas

Twin towers of the Arlington Hotel and spa rose into the soft blue Arkansas sky. David looked up at them through the windshield of the cab with just a passing interest; his attention lay elsewhere. The cab stopped directly in front of the grand entrance. Irish helped both ladies out of the automobile with surprising panache from the middle seat.

Stepping out on the redhead's side, he whispered into her ear. She threw back her head with beckoning laughter. David was bewitched by the auburn beauty with alabaster skin.

"Hi, my name is Nancy," said a voice behind him.

Startled, realizing he had been caught staring again, he turned and took the blonde's outstretched hand, stammering his name in response. She smiled sweetly at his naiveté. Her platinum hair and red dress gave her the look of a movie star. Its tight fit left little doubt what ecstasy lay beneath. Yet he still stole glances at the redhead; she was captivating, intoxicating.

"I'm sorry," said Irish, "my manners—how remiss of me. David, may I present Alexandria and Nancy. Ladies, this young squire is David Brennan, student aviator extraordinaire."

Alexandria stalked around the cab and took his hand, pulling herself close. She pressed her body against his as she kissed him on the cheek, whispering in sweet breath: "Hello, David."

"Hello," he somehow managed, hypnotized by her green eyes. His aviator's scan had registered her face in an instant; she wore only enough makeup to accentuate her natural beauty. They locked eyes for a long moment, not with the innocence of love but the hunt of passion. David was not the hunter.

Irish observed with amusement. He cleared his throat and spoke to re-establish his schedule.

"I have reserved two adjoining suites in my name," he told the two women. "Please make yourselves comfortable. Freshen up, and we will meet you in the lobby bar for a cocktail in one hour."

A bellman joined them on the driveway. Irish tipped him with a ten-dollar bill and pushed David back into the cab. He ordered the cabbie to their first stop: a local haberdashery. Since David didn't know what a haberdashery was, he didn't question the trip until they stopped in front of the clothing store.

"Why are we stopping here?"

"Because you need a wardrobe," replied Irish. "Sneakers, jeans, and T-shirts aren't cutting it."

Irish quickly ushered him in the door where they were immediately met by a handlebar-mustachioed man in his fifties, wearing a tweed suit.

"Captain Myers, how nice of you to visit us, how can I help you?"

"Good evening, Whadingham, great to see you. I have a rush job for you. This is my godson, David. He needs the works, from swim trunks to dinner jacket. Any chance we can do it in forty-five minutes?"

Whadingham looked at David closely.

"We may get lucky," he said. "He looks to be a 40 slim, exactly."

"Splendid," replied Irish. "Oh yes—he will need a set of luggage as well."

"As you wish, Captain." Whadingham snapped his fingers and two assistants scurried out of the back room.

"David, do what you are told here," instructed Irish. "I'm off to the jewelers and the florist. Questions?" David shook his head.

"Outstanding, I'll be right back." Irish was out the door and into the taxi in a flash. Whadingham shook his head in amusement.

"Big dates tonight, eh?"

"I guess so," replied David, still trying to stabilize in the whirlwind of Irish Myer's wake.

07:15 Local, 06JUL (23:15 GMT, 05JUL)
The Jungle, The Philippines

Nogushi was fighting to maintain composure; his men were rattled and so was he. He didn't dare split his men again, so he ordered them to don their rucksacks and all their gear. They had already cut down the five bodies and hurriedly buried them without ceremony. They moved out immediately, in a tactical formation, in the direction the fleeing Negrito had taken.

Butler and Donnelly watched them from the opposite side of the Japanese camp. They had doubled back after the grenade attack.

"They are going to be moving slowly with all that gear," said Donnelly with a smile.

"Yes they will," replied Butler, handing him his canteen of black jungle water. Donnelly took a long pull.

"How long are we gonna let them flail around out there?"

Butler smiled.

"I've got a couple of the Negritos leaving an obvious trail—uphill, of course. We'll let them wear themselves out. Let's get out some chow for the men and relax."

"Yes sir. So what's the plan, Captain?" asked Donnelly as he stood up.

"We will hit them again tonight—one hit, the company sergeant—then withdraw."

"I mean the big picture," said Donnelly. "They still outnumber us three-to-one."

Butler reached into his rucksack, pulled out a small C-rat can of Vienna sausages, and began to ratchet his church-key can opener around the edge. Prying the lid open, he fished one of the little grey-pink sausages out and offered the can to Donnelly. The sergeant took one, popped the whole pasty mass into his mouth, and sat back down.

"Did I tell you what my major was in college?" Butler asked between smacks.

Donnelly nodded as he took another offered sausage. "Military history."

"Actually, I had a double major. Psychology was the other."

The sergeant shrugged, washing down his meal with jungle water, straining the grit with his teeth, and then spitting it.

"So?"

"So, have you read any history about battlefield routs—I'm talking total decimations?"

"Yeah," said Donnelly. "They usually came from being outnumbered."

Butler laughed.

"Actually, many times the smaller force was the victor. What was a constant was panic."

"Panic?" Donnelly asked, taking another drink from the canteen.

"Yes, panic—primordial fear, a total loss of control and military bearing." Butler took another grey meat stick from the can. "We will spook them, get them to run."

Donnelly plucked out another meat morsel.

"And then what?"

"We will shoot them down like dogs."

19:45 Local, 05JUL (23:45 GMT, 05JUL)
Arlington Hotel

Irish and David swept into the bar dressed to the nines. The place was more intimate than luxurious, brighter than most bars. It was alternately lit by soft white light emanating from small brass lamps at each table as well as indirect lighting overhead. The ladies sat in a quiet corner bathed in the clean illumination. Alexandria presented her hand like a prima ballerina, and Irish dutifully kissed it.

"You boys clean up well," she quipped.

"It's all about the inspiration," he replied. "And might I add, no man has been as inspired since Michelangelo carved the Venus de Milo."

Alexandria surrendered her catlike smile. "Irish, you are a silver-tongued bastard, aren't you?"

As they sat down, a waiter joined them and Irish ordered for the group. For the next two hours they snacked on shrimp and caviar, enjoying tasty cocktails as well. At 20:30, Irish called for the group to adjourn to the hot mineral pools of the spa.

Irish and David arrived first and hopped into the water in their brand new swimming trunks. Again, a waiter appeared instantly. Irish ordered a magnum of French champagne with four glasses and settled into the water up to his neck. Alexandria and Nancy made their entrance, hair down, in flowing terry cloth robes provided by the spa.

Alexandria walked elegantly, one foot directly in front of the other like a New York model, toward the pool. Stopping at the edge, she let the robe fall away revealing a form-fit black swimsuit. Intoxicated by Alexandria's aura, David didn't even notice Nancy's equally provocative red swimsuit.

The pop of the champagne cork broke the spell. Alexandria accepted a glass from the waiter and slipped gracefully into the magic water. Irish rose and lent his hand to Nancy as she joined them. The warm water soothed their flight-stiffened bodies, and the champagne added a medicinal quality that bordered on euphoria.

"Nancy, how goes the dissertation?" queried Irish.

"Oh, it's half-political, Irish," she responded. "You know how that is."

"You good ol' boys don't like the competition," Alexandria quipped.

"Hey, don't count me in that group," he said. "Dumb women bore me."

David looked up from his champagne, confused.

"What's a dissertation?" he asked.

"Nancy is studying for her doctorate in American Literature," Alexandria purred with pride, her mouth just barely above the water level.

"A doctor?" asked David in surprise.

"Not a medical doctor, David," replied Nancy, "a PhD. I'm studying to be a professor of American Literature."

"Nancy has a photographic memory," beamed Irish. "She was a child prodigy, truth be told."

Nancy shrugged her shoulders and slipped deeper into the water. "I just have the ability to see what I've read in my mind, that's all."

"Not by a long shot," Alexandria shot back. "Don't believe it, David. Her insights and interpretations of literature are quite respected in academia—reluctantly, in most cases." There was a hint of irritation in her voice.

"How did you all meet?" asked David.

"We are all Rhodes Scholars," Nancy replied, looking a bit sheepish.

"That's our little secret, sport," Irish added.

"Wow—I didn't think such beautiful women could be so smart," David blurted as the champagne took effect. Then he blushed, embarrassed, and Alexandria smiled at his boyish charm. David changed the subject quickly in an attempt to cover his clumsiness.

"What school do you go to, Nancy?"

"University of the Ozarks. It's about a hundred miles from here."

"Presbyterians, they run this country, you know." Irish winked at David, goading Alexandria. "They have all the big money."

"That's not what Hitler says," David replied.

"Hitler is an idiot, a paperhanger," Irish sniffed. "Flunked out of art school, for God's sake."

"I'd remind you," Alexandria countered, "that idiot has taken over half the world, Irish."

"So he's a savant; we will fix that. Just give us a little time." Irish grew defensive.

"Really, a world conqueror is an idiot savant? Alexander the Great would be so disappointed, not to mention Napoleon, Charlemagne, Caesar, Genghis and Kublai Khan—"

"Okay, okay, Alexandria," Irish put up his hands in mock surrender. "You proved your point." He sank deeper into the mineral pool.

Alexandria smiled in victory. "Back to the original subject: it is the oldest university in Arkansas, David. It was founded in 1834—indeed, by Presbyterians," she shot a hard glance at Irish. "Nancy is on the faculty."

After another hour of intellectual discussion that at times grew animated, Irish knew he must move the group along or it would be an early night. He coaxed them from the luxurious water. As Alexandria was stepping out of the pool, she slipped, falling backward into David's arms. He caught her, cradling her supple body with his. David's body tingled with excitement as his blood pressure soared, coursing through his body and nudging Alexandria with the consequence. He quickly set her on the edge and retreated into the water. Her predatory smile returned and she winked at David.

The Fountain Room was the quieter and more discreet of the two formal dining rooms; the Venetian was the place to be seen in Hot Springs—definitely not an option. Irish preferred the Fountain Room anyway, for its intimacy. He felt comfortable in the European-accented décor and loved the gourmet food. He perused the menu intently as the others sipped cocktails, then picked up the wine list and studied it. Finally satisfied, he waved the waiter over.

"My good man," he intoned, "we'd like to start with lobster bisque and then move on to the Peking duck. And for the main course, filet mignon with Béarnaise sauce. The wine list is quite nice; we'll start with a Saint Château 1936, and then with the main course a fine burgundy. Pick your favorite for us."

As expected, the dinner was exquisite. David followed Irish's lead on everything from fork choice to wine swirl. Shy by nature, David was impressed with the ease and panache with which Irish operated. He was trying to be careful and not get drunk, trying to be calm and cool like his mentor, but he couldn't hide his boyish enthusiasm. He had never eaten food that tasted so good or been with women who looked so beautiful.

Alexandria watched with a wry smile. After dinner, Irish ordered cognac and Cuban cigars. She didn't wait. She eased out of her chair, stopping behind

Irish to whisper into his ear. A lock of hair fell across her forehead as she leaned down. Her eyes held David's.

"I'm going to release this butterfly from his chrysalis," she murmured.

David fought to maintain Alexandria's gaze as her dress's neckline opened, revealing what was beneath. Irish cackled loudly as she walked to David and led the tipsy boy away from the table by the hand.

23:48 Local, 06JUL (15:48 GMT, 06JUL)
The Jungle, The Philippines

Butler jerked awake, still seeing the accusing eyes of the young Filipina. She came to him often now in his sleep. He touched the crucifix that hung around his neck and sat up amid the jungle foliage. Sergeant Donnelly sat three feet away, legs crossed.

"You okay, Captain?" he asked in his thick South Boston accent. "You're not getting twitchy on me, are you?" He tossed a can of Spam to Butler, who caught it even though the only light was from a partial moon.

"It's open," said the sergeant, "but I haven't knocked the can-snot off it yet."

Butler pulled out his KA-BAR fighting knife and sliced off a chunk of Spam, flinging off the fatty slime with his finger.

"Oh—I'm sorry, Sergeant," he cracked. "I should have saved that for you."

Donnelly laughed, looking at the glowing hands on the dial of his watch.

"We should be hitting them any minute," he said. "Question."

"Go ahead," Butler replied between chews.

"Why the silent kill? Why not just toss another grenade and really rattle their cage?"

He could see Butler's teeth as he smiled in the dark jungle night.

"You think waking up next to a dead man isn't going to rattle that Jap captain? He's the key—we have to get to him. Waking up next to his dead sergeant will let him know we can get to him any time we want. Now it will be personal. You got any crackers?"

Donnelly tossed over a can.

"They're limp but edible."

CHAPTER 16

11:48 Local, 06JUL (17:48 GMT, 06JUL)
Hot Springs Regional Airport

As the Pratt and Whitney Junior Wasp R-985 engines popped to life, David didn't seem to notice. His full attention and focus was on the statuesque lady standing by the cab. He waved a childlike wave; she smiled wide and blew an exaggerated kiss. He realized then that he would never see her again, certainly never be with her again, but she would inhabit his memories and dreams forever.

"Who is she?" David asked above the rough idle of the engines.

"Who?"

"Her!" David nodded toward Alexandria.

"Oh, you mean the governor's wife?"

As David's face went pale, Irish laughed heartily.

"Don't worry, knucklehead, he doesn't care. Rumor has it he doesn't like women at all—know what I mean?"

David looked at Irish, wild-eyed and clueless.

"Never mind, sport. It works for them. She's discreet and he's still the governor. Did you learn any new tricks?"

"I learned tricks I did not know existed, Irish."

"So how was it?" Irish pried.

"It was…wonderful!" David turned and faced Irish. "I don't think I'll ever be the same."

"I expect not, David," Irish said between laughs. "I truly expect not. That is the best part of associating with really smart women, young man. They are not inhibited by societal norms; they are free!"

As the twin Beech lifted off, Irish wagged the wings in good-bye. David sat quietly, lost in thought.

"Hey, snap out of it!" Irish yelled over the noise of climb power. "You got it—take us to Rolla, Missouri."

"Rolla? Why Rolla?" David asked as he took control of the aircraft. "What could possibly be there?"

"I've got a cousin there. She works at a little radio station—K-HITs, or something like that."

David laughed and shook his head.

"Hey, I'm not kidding," said Irish. "Bunni is my first cousin."

"Bunni? Yeah, sure, Irish."

"Just drive, Romeo. You are starting to piss me off!"

13:32 Local, 06JUL (18:32 GMT, 06JUL)
Washington, DC

C.R. Smith and J.T. sat in a small, cramped office in the damp basement of the White House. They were poring over documents: aircraft orders, manning requirements, all the administrative requirements to build an Air Force from scratch. Stacked on the corner of the simple metal desk were the officer records of over twenty Air Corps colonels.

Setting down an aircraft order to the Douglass Aircraft company, C.R. asked, "Did you get a chance to look through the records for a wing commander?"

J.T. glanced at the stack. "Yep."

"What did you think?"

"Spit and polish, a bunch of seagulls"—aviator slang for a pilot that rarely gets off the ground; you have to throw rocks at them to get them to fly—"not 1,000 hours of flight time for any of them."

C.R. nodded in agreement. "What do you suggest?"

J.T. slid back in his chair, one of the rusty wheels squealing in protest, and looked his old friend squarely in the eyes. "What do you want me to suggest, boss?"

C.R. didn't reply. The men knew each other far too well to dance around a subject.

"I want my own deputy and chief of maintenance," J.T. said, breaking the silence.

"Who do you have in mind?"

"Irish and the Chief."

C.R. smiled.

"Are you going to leave anyone at American Airlines?"

12:53 Local, 06JUL (18:53 GMT, 06JUL)
Mississippi River Valley

Irish had plotted a route up the great Mississippi River valley. It was truly a God-given day; the vast sky was absolutely cloudless, not a speck of dust or haze hung in the atmosphere. The jagged, meandering path of the river surprised David. Oxbow lakes littered the valley. He could sense the power of the expansive river. Hundreds of yards across, it snaked through a valley that was miles wide. White bluffs bordered the river valley on both sides, its bountiful, flat bottom land bursting with fields of grain and vegetables. Texas rivers of David's youth were creeks by comparison.

"It looks like the river could fill this whole valley if it wanted to," he said.

"It can," Irish replied, "and has."

"What about the farms and towns?"

"They wash away."

David looked up and down the valley. "Then why would you live there?"

"River towns have to be on the water to survive. This watery highway moves grain, timber, whatever to New Orleans and through it to the rest of the world. An occasional flood is a small price to pay for a flourishing town."

David was not convinced. "That's stupid!"

"So is screaming through the sky at 200 miles an hour," snapped Irish.

David offered no comeback. They got a time hack over Cape Girardeau and pressed on toward St. Louis. Twenty minutes later Irish pointed to the horizon.

"There it is: River City."

"Why River City?"

"French trappers settled in the area where the Illinois and Missouri Rivers join the Mississippi." Irish pointed north. "See where the Illinois joins from the east and the Missouri from the west?"

"Yeah, I see them."

"Head toward the Missouri. We are going direct to Rolla from here."

Irish reached down to the coffee crank-type handle of the NDB radio and ground in 1120 on the dial. A sports announcer's voice reverberated through the overhead speaker.

"Hey, hey," Irish said. "There is a Cardinals game on. Excellent, we can listen all the way to Rolla. I love Stan the Man."

"You like baseball?" asked David.

"I'm called Irish, but I'm American now—red, white and blue. This is a country of fresh starts. Look around you, young man, this is America."

06:06 Local, 07JUL (23:06 GMT, 06JUL)
The Philippines

"They're on the move again, Captain. Kind of frantic, too." Sergeant Donnelly beamed with a most devious grin. "I think you are starting to get to them. Shall we hit them now?"

Captain Butler stood, stretching his back.

"No, not yet. Let's run them around some more and get 'em good and tired."

"Yes, sir. I'll get the Negritos on it. You want another circle?"

"Yeah. Why should we tire ourselves chasing them? Let's run them around and bring them back to us."

"Done deal, sir." Donnelly disappeared into the jungle, leaving Butler to squat with his ghosts.

CHAPTER 17

09:40 Local, 08JUL (15:40 GMT, 08JUL)
American Airlines Operations Office, Dallas, Texas

Hass-man and J.T. literally bumped into one another in the doorway of the American Airlines operations office. Both wore the uniform of an Army Air Corps officer—Hass-man with the rank of captain and J.T., the birds of a full colonel. Each also wore a look of surprise.

Gathering himself, Hass-man snapped off a salute that J.T. returned, shaking his head with an approving smile.

"I don't know why I'm surprised," he said. "Where are you headed, Captain Hass?"

"Eighth Air Force, European theater. I'll be flying the new P-47 Thunderbolt."

"See you there, hombre. I'll buy you a beer in London."

"And I'll buy you one in Berlin."

"Deal, Hass-man!"

16:00 Local, 09JUL (22:00 GMT, 09JUL)
Atlanta, Georgia

Day two and three of the cross-country trip were devoted to training. Irish and David had spent both nights in luxury hotels but by the time they ate dinner it was time for bed. In Memphis, they watched the ducks march through the lobby of the Bradbury Hotel. In Atlanta, they stayed at the grande dame of Peach Street, the Georgian Terrace Hotel. Its stone terrace dining area provided an enchanting setting that made David think of Alexandria and how she fit its ambiance—and how he did not.

On day four Irish arranged for a late checkout at the Georgian Terrace, and they slept in. David thought it was a sign his tutelage was nearly complete. He was wrong. When they arrived at the Atlanta airport he noticed two changes in the routine. First, there was a canvas bag rigged up on his side of the cockpit, suspended from the overhead panel and covering all the windows. Second, they had a comely passenger waiting for them.

David looked in the cockpit, inspecting the bag arrangement. He didn't like the looks of it. "How am I supposed to see?"

"You're not." David definitely didn't like the sound of that. Irish either didn't notice his discomfort or didn't care.

"You will navigate by reference to your aircraft instruments only." Before David could respond, Irish went off to tend to his passenger.

Lined up on the runway, engines idling, the UC-45J sat motionless even though it had been cleared for takeoff.

"You have got to be kidding me, Irish!"

"I most certainly am not. Now roll this crate." David eased the power up slowly.

"Stay on the runway center line by referencing your compass card and maintaining a constant heading. We're holding up traffic—let's go!" Irish demanded.

The UC-45J snaked all over the runway, finally struggling into the sky just in time as it neared the runway edge. David's control inputs were rough and uncoordinated. "Hey, David," Irish advised, poking his head into the canvas bag, "you don't fly it any different. Use the artificial horizon like you would use the horizon of the Earth. It's the same, just smaller. Power plus attitude still equals performance. Six degrees nose up, with climb power set, will give you climb-out airspeed if you keep the wings level and the aircraft balanced. As a bonus you will hold a constant heading. Sweeten them up by scanning each instrument individually, rapidly."

David poured out sweat as he fumbled with charts, changing NDB, non directional beacon, frequencies and flying the aircraft. He didn't seem to have enough time or hands and was consistently behind.

Adding to his nightmare, Irish had multiple practice approaches planned en route. He would fly to the field's radio navigation aid following the needle on his compass. When it swung off his wingtip, it meant they were overhead, and he would then fly outbound on a pre-set course, holding the tail of the needle on that specific compass bearing.

Irish incessantly chirped out directions in the background: "Head of the needle falls, tail rises—push the head of the needle to your desired course, pull the tail. Did you start the clock?"

After a minute-and-a-half outbound, David turned thirty degrees off the course for the procedure turn, timed another minute as he descended to the charted altitude and turned back toward the final course to intercept it. Once past the final approach fix, he would configure the aircraft for landing and then descend to the MDA, minimum descent altitude. After a predetermined elapsed time, if they didn't see the runway, they would perform a missed approach and divert to another field.

Normally an aircraft would descend out of the overcast already configured for landing, pick up the runway visually, and land. However, the large canvas bag blocking David's vision guaranteed that the norm was not possible. So, each of his approaches ended in the most work-intensive procedure of instrument flying: a missed approach.

First order of business was to get away from the ground, thus a climb was initiated. Next, he had to reconfigure for cruise flight and turn toward the divert field. Radio transmissions were required as landing gear and flaps were retracted. It was always a handful, even for an experienced crew.

David did the drill over and over again as they made their way to the east coast. Finally just above MDA going into Washington National Airport, Irish took down the bag. It was dark. David had hardly noticed, under the bag for the last five hours. To his left was the Capitol, defiantly lit in the face of war. He saw the Lincoln, Washington, and Jefferson Memorials—even the Capitol dome was bathed in white light.

Irish brought him back to task. "OK, land and let's get something to eat."

Famished and wrung out, David was more focused on a burger and fries than flying the twin Beech. Twenty feet above the runway, his airspeed began to decay.

"Watch your speed, Junior," warned Irish, but his caution came too late. They dropped like an anvil onto the runway.

"Shit!" David exclaimed in surprise.

"Can't stop flying just because you are tired," observed Irish.

21:47 Local, 09JUL (02:47 GMT, 10JUL)
Washington, DC

With the most delicious hamburger he had ever enjoyed digesting slowly in his belly, David sat in the claustrophobic cockpit of the Beech. He was beginning to hate the aircraft. In fact, he was questioning his decision to fly in the first place.

Instead of reinstalling the canvas bag, Irish folded it and threw it behind the aft seat. He joined their passenger in the back and snapped closed a curtain just behind the cockpit.

"Take us to New York, my good man, and don't conserve fuel."

Carefully lining up on runway 1-9, David ran up the power smoothly once cleared for takeoff. As he raised the landing gear, he heard the distinctive sound of a Champagne bottle popping its cork in the passenger compartment. The effervescent release of the bubbly was accompanied by high-pitched giggling, barely audible over the roar of the engines. As the gear retracted into the wing, he began a tight turn over the city to a northerly heading, direct to the Big Apple.

"What altitude do you want, Irish?"

"Anything above five thousand. We are joining the mile-high club!"

Gladly trading the dark night for the claustrophobic confines of the canvas blind, David comfortably trimmed the aircraft for a steady climb to altitude. He was quite content to fly without a critic sitting next to him, especially in the smooth, clear air of the eastern seaboard.

Clear skies began to give way to cirrus, then stratus clouds near Philadelphia. Obscured by a dark cloud deck below him, the ground would provide no navigation for his flight. Pulling out the charts, David quickly put the frequency for Philly in the NDB. Soon the stars were obscured by high cirrus as well—he now knew why Irish had not insisted on the bag. There would be no cheating now that he was under instrument meteorological conditions.

It was dark, real dark, as the clear area between the layers began to close off. In the distance David could see lightning throbbing in large cumulous clouds. A choppy ride began to deteriorate even further as they progressed toward New York.

"Irish," he called, "it is getting kind of ugly up here."

"Shut up boy, I'm busy."

A trickle of sweat rolled down David's back as the ride, buffeted by turbulence, began to turn violent. Lightning cracked, filling the cockpit with a blinding flash, and his night-adjusted pupils were shocked into blindness. He fumbled to find the thunderstorm lights, seeking their bright illumination to save all of their lives. As the turbulence turned severe, he let out a cry for help.

"Irish!" he begged.

"Just hold a constant attitude." Irish's voice was irritated. "Don't chase the altitude."

Giggles came from the rear again. David was furious. He couldn't believe their passenger had no clue how close to their demise they were. Hammered by rhythmic waves of rain and turbulence, the aircraft writhed near disaster as the giggles gave way to an almost inaudible moan. Just when he thought the aircraft would surely break apart, they were slammed with one last jolt and thrown free into clear smooth air.

Irish startled David by jumping into the co-pilot seat. "What are you whining about? It's beautiful out there."

David had to laugh, shaking his head and looking southwest at the back side of the cloud giants who had conspired to kill him. A line of them stretched to the northwest. Awe-inspiring, they were the Titans of nature, and menacing. Firing lightning bolts at each other, they fought violently for the sky—and still, he had defeated them. They had thrown their worst at him and he had emerged alive, victorious! David was ecstatic. He had cheated death and deprived the Colossals their sacrifice.

His reward was New York City at night, from the air. The sight astounded him—he never knew cities like this existed. Irish had planned an approach up New York harbor and past the Statue of Liberty. Pictures from David's grade school books didn't come close to capturing her splendor. Lady Liberty's verdigris body was a sensual beacon to all mankind. David flew close to her glow.

Turning toward Manhattan, he could see the bridges linking the island to Brooklyn, recognizing the Brooklyn Bridge from pictures. As they flew up the Hudson River, Newark was on the left and New York, the right shoreline. Both cities went right up to the edge of the river. At night the sins of overcrowding and pollution were hidden by the dark and cleansed by the city light. Like the universe, only the starry grandeur showed. Asteroids and meteors, the celestial trash, was lost in dark space.

Manhattan Island had buildings on every inch, it seemed. Surrounded by an ebony border of water, it looked like a city of the future. Descending down to 2,500 feet, they went north of the island and turned east on the base leg of their approach to New York's newest airport and the new headquarters of American Airlines: New York Municipal Airport. The local press had nicknamed it LaGuardia Field due to Mayor Fiorello LaGuardia's staunch support of the grandiose facility.

Rolling wings level on final approach to the southern-oriented runway 2-2, David couldn't help but be distracted by the backdrop of mountainous skyscrapers, shining against the night sky. In only a few hours, he had flown from God's towering edifices, pulsating with the power and fury of nature, to mankind's, illuminated with artificial light. At a glance it was a dichotomy, but beneath a cosmic segue, a true connection. David felt the tingle, the power from both the raw and harnessed electricity. This night held answers to questions he could not fathom.

"You gonna put the landing gear down, Junior?" Irish snapped.

Irish had the trio whisked into Manhattan in a black limousine, arriving at the Waldorf Astoria in record time, thanks to the motivation of a large tip. He acquiesced to an hour of prep time only after surrendering to the pouting of their pretty passenger. Their suite was so impressive David did not want to leave it, but then decided he must celebrate his victory over the thunderstorms. While he wandered around the glamorous rooms, Irish meticulously picked out a suit and tie for David to wear from his new wardrobe. After a steamy shower, in a bathroom bigger than his bedroom back home, David put on the clothes Irish had chosen for him.

In the hallway, he glanced into a mirror and was surprised how sophisticated he looked, his age hidden by the dim lighting. He felt quite confident—until they hit the prying, bright lights of Times Square. Under the revealing lights, he felt exposed, a country rube in a borrowed suit.

As they journeyed from nightclub to nightclub, David couldn't shake the fear that he would be found out, exposed as a fraud and physically thrown from the establishment. He stuck close to Irish throughout the night. What a night it was; Irish knew every nightclub in Manhattan. When the night grew long, he shifted to Irish pubs, even speaking Gaelic to the patrons and owners.

Having sortied to their max range, David realized they were now going to RTB toward their hotel. He was amused how much his thought process had changed, recognizing how Irish had planned a route out to a point, then back, ending up across the street from the Waldorf right at closing time.

CHAPTER 18

10:25 Local, 10JUL (15:25 GMT, 10JUL)
Waldorf Astoria Hotel, New York, New York

A clanging cart arriving with room service onboard announced the coming of a new day. David awoke but retreated immediately by closing his eyes. Irish banged a sterling silver serving spoon on the domed server.

"Breakfast is served. More of a brunch, actually."

The grandfather clock chimed eleven times as David surrendered, more to the glorious smell of the food than the noise. He got up and made his way to the parlor. Breakfast looked and smelled fantastic. He realized they hadn't eaten since Washington, DC As their passenger feasted on plump strawberries, he also realized that he had no idea what her name was.

New York strip steaks, Belgian waffles, French toast, thick maple-flavored bacon, eggs Benedict, and three different juices filled trays littered with strawberries. David poured a large glass of grape juice and attacked the breakfast cart with passion. Irish smiled, and his companion shook her head in amusement, as they looked on.

11:15 Local, 10JUL (16:15 GMT, 10JUL)
Perdido Key, Florida

First Sergeant Paillou squatted on the pure white beach, staring out to sea. The sand looked like granulated sugar. The soft blue ocean licked at it as if trying to take a taste. Silent—except for the soft hush of the surf, the beach was desolate. Overhead, an occasional Navy training aircraft buzzed like a fly in a quiet room.

Behind Paillou stood a small, three-bedroom house. The extra rooms sat empty, at the ready, even though he knew it was unlikely his wife and children would fill them. When things had begun to get crazy in China, he had sent them to the interior to live with her grandfather. He thought they would be safe, but the Japanese had moved so rapidly he did not know if they reached safety or not. To complicate their escape, his son was from his first wife, an American. She had died when the boy was two, and now he feared that his son would meet the same fate, along with his Chinese wife and their daughter. He prayed his worst fears would not be realized. He must get back to the Pacific, but to do that he had to get back into fighting shape. The Corps had damn near medically discharged him in Pearl due to his wounds and the flaring of malaria. They weren't too thrilled when he checked himself out of their little hospital either. Tom Shelby had covered his ass, but he had to lay low for a while.

This candy-ass tour would allow him to heal and get back into the fight. If he got lucky, he might even get into China to look for his family.

13:30 Local 10JUL (18:30 GMT, 10JUL)
LaGuardia Field, New York

Irish's traveling companion had stayed in New York City. Just as well, thought David, I can use a few less distractions. He glanced over the runway from the American hangars, watching as a Pan Am Clipper emerged from the water on the seaplane ramp. Wondering where it was coming from, he glanced over at Irish erecting the bag again, and knew where they were going. Irish flogged him all the way to Savannah, Georgia. The UC-45J's extra tanks allowed them to stay in the air for five hours; he was drained.

"Get in the back and take a nap, Davy-boy," said Irish. "We are only halfway to our destination. I'll get us fueled and get some chow."

David wasn't a napper and didn't think he would fall asleep, but instrument flying was so physically and mentally exhausting that he closed his eyes just to rest them for a minute. Irish woke him an hour-and-a-half later by handing him a ham and cheese sandwich.

09:10 Local 11JUL (01:10 GMT, 11JUL)
The Philippines

Donnelly shook Butler's shoulder, cautiously holding the muzzle of the captain's Thompson machine gun to prevent an accidental shooting: his own.

"Sir, wake up."

Butler sat up, dazed. The jungle was alive with sound; birds and monkeys chattered, calling out the warning that man approached. It didn't make sense. Too soon, he thought. Then he looked at his watch.

"I've been asleep six hours?"

"Yes, sir. Didn't see much point in waking you any sooner."

He hadn't slept that long in weeks, maybe months. Now, his mind was clear and vengeance its focus.

"How far out?" he asked.

"Two, maybe three miles. The lads say they are pretty rattled."

"Okay. Let's end this now, Sergeant."

Butler spread a map on the jungle floor, pointing at it with his KA-BAR fighting knife.

"We will hunker down the main force here, have Rubio and two of the Negritos get around behind them, hitting them here. That should put them just in front of us." Again, he pointed with his knife.

"Hit them with grenades again, but this time, hold them with automatic weapons fire. Give Rubio and the Negritos the two BARs, Browning Automatic Rifles, and make sure they keep them facing the threat axis. After five minutes, have Rubio shoot into the trees overhead."

"Then what?"

"We will form a skirmish line to the Japanese rear and simply walk up from behind and kill them."

Butler's men squatted in the jungle. They could hear as the Japanese troops closed in. The jungle life that had announced their pending arrival now fell silent. Like the warriors below them, the creatures did not want to reveal their presence. Both groups awaited with anticipation the coming carnage. All eyes in the jungle, be they human or beast, looked toward the Japanese intruders.

The concussion from grenades shattered the silence, and shrieking from the wounded joined the renewed jungle cacophony. Staccato of the automatic fire that raked the Japanese position echoed through the trees. Wild shrieking continued to build, rising to a crescendo as heavy, 7.62 caliber rounds were directed into the canopy overhead.

Butler jumped to his feet.

"Move fast," he ordered. "Leave no one alive."

The Japanese soldiers had lost all discipline, lying prone and shooting toward the perceived threat with no one watching their flank. Only one soldier noticed them emerge from cover. Butler put a single round between his eyes before walking right on top of the Japanese, shooting left and right. Dead birds and monkeys fell among them as they moved through the Japanese like a scythe. Blood flowed. The jungle floor welcomed it equally, from man and beast.

Butler was quickly upon his Japanese counterpart. Sensing his presence, Captain Nogushi turned just in time to see the butt end of a Thompson smash into his face. The ravenous jungle fell silent, satiated for the moment.

20:12 Local, 10JUL (01:12 GMT, 11JUL)
Miami, Florida

Moonlight glanced off the Atlantic, showing whitecaps and outlining Miami Beach. Irish looked jubilantly at the lively resorts that beckoned below.

"Take off that damn bag," he snapped.

"Gladly," David shot back.

"Thar she blows, laddie!" Irish's tone had softened and his boyish giddiness had returned.

"There's what?" asked David, clearly still irritated as he wrestled his heavy canvas nemesis into the backseat.

"South Beach, Davy-boy, only the wildest resort town this side of Havana. I'm talking Miami, boy!"

David shook his head, bone tired. "Count me out. I'm going to bed."

"Sleep when you're dead, knucklehead. Tonight, it's salsa. Besides, that is our hotel—you won't get any sleep anyway."

Irish pointed to a large resort with colored lights on a patio that even from their altitude of a thousand feet could be seen writhing with activity.

"Let's bump up the speed."

* * * *

David sat like a zombie on the edge of his bed. It was covered in pastel: blues, pinks, and corals that matched the décor of the room. The appealing colors had no effect on his mood. Already dressed, he combed his hair slowly in the mirror that hung on the wall.

Irish burst into the room carrying a silver service tray. He yanked off the servers, revealing Cuban flank steak, black beans, and rice with fried plantains on the side.

"Wa' la, mon ami," he said in a thick French accent as he bowed at the waist. He grabbed a large coffeepot, pouring two very dark cups. "This is Cuban coffee, son. It will get you back in the game. Here, take a bite."

As always, Irish was right. David was rejuvenated after their snack. He stood up, pulled his necktie tight, and nodded toward the door. Irish bolted out of it with David closely in trail.

09:59 Local, 11JUL (01:59 GMT, 11JUL)
The Jungle, The Philippines

Captain Nogushi sat on an ammo crate with his hands securely tied behind him. He wiped the blood from his mouth onto the shoulder of his rotting uniform and spat more onto the jungle floor. Watching it absorb, he looked with resignation at the hangman's noose that hung over his head. He was in no doubt of his fate. Serenity swept over him as he gazed around at the remains of his men, already being slowly, perceptibly consumed by the fetid soil.

Having failed the Emperor, Nogushi welcomed death, but he couldn't expect these American gangsters to allow him the honor of seppuku. Their ferocity and that of their fellow barbarians, the Filipinos, had surprised him. He thought of that as he was stood on the makeshift gallows.

Butler put the noose over his head and their eyes met. A glint of sunlight drew his attention to the crucifix around Butler's neck. Recognizing it, his eyes widened, and Butler's eyes narrowed as he kicked the ammo box from beneath the Japanese captain. Stretching tight, the rope choked Nogushi, finally breaking his neck as he flailed, and the jungle silently applauded.

22:48 Local, 10JUL (03:48 GMT, 11JUL)
South Beach, Miami, Florida

Supercharged music filled the air. David loved it; he couldn't keep from tapping his toes. Switching seamlessly between Cuban music and Glenn Miller, the Latin beat banged out on the tall, thin drums intrigued him.

While he enjoyed the band, Irish was on the prowl. Apparently, he had decided to go with the thrill of the hunt in the target-rich area rather than call one of his many acquaintances. In no time, he arrived at a table with two Latin lovelies in close formation.

"David, meet Carmen and Maria."

"Good evening, ladies," David shouted over the music as he stood.

The women chatted in their native tongue, speaking too fast for him to catch a single word with his high school Spanish. Irish waved over a waiter, ordered a round of cocktails, then turned and held out his hand to the tall, slender Carmen.

"Would you care to dance, my dear?"

She purred as she took his hand, allowing him to pull her from the seat onto her high heels.

"Do you dance, Da-vid?" Maria asked in an enticing accent. Petite and younger than Carmen, her bright yellow dress and matching hair band projected an innocence that her companion did not.

"Not really," he smiled in return. "Say, Maria, what do you call those tall drums?"

"Congas, Da-vid. Let me teach you to dance to their beat."

11:52 Local, 11JUL (03:52 GMT, 11JUL)
The Jungle, The Philippines

At the edge of the clearing, the Japanese captain hung lifeless. His head was at a grotesque angle. His body already appeared to be decomposing. Butler stared from across the clearing. From his vantage point, the jungle was closing around the corpse, green tentacles outstretched, waited to feed on the carrion.

"Captain, what do we do with the one still alive?"

Butler, still captivated by the optical illusion, mumbled an unintelligible response.

"Say again, sir?" Donnelly asked.

"Cut him loose."

"Cut him loose?"

"Affirmative, give him this letter and cut him loose."

It was Donnelly's turn to stare. "Do you mind if I ask what is in the letter?" He stood fast, ready for a showdown.

Butler stopped looking over his shoulder, giving him full attention and the envelope.

"It is a summary of his trial and execution," he replied, nodding toward his Japanese counterpart, "signed by me with a warning that future massacres will be dealt with similarly."

Sergeant Donnelly's eyebrows rose in disbelief. "Holy shit, Captain— they'll send the whole Jap army after us! This will have the exact opposite effect you want. Patrols will go into the villages more, not less. It will be a blood bath—"

Butler cut him off. "Did you look closely at them?" He pointed to the corpses succumbing to the jungle floor.

"Yeah. They are dead. Like we will be if you send that letter. Let me cut his throat and let's get the hell out of here."

"Follow me." Butler turned and walked toward the fallen Japanese, where his troops searched the bodies. "Look at their belts."

"Captain, with all due respect, we don't have time to play Twenty Questions."

"Paul, look at their damn belts!"

Sergeant Donnelly dutifully walked over and saw what his captain was trying to show him. Moving from Japanese to Japanese, he rolled the bodies over to inspect their belts. Every single belt had been adjusted tighter more than once; the marks from past settings were evident. He turned to his corporal, who was emptying the rucksacks.

"Kowalski, what kind of supplies are you finding?"

"Not much, Sarge, some of our old C-rats and rice, mostly rice. Looks like the same local stuff we are getting."

"Anything with Jap writing on it?" Donnelly asked.

"Nope."

The sergeant moved back to Butler. "They aren't being supplied; they are foraging."

Butler nodded. "They will be in the villages more and more, and we need to send a message."

The captain walked back to where the patrol leader hung from the tree, skin pulled tight and dead, dark eyes fixed, unblinking, like a shark's. What little humanity that had remained in him was gone. Butler bent down to pick up his samurai sword. Turning, he walked directly to the bound private, whose eyes grew wide in fear.

Oblivious to all else, the young soldier focused on the barbarian captain as he closed on him, pulling the sword from its sheath. He bowed his head, his bowels and bladder involuntarily voiding, and prayed for a clean strike. He had witnessed the agony of a sloppy decapitation.

Head down, he waited for his own. Instead, he felt the ropes cut from his wrists. He raised his head to face his executioner as the barbarian sergeant and Filipino jerked him to his feet. Inexplicably, the American captain snapped the sword into two pieces over his knee, handing him the piece with the handle. Butler spoke through Rubio to the private.

"Take this to your commanding officer with this letter. Tell him what you saw. Tell him there are many more units like ours. Any atrocities will be answered in the same manner. Now leave."

CHAPTER 19

09:00 Local 11JUL (15:00 GMT, 11JUL)
Dallas, Texas

Kate Dobbs sat at her white, French provincial makeup table, putting the finishing touches on her mascara. She heard J.T. pull into the driveway outside and glanced into the mirror, looking at her packed suitcases strewn across the perfectly made bed. Surveying the rest of the room through the mirror, she couldn't help but smile to herself. She knew that the French furniture, silk bedspread, and matching curtains made J.T. noticeably uncomfortable. That was the desired effect; this was her domain. His was the cockpit, and he ruled it like no other, but here in their bedroom, she ruled.

Quietly, self-consciously, he stepped into the room, scanning instantly from the white suitcases to the looking glass. Kate's eyes awaited his. Her defiant glare meant one thing and one thing only: he would have company. She pulled her chiffon neckerchief tight with authority, stood, and without a word walked from the room. J.T. picked up two of the custom bags and followed behind her. *I better get a nicer room in DC,* he thought.

10:00 Local, 11JUL (15:00 GMT, 11JUL)
Miami, Florida

A pillow impacted his head at precisely ten o'clock in the morning.

"Get up, Da-vid," Irish begged with the same Spanish lilt as Maria. "Come on, it's graduation day."

"I'd rather sleep," he mumbled, and rolled over.

Irish flipped over the bed, sending the sleepy young pilot tumbling to the floor.

"Move it! I need to get this Beech to Naval Air Station Key West—today."

Airborne by eleven, they had to skip the luxury of room service to which David had become quite accustomed. Retracting the gear and accelerating, they headed out to sea.

"Where are we going?" asked David.

"Today we are doing post-graduate work. Navigation over open ocean."

"That's ridiculous—how can you navigate over water? All you can do is run a DR plot and hope for the best."

"Oh contraire, my wet-nosed little friend! Behold, seven-eighths of the world's surface." Irish swept an arm toward the windscreen and the endless sea beyond.

Absorbing the view in front of him, Irish wore a clear look of content. He could not hide his love of flight. It was one of the few emotions David had learned to read from him, and the only one he would give freely.

"I won't bore you with the importance of time, heading, and speed control," he said. "We have already learned that. Nor will I reiterate weather and its serious implications. Review is over."

Unconvinced, David sat with a scowl on his face.

"To unlock the mysteries of ocean navigation," Irish continued, "all we have to do is look."

David shrugged dismissively, seeing nothing but water.

Irish grew irritated. "Where is the damn sun?"

That was easy; David was squinting because of it.

Irish didn't wait for an answer. "High, but still in our face. It is eleven, so we are going basically east. As it moves to afternoon, we will cast a shadow on the water. That shadow will point east."

Reluctantly, David had to acknowledge the obvious, surrendering only a nod.

"How do we know if the weather guessers were correct about the forecast winds?" Irish asked.

Not knowing the answer, David knew better then to respond at all. He was tired and reaching his limit on cognitive function. He sat staring out the window.

"Look at the waves! What do you see?"

All he saw was blue and said so, with sarcasm. "Blue."

"Wrong," boomed Irish, his voice overpowering the roar of all 900 combined horsepower from the Pratt and Whitney Junior Wasp engines.

"They have whitecaps—look closely."

Sure enough, they did.

"See how they form lines with troughs and peaks?"

David relented, nodding in acknowledgement and letting go of his sarcastic funk.

"Those peaks come to points," Irish continued. "Those V-shaped points are arrows that show the direction you are being blown. Compare that with your weather brief and if they are significantly different, you must adjust."

Irish reached into his navigation kit bag and pulled out an oceanic chart. After folding it several times so that only the area they were flying over showed, he tapped it.

"Do you see the lines on this chart?"

David nodded cautiously.

"They are shipping lanes. Now look behind the ships out there. Those wakes they generate can stretch for miles, especially on a calm day."

David looked closely, surprised by how many ships were indeed on the ocean.

"In constricted waters with shallows or island channels," Irish went on, "the lanes can be surprisingly narrow. Put an intermediate time-check point in the middle of the shipping lane. It is only ballpark, but might be all you have. It can be surprisingly accurate. The main point is that you have to use every means available to maintain situational awareness. It's important—do you understand?"

"I guess so."

"Negative, negative! A guess is never the correct answer in navigation or aviation in general." Irish glared in frustration at David, who stared back in confusion at what he considered an esoteric line of questioning.

"Son, what I'm trying to teach you is to think. For example, let's just say you are someday looking for a big ship: look for a big wake." He pointed out various-sized ships and their wakes.

David looked at the correlation that seemed elementary now. "I guess you are out of luck at night."

"Not true—night is the easiest! At night you have what our ancestral navigators circled the globe by: the stars."

"But on an overcast night," David objected, "you sure wouldn't have the shipping lanes."

Irish broke out in his biggest I-got-you smile. "In warm waters, micro-organisms glow when they are churned by the screw of a passing ship. They glow, and so does the wake."

David had heard enough. He was calling his mentor on this one, quite sure his leg was being pulled.

"No way! That's a tall tale and I'm not biting on that one. What do they have, little batteries?"

"So you have never seen a lightning bug?"

Irritated at being set up again, David turned his attention to the vast ocean. Picking up on his irritation, Irish changed the subject.

"So what did you and Maria do last night?" he asked with the prying smirk of a lecher.

"We just walked on the beach and talked. She's a very nice girl; I liked her. It was a beautiful night under the stars."

Irish shook his head and laughed in disbelief. "Son, son, son. What a wasted opportunity."

"How do you keep them all straight, Irish?"

"Let me ask you something, David: when you go into the candy store, do you get the same thing?"

David thought about it. "Yeah, I usually do."

"Oh, my gawwd, boy!" Irish bellowed good-naturedly. Changing his demeanor, he patted David on the back. "That's good. You will be content and happy in life."

"What do you mean?"

"Forget it, just fly."

Irish was tired of competing with the engines. He settled into his seat and himself.

11:42 Local, 11JUL (17:42 GMT, 11JUL)
Recruiting Depot, Dallas, Texas

First Lieutenants Hass and Piffel stood in front of the out-processing desk in the austere office. An Army Air Corps major looked at the induction orders again and then Hass's uniform. It didn't jibe.

"You want to tell me where you got the air medals and campaign ribbons?" His voice was skeptical.

"Classified," came the one-word response.

"Classified, Lieutenant? I'm a major. I can determine what is and isn't classified."

"Apparently not," shot back Hass.

"Sir, I was Lieutenant Hass's recruiter," intervened Piffel. "He was in a black project. If you have a need to know, you can contact General Smith. I have the number if you'd like."

There was a pause.

"I have the general's number," the major lied. "I'll call him later. You two just make sure you are on that train to Maxwell. Dismissed."

With parade field precision, Hass and Piffel rendered perfect salutes, executed an about-face, and exited.

12:48 Local 11JUL (17:48 GMT, 11JUL)
The Bahamian Islands

Rolling into a thirty-degree angle of bank over their first checkpoint, David noted the time and snuck a peek at the island below. One of the many small islands in the Bahaman chain, he was surprised by how desolate they all were. A mere sixty miles from Miami, and yet no sign of civilization was present. Continuing his turn to the southwest, he steadied up on a course for Cuba.

After a while, Irish had him climb. Passing through 10,000 feet of altitude, they donned their individual oxygen masks. David hated wearing the uncomfortable contraptions. Irish's metallic voice came over his headset, transmitted by the microphone in his mask.

"When—not if—you get lost," he instructed, "climb, conserve, and communicate."

David nodded, not wanting to hassle with the cumbersome inter-communication system (ICS). His instructor's regenerated voice continued in his headset.

"We have to wear the O2 masks to keep our wits, and as an added bonus, it improves your vision, especially at night."

Again, David nodded his response.

"We climb first, to allow us to do the other two items," his mentor continued. "At altitude, we can lean out the mixture and conserve fuel. Plus, the higher we go the more range we get out of our navigation and communication radios. It also allows us to see a lot further."

Irish pointed to their plotting board with a grease pencil and matched their course to the chart, moving the pencil further southwest and tapping on Cuba. Next, he pointed out the front windscreen. In the distant haze, David could see the island of Cuba.

They flew to a checkpoint ten miles off the Cuban coast and turned north for Naval Air Station Key West. NAS Key West was located on Boca Chica, the second-to-last major key of the chain that stretched 130 miles to Miami. The Navy had rapidly built the NAS to put patrol aircraft over the shipping lanes of the Caribbean. PBY Catalina flying boats were already hunting submarines in the shallow waters.

Fifty miles out, Irish told David to descend. At 10,000 feet, he pulled off his mask, tuned the radio, and picked up the handheld microphone.

"Coastal defense Navy 5-7-6, a single UC-45J, forty south, for landing Key West."

A scratchy reply came over their headphones. "Navy 576, state your mission and departure point."

"Navigation training, Miami."

"Roger 576, continue, switch Navy Key West at ten miles."

David studied the Keys that stretched in a crescent string all the way to the tip of Florida. Something was different about them. Finally, he realized what it was: no beaches.

"Why no beaches?"

"Coral reef, only one in US waters," replied Irish. "There have been a lot of shipwrecks over the years. That is why Key West is here."

"Rescuers?"

"No, salvagers—some would even say pirates. This little island had the highest number of millionaires per capita not that long ago."

"How do you know so much about the Keys?"

"I used to spot shipwrecks from the air in a float plane and land salvagers as close as I could. First salvager gets to claim the cargo."

"Is that legal?"

"Law of the sea, my boy. Unless the captain goes down with the ship, it is open booty."

David stared at Irish. The more he learned about him, the more larger-than-life he proved to be.

He waited at the airplane with the bags while Irish did the transfer paperwork for the Beech. Irish returned in a grey jeep, which should have surprised him but didn't.

"I found an old friend to drive us to town," said Irish. "Jump in."

David threw the bags into the back and climbed on top of them.

As they drove off base, David recognized the second class petty officer at the wheel but could not place the Navy man. With the windshield of the new jeep folded down, the warm Caribbean air flowed through their hair. He leaned back, basking in the late afternoon sun. All too soon, they squealed to a stop in front of a large, square Victorian house with porches on all four sides.

While he was struggling with the bags, David became alarmed when a large, bearded man came at Irish, full-bore. Grabbing Irish in a bear hug, he bellowed his name as he lifted him off the ground.

"Papa, long time no see!" Irish exclaimed.

"Barcelona, 1937," said the bearded man. "You got your ass shot down."

Irish grimaced. "Not in front of my protégé, Papa. I'm an air god to him."

The big man winked at David. "No doubt, Irish, no doubt."

"Hey, David, here are your bags."

David turned to face the sailor who drove the jeep.

"I'm sorry," he said. "I recognize you, but I don't remember from where."

"I was in India with your father and brother—Joe Butler."

They shook hands, and David sensed he was uncomfortable.

"I have to get the jeep back," said Butler. "See you tonight, Irish."

Papa had watched the awkward exchange, raising an eyebrow in question. Irish waved him off with a glance and slight shake of his head. Moving toward the porch, Papa called out to several men sitting there.

"Boys, these are friends of mine. Irish is a fellow warrior from the Lincoln brigade. We fought against fascism in Spain together."

Irish helped David with the bags as the younger man looked warily at the eclectic group on the porch.

"Geez, Irish," he whispered, "those guys look like pirates."

"Some of them are, sport. Best not to ask questions—*capiche?*"

"Yes, sir."

Papa showed them to a guest room on the second floor. "It's Saturday night, fight night at Reds. You want to box, Irish?"

"No, thanks, I'll watch."

"Okay, you boys freshen up and join us on the porch. It is great to see you, old friend." He slapped Irish on the back and returned to the front porch.

David was taken aback by the events on their arrival. Finally, he spoke just one word: "Boxing?"

"Yeah, boxing," said Irish. "Papa loves to box. Don't get in the ring with him—he's a bruiser."

"Roger that," mumbled David. "What does he do, anyway?"

"He's an adventurer, writer, warrior, lover of wine, women and song—an all-around wild man."

09:11 Local, 12JUL (14:11 GMT, 12JUL)
Key West Airport, Florida

Inside the pilots' planning room at the airport, Irish sat quietly at a charting table. He opened a logbook and began to meticulously fill it out. David sat quietly, looking out the window at the aircraft coming and going. Finally Irish finished, handing David two wallet-sized cards.

"Graduation day, young man," he said, beaming. "Congratulations, you've done well."

David read the cards. One was a commercial license; the other, an American Airlines identification card. He stared at the AA ID card and spoke slowly.

"I appreciate this, I really do, but I, ah..." He stopped gathering his thoughts, suddenly blurting out, "I want vengeance!"

Irish leaned way back in his chair. "Vengeance is mine, sayeth the Lord. Who are you, the Archangel of Texas?"

David stood on the balls of his feet, fists clenched, eyes burning with intensity.

"Easy, boy," Irish raised his hands in mock fright, then added, "C.R. has you in a class Monday and—"

"I already talked to a recruiter. He said I was too young. But with this," David waved the commercial license, "I'm off to Pensacola."

Irish returned to his dramatic flair, feigning hurt. "Why, David, you used me."

Not picking up on the subtle sarcasm, David hung his head, shamed by the comment. It caused Irish to laugh out loud.

"Son, how many routes does AA have over water?"

David shrugged.

"I'll tell you how many: none. Hell, we knew what you've been up to. The only question was which branch of the service. J.T. had his money on the Navy—guess he was right. You didn't really think dogfighting was part of the commercial syllabus, did you?"

"No, I guess not."

"Exactly. You will start your celestial navigation course on Monday. You will complete it in approximately one month. After that, you can take a military leave of absence and have your seniority number waiting at American Airlines upon your return."

"What is the big deal about a seniority number?"

"Oh, out of the mouths of babes!"

David sat back down and looked out the window at an Eastern airliner landing. Irish looked up and watched the DC-3 roll to a stop. He began to gather his papers and logbooks.

"Why did we go on this cross-country, Irish?"

"So you could see what you are fighting for. A lot of young men are going to die, most never having lived—children, really, fresh off the farm or out of some big-city slum. Doesn't really matter; they will be gone, never having known the joys of life or seen the country they died for."

"I don't need any motivation."

"You will find it hollow, David."

"I will find it often."

Irish nodded, a sad look on his face. "You have to live life, not avenge death."

They ambled across the ramp, headed for the Eastern aircraft which was now parked and shut down.

"Okay, David. Act like you've done this before, and let me do the talking." Irish walked directly to the Eastern captain, who was observing the servicing of his aircraft.

"Good morning, Captain, I'm James Myers with American. Can my FO and I catch a ride to Miami?"

"Myers," replied the pilot. "Irish, isn't it?"

"In the flesh, and this is David Brennan."

Studying him for a few seconds, the Eastern captain asked, "Are you Charles Henry's boy?"

"Yes, sir," David answered with pride.

"I flew mail with him in the twenties; he was a good man. Hell of a thing."

"Yes, sir, I guess it was."

"Tell your mother Mike Tado sends his best. She and my wife were friends."

"I'll tell her you both said hello."

Captain Tado shook his head and looked out at a seagull floating to a landing on the coral taxi way.

"She passed away two years ago."

"I'm sorry," David said, embarrassed.

"Don't be. Life's not fair, young man. Enjoy what you can while you can. You just don't know what's around the corner. Grab a couple of seats, fellas, and get comfortable. We'll get you to Miami."

As the DC-3 moved up the island chain, the natural beauty outside the aircraft was juxtaposed against the deep melancholy that filled it within. From Miami, they picked up a Delta flight to Atlanta, where they picked up an American Airlines flight to Dallas.

It had been a long day by the time Irish pulled up in front of the Brennan home. He grabbed David by his collar as he started to get out, and pulled him close.

"The week's details will be our little secret. What goes on the road stays on the road."

"Okay, Irish."

"I'm not kidding. Not even a hint, or your mother will skin us both alive."

"Hey, I'm the one living here. Do you think I'm stupid?"

"Good point, Junior! One more thing, I will be leaving in a couple of days to join J.T. in DC, then points beyond. I won't be here to drag your butt to celestial navigation school. I want your word that you will complete it. Not just attend it and bug out—complete it. Then you can go kill Japanese."

David hesitated, not wanting to be pinned down. Irish pulled him closer, glaring at a very uncomfortable range.

"Okay," David said at last. "I give you my word."

"Outstanding—see you after the war! Now, go tell your mother what a boring time you had with old Irish."

David stared at Irish with an incredulous look.

"No, no, you are right. She won't buy that. It will make her more suspicious.

Just shrug a lot and use monosyllables. She will eventually give up."

David shook his head, laughing out loud as he made his way up the sidewalk to the house. Irish sat and watched him, thinking, *Good kid. Lord, I hope he makes it home.*

CHAPTER 20

07:10 Local, 12AUG (20:10 GMT, 11AUG)
Guadalcanal

A dark navy blue F-4U Corsair slashed through the bottom of the cloud deck, made a violent course correction, and spit fire from its wings. Six .50-caliber machine guns spewed glowing rounds. The marine aviator at the controls held the piper of his gun sight on an A6M2 Mitsubishi Zero that exploded after a surprisingly short burst. Without releasing the trigger, he walked the tracers from the flaming Zero to its flight lead. Again, the aircraft immediately exploded.

Major Sean "Thumper" McDonald, USMCR, instantly snatched on six G' as he mentally thanked the Imperial Japanese command for trading armor for performance. Executing a high-G barrel roll, he craned his neck to make sure no bogeys had gotten on his six o'clock position, directly behind. Thumper always finished his kills with an evasive maneuver.

To shoot down another aircraft required the attacker to be predictable and focused on what was in front of him, not behind. It is what is behind a fighter pilot that will kill him. The aircraft in front of him are vulnerable, neutral at worst, with the potential to provide him the glory of aerial victory. What is behind can shame him with defeat. The caveat is that many fighter pilots will try for a face shot in a head-on pass. In air combat there are no absolutes. The closest thing to an absolute is the fact that ninety percent of kills are unobserved—like the two Thumper just got: they never saw him.

That was why he always finished his kills with an evasive move. It had been a while, a long while, 24 years, in fact. He was an old man, 43 years and counting. To add insult to injury, he was a staff puke. His wing commander would be pissed when he found out. He had no business being out here. In his head he knew this, yet in his heart he didn't care. He was a fighter pilot, not a paper pusher. Besides, he just got two victories and if he got the brand new Corsair on the deck without bending it, maybe the colonel wouldn't go nuts on him.

19:12 Local, 11AUG (20:12 GMT, 11AUG)
Off the Irish Coast

This, the last leg of their journey, was shaping up to be the most brutal. They had taken off from Cork, Ireland, and never climbed, staying low to avoid German fighters as they approached England. The low-level air mass over the Irish Sea was very unstable; turbulence hammered them as they crossed St. George's Channel.

Kate tried in vain to keep her composure and her lunch. Finally, she could do neither. Grabbing a bag, she moved aft, away from her fellow passengers. J.T. followed, holding her thin body as she retched. There was nothing else he could do.

Irish bounced from window to window, trying to get one last glimpse of his homeland. Giving up, he joined J.T. and Kate in back with the cargo.

"How's the happy couple? Are we having fun yet?"

J.T. glared daggers. Kate straightened, took the offered handkerchief, wiped her mouth and then handed it back to Irish along with the bag.

"Dandy time, ol' boy," she said. "Do take care of that for me."

Irish bowed, having been one-upped, and disappeared forward with the bag and its contents.

"Sorry about all this, Kate," J.T. shouted over the engine noise. "C.R. promises the apartment he got for us will make it up to you."

She looked around the well-worn cargo compartment full of wooden crates and incredibly uncomfortable wood-slat seats.

"You will forgive me," she replied, "if I don't hold my breath."

J.T. laughed and escorted her back to her seat.

While this ride was indeed unpleasant, it hardly compared to the trans-Pacific flight he and his fellow AA pilots had made to India for Project 7Alpha. Of course, he was smart enough to keep that little observation to himself. He pulled out the message C.R. had transmitted to Cork.

TOP SECRET

DTG: 0040Z12AUG42
FROM: COMAIRTRANSCOM
TO: COMTROOPCARRIERCOMMAND 8th AF
SUBJ: UPDATE
TEXT: COMMAND HAS SECURED ALL CONTRACTS FOR
BUILDUP OF C-47 FLEET. WILL BEGIN ARRIVING 5 PER/
MONTH THEN RAMP UP. NEED PLAN TO PUT INVASION
AIRBORNE FORCE ON CONTINENT WITHIN 2 YEARS. MORE
TO FOLLOW. C.R. SENDS

TOP SECRET

08:45 Local, 12AUG (21:45 GMT, 11AUG)
Henderson Field, Guadalcanal

Major McDonald stood at rigid attention in front of the desk of Colonel Miguel "El Toro" Rojas, wing commander of the Cactus Air Force. Sweat ran down his temples as he watched the clock behind the colonel mark the tenth minute since he had assumed his statue-like position.

The tent was stifling, its air so thick and pungent Thumper was sure he could feel microorganisms being drawn into his lungs. After what seemed like an eternity, the colonel looked up from his paperwork.

"You are a staff officer," he said, holding up a short stack of files for punctuation. "Stay out of the air."

Rather than acknowledge the order, Thumper stood silent, surmising that there was no point in pretending that he would. El Toro let him sweat for a while longer, sure that his major would, in fact, take to the air again. This battle of wills was more about minimizing than preventing more aerial exploits.

"Dismissed, Major." Thumper fled the sauna-like tent immediately.

21:47 Local, 11AUG (21:47 GMT, 11AUG)
London, England

As the moon rose, an Army Air Corp C-47, the military version of the venerable DC-3, plunked onto the runway. Turning off the active, it fast-taxied to the transient line at base operations. A green staff car pulled all the way up to the aft door of the aircraft. Immediately exiting the car was a large man with a grey, flat-top hair cut, wearing the uniform of an Army Air Corps major.

Gregory Scott, major of the US Army Reserve and currently on leave from American Airlines, helped Kate out of the C-47 and into the car. J.T. began handing down bags, including the white Gucci bags of his bride. Better known as Chief, Scott had run maintenance for Project 7Alpha in India.

"I heard a rumor," he said, "that you might have that Irish knucklehead with you?"

"That's Lieutenant Colonel Knucklehead to you, Major." Irish's voice floated out of the fuselage, laced with glee. He appeared in the door, luggage in both hands, still able to brandish his shiny new rank.

"Oh great," moaned the Chief. "Just great! Let's get out of here."

After quickly loading the trunk, they jumped in the car with Kate. Irish found an ice chest full of British stout in the front seat. He opened four bottles, using the locking mechanism of the door, as the Chief looked on in disgust.

"You know, I got one of those new-fangled devices known as a bottle opener, Lieutenant Colonel."

"No need, ol' boy."

"You keep misusing my machine and we will have a little chat behind the hangar."

"Now, now, boys. Play nice," Kate interjected from the back seat, as the Chief reluctantly took the offered beer with an abrupt tug. He eased the big staff car into gear and headed toward London's center.

"Hey," he said, "What's this I hear about Charles Henry's boy running off to join the Navy?"

"I'm afraid it is true, Chief," replied Irish. "He is off to flight school any day now."

Chief shook his big head and held up his beer in a toast. "Well, here's to the little dumb shit. Landing airplanes on boats; what the hell was he thinking?"

C.R. had not let Kate down. The flat was spectacular. She gushed as she swept through the classic Victorian apartment. She settled the men in the library, serving each a beer from the icebox, and they smiled at each other as she rushed from room to room in jubilation. Then, just as she came into the library to join them, the air raid sirens began to wail.

"Down to the cellar," said Chief as he stood.

"Come on, do we really need to?"

"Absolutely, Irish, the Gerries will bomb everything and anything. Let's move."

Irish grabbed the icebox full of beer as J.T. picked up Kate's luggage and the four scurried toward the steps. They weren't in the basement for ten minutes when the bombs began to explode all around them. Terrifying concussions grew closer. The noise was so loud, it was disorienting. Kate buried her face into J.T.'s chest as the lights flickered and went out. The air was knocked out of their lungs as the building collapsed.

Thick dust filled the cellar air. J.T. put his tunic over Kate's face so she could breath. He balled up his handkerchief and popped it in his mouth, breathing through it. Kate began to shake, and he pulled her tight.

As the dust began to settle, the Chief's voice rang out.

"Anyone smell gas?"

"Only my own," quipped Irish.

The Chief ignored him and lit his Zippo. Holding it over his head like a torch, he scrounged around until he found a candle. Its glow was dimmed by the dust, but the illumination was better than nothing. As he moved back to the others, Irish began to laugh.

"What is so damned funny?"

"You," Irish could hardly get out between spasms of laughter.

Covered with black soot from head to toe, the Chief looked like one of the Three Stooges. J.T. and Kate couldn't help but join in.

"Well, you all look the same," he grumbled as he moved toward the steps. "Shit, we are buried."

Irish rushed over to the Chief.

"Great," he moaned. "J.T., how about you leave me out of your next little adventure."

"Anything you want, my Irish friend." J.T. continued to giggle, happy to be alive.

"I'll tell you what else I want." Irish's voice grew a little shrill.

J.T. tried to stop laughing but couldn't. He knew Irish had a touch of claustrophobia.

"What else do you want?" he asked.

"I want to know what the hell J.T. stands for. Your name is Dane Dobbs."

"Childhood nickname," he replied. "Short for Just Trouble."

"Oh, how apropos!"

07:32 Local, 12AUG (23:32 GMT, 11AUG)
The Jungle, The Philippines

Haunting visions flashed, one after another, each more disturbing than the last. Always, they settled on the young girl's eyes, staring at him, begging him to ease her pain. Then she would slowly be pulled into the foliage, sinking into its depths.

"Sir, sir—wake up."

Butler opened his eyes, and the triple-canopy jungle came into focus. It framed his daily life and now, his dreams. He blinked as the canopy descended on his consciousness, its myriad colors each perceptible to him. Initially, they had merely been green. The difference in hues had since moved from subtle to stark.

"Captain," Donnelly prodded.

Butler subconsciously rubbed the crucifix between his thumb and forefinger and abruptly sat up.

"Man, you sure have gotten used to sleeping in the jungle, Captain. I can't sleep more then a couple of hours to save my soul."

Butler stared at his sergeant, alarmed by the comment. "Yeah, jungle coma. What's going on?"

"Rubio says we stepped in it again. Japs are moving, and they seem very pissed. Their units are no smaller than company strength, a couple hundred guys minimum. Anyway, Rubio wants to move deeper into the jungle."

"Deeper." The captain's voice shuddered slightly.

"Yes, sir, up into the Sierra Madre mountains. It will be a lot harder for a big unit to follow us up there."

Butler's face narrowed in thought. "Okay, but let's leave a trail in the opposite direction. Do we still have that TNT we found at that old mine?"

Donnelly smiled. "Yes, sir."

"Roger that, no point lugging it uphill. Rig a little booby prize for our pursuing admirers."

"Always thinking, eh, Captain?"

"I wouldn't want our Japanese friends to think I was ignoring them. They should always know we are ready to receive them in the jungle with presentos."

Donnelly and Kowalski set the trap by individually taping five sticks of dynamite to each of three grenades. They set a trip by twisting a wire on the pin of one grenade, and stretching it across the trail to a tree. The other two bombs were off the path, set so that as the troops sought cover, they would trip the secondary devices.

As the men moved up the trail toward the mountains, a distant explosion gave the jungle its voice, shrieking approval. Secondary and tertiary muffled booms echoed behind the first through the mountain valleys, taunting the survivors.

02:42 Local, 12AUG (02:42 GMT, 12AUG)
London, England

The British rescue team was quite surprised, after finally breaking through to the basement, by the jovial mood of the Americans who had just been entombed by the collapsed building. They were equally surprised that one of the colonials actually had luggage.

Passing through the rubble in the darkened streets, the inebriated group was sobered by the destruction. Kate couldn't believe the scene into which they had emerged. Small gas fires, emanating from buckled buildings, illuminated littered roads. The effect was medieval. She felt like an intruder at an ancient funeral rite. Her unease grew as they moved through the ruined streets. Crushed by her lovely apartment, the staff car would have been useless anyway. They moved on foot.

The Chief led them east. "It looks like a south-to-north bomb run. We should be out of the area in a couple of blocks."

Just a few blocks later, they were standing on a bustling London street. The only sign of the carnage they had left behind were the emergency vehicles rushing to the area. Kate felt as if she had been delivered from hell.

20:42 Local, 11AUG (02:42 GMT, 12AUG)
Fort Worth, Texas

David had kept his word, completing the course as promised. It was the hardest course he had ever taken by a factor of ten. He would never look at the stars in the same way again. Strangely, it would be with more awe, not less, now that he had learned a few of their secrets. Their mathematical precision intrigued him. Standing on his mother's back porch, he looked up at the celestial map overhead. It revealed north, south, east, and west to him at a glance. His exact position on the planet could be plotted with the use of a sextant and tables. The immensity of the stars was overwhelming; he longed to be among them.

"What's wrong, David? You were more quiet than normal at dinner." Laura's voice stirred him; he had not been able to summon the nerve to tell her about the orders that lay on his dresser.

"I need to talk to you, Mom."

She sighed, anticipating what was unfolding. "Come inside then, and let's talk"

They stepped back into the bright kitchen; its yellow-and-white tile and paint caused him to squint as his eyes tried to adjust. David went to his room to retrieve the orders and then sat at the small dinette set. He laid the reporting orders as a student naval aviator on the clean Formica tabletop.

Laura didn't look at the orders; she didn't need to. David's sister and brother were at the sink, Kaitlyn washing dishes and William drying.

"Kids," said Laura, "David wants to talk to us. Come over here and sit down."

The unusual respite from chores was met with silent stares. Without a word, they took a seat at the table that only recently had the leaf pulled out and two chairs put into the storm cellar.

Rather than prolong the discomfort, David got right to the point. "I joined the Navy. I leave for flight school in Pensacola three days from now."

William's eyes welled up with tears.

"Who will be here for me? Everyone is always leaving me and they never come back!" he cried out and ran from the room. Silence fell over the others. David's guilt seemed amplified by the brightness.

"Davy," Laura spoke quietly, "you can kill them all, and it won't bring your father and brother back."

He stared at the random pattern in the Formica, likening it to the stars overhead.

"Go talk to William," his mother suggested. "He doesn't understand."

David found William in his room, face down in his pillow, weeping quietly. Ding, the adopted family dog, lay next to him with his head on William's shoulder. Ding had been the squadron dog in India; J.T. had given him to the Brennans when 7Alpha returned from the war. The dog had taken to William and followed him around day and night. It was truly an ugly beast, but sweet and loyal.

"Hey, Willy-boy, how are you doing?" said David.

William kept his face buried in the pillow. *Thump, thump, thump.* Ding's tail pounded the bed.

"Don't worry," David went on. "I'm coming back—I'm going to be a Navy fighter pilot. The Japanese are the ones who should worry."

William didn't respond. The only sound was Ding's scruffy tail wagging against the covers.

"I've got something for you. It was Dad's."

William's face slowly turned. David was holding their father's leather flight jacket.

"It's yours now," he said. "I'll be getting my own soon."

William reached out and pulled it close, hugging it. He began to weep harder. Ding sniffed his cheek and licked him gently.

David sat on the edge of the bed. "I miss them too."

Even Ding's tail fell still as the brothers shared their grief in the dark room. Laura entered and turned on a small lamp, its cast revealing the mementos of a twelve-year-old boy: baseball banners and pictures, mostly of the Yankees. Then she noticed that airplane models and pictures had started to become a priority, and sighed.

"Boys," she said, "I have ice cream and cake. We can eat it while we listen to the radio. *The Shadow* is on in a few minutes, William."

Ding sprinted to the lead as they left the room. Laura had temporarily lightened the mood with vanilla ice cream and angel food cake. It soured again when a war bulletin interrupted the programming with news of the battle for Guadalcanal.

CHAPTER 21

15:38 Local, 14AUG (21:38 GMT, 14AUG)
The Sunset Limited, Louisiana

Smoke billowed from the stack of the Missouri Pacific Railroad's Sunset Limited locomotive. Whiffs passed periodically past the window where David sat. He had boarded the Rock Island Line's Texas Rocket that morning in Fort Worth, switching trains in Houston. Thus far, the ride had been excruciatingly lonely. He was seriously questioning his decision. Already, he missed his family intensely and couldn't shake the feeling that he had abandoned them.

David had told his mother he would send her money but she had refused, reminding him of Irish's generosity. It had caused him to think about what Irish had told his mother about his father that night. An ace, and a very brave one at that, his father had been a true hero. How could he possibly think that he could measure up?

His thoughts swirled in circles like the smoke rushing past his window— faster and tighter, always focusing on the same notion: vengeance. His thoughts of retribution were beginning to dominate his subconscious as well; his dreams were no longer a refuge.

David shifted his gaze from the smoke to the telephone poles clicking by, but the scenery was still a blur behind them. Finally, he noticed the bayou passing in the background and realized he was close to New Orleans. After a stop, with hours to go before his destination of Pensacola, he decided to seek out the dining car. Weary of being taunted by his own mind, he welcomed the distraction.

The rush of hot air and noise between train cars revived him as he struggled with the door to the dining car. Once inside, he could see it was packed. Natural light flooded in from the large windows, reflecting off the modern décor's ample use of chrome. He searched for an open, red Naugahyde seat. As he looked around, he noticed most of the patrons were young men. He headed for a table for four with an open seat.

"Do you guys mind if I join you?"

A blond-haired young man gave him the once over, pausing to read the large yellow envelope in David's hand.

"Sit down, classmate."

David looked confused. "What?"

All three held up the same type of envelope with the exact same number written in large black marker on the front.

"We figure 36/42 means the 36th class of 1942. I'm Paul Bement." The young man held out his sturdy hand.

David took the offered hand and replied, "David Brennan." He sat down at the table, putting the envelope on the floor.

"Where are you from, Brennan?"

"I grew up in Fort Worth."

"Well, I'm from Webster Groves, Missouri. This here is Andy Levine from Skokie, Illinois." He pointed to the young man next to him with his thumb. "He's Jewish, so no jokes."

"I ... ah ... don't know any...."

Nodding to the fourth classmate, Bement continued, "And that's Steve Crane from Ventura, California."

Andy shook his head, laughing at the introduction.

"I've been with Paul since Union Station in St. Louis. Don't worry, David, you will get used to him," he said.

"I just met him, and I'm not so sure," added Steve.

David was relieved to be in the company of young men in the same boat: far away from home, family, and friends, plunging into the unknown. At least now he would have company.

"So what do you want to fly, Brennan?"

"I want to fly fighters, hopefully the new Hellcat."

Bement nodded approval.

"So do these two. Not me—I want to fly dive bombers."

"Why?" asked David.

"Because I want to blow shit up." Bement grinned. "Besides, I got four brothers in the Marines. I figure I can help them out more by dropping bombs."

They chatted all the way to Pensacola, a pleasant trip with good food and company. It was in stark contrast to what awaited them.

07:42 Local, 15AUG (23:42 GMT, 14AUG)
Sierra Madre Mountains, The Philippines

They moved for six days, higher and deeper into the jungle. Butler grew more detached with each step. Donnelly noticed and assumed his captain was merely letting down his guard a little as the threat diminished. The platoon had been on the ragged edge of combat far too long. They were all exhausted.

Resting in a dried-up stream bed, Butler sat with the Negritos, intently studying a frond he had picked up from the forest floor.

Rubio was worried. "We must find water."

"I know where the water is. Follow me," Butler said as he rose and moved silently into the jungle. Kowalski looked at Donnelly, who shrugged and moved out behind the captain.

Moving with purpose—he was not wandering—they went up the mountain until they found a game trail. Once on the trail, they moved laterally across the mountain until they came across a small clearing with a stream and a pool of fresh water.

Donnelly stood next to Butler, looking at the oasis. "How did you know, Captain?"

"Kind of obvious, don't you think, Sergeant?"

"No. No, sir, I don't!"

19:22 Local, 14AUG (01:22 GMT, 15AUG)
Naval Air Station, Pensacola, Florida

Chaos, absolute chaos, reigned in front of the Battalion One (BAT I) building. Newly arrived civilians were trying to line up in some semblance of a military formation in the last remnants of the day's sunlight. Marine Corps drill instructors darted in and out of the gaggle like piranhas in a feeding frenzy. And like piranhas, they would single out and encircle a victim, each taking a bite of hide from different directions.

"You miserable maggot, stand at attention," one screamed at Levine, then appeared in front of Bement as if by magic. "Wipe that smile off your face, you piece of shit! My God, did your parents have any children that lived?"

Bement tried with all his might not to smile but failed. The large gunnery sergeant stabbed a fist into his solar plexus; Bement went down with a flop. Gunny Talbot put the heel of his boot on Bement's ear and ground it.

"Is this funny, boy? Give me twenty pushups, a count of four, begin the exercise!"

Bement began the pushups; Talbot put his boot on his buttocks.

"Get that big butt out of my sky."

He pushed Bement hard to the ground. Instantly, he was standing in front of David.

"You gonna cry, momma's boy? What are you, twelve? I swear to the Almighty if you cry, I will rip out your spine!"

David involuntarily shifted his glance, making eye contact with Gunny Talbot.

"You eyeballing me, momma's boy? You eyeballing me?" he shrieked like an out-of-control madman.

All ten DIs continued to sow fear and confusion in the officer candidates, verbally assaulting them from every angle.

Suddenly it was silent. Out of his periphery, David could see a short bull of a DI in full uniform. All the other DIs wore freshly starched battle fatigues, drawn in at the waist by a shiny black leather belt. Each, including the DI in full uniform, wore a Smokey the Bear hat. His green wool uniform tunic was accentuated by row after row of decorations for bravery in combat. The other DIs deferred to him with respect.

"I am First Sergeant M.L. Paillou," he announced. "Your soul may belong to Jesus, but your ass is now mine." Standing at rigid attention, only his jaw moved. His tie and khaki shirt were so stiffly starched, they seemed carved from stone. He observed the area with contempt.

"Whose gear is adrift on my parade deck?" he bellowed, instantly reactivating the pack of piranhas. They set upon the officer candidates with renewed vigor.

"Get those candy ass civilian suitcases off the first sergeant's parade deck! Pick them up! Pick them up, you idiots!"

The young men stood holding their bags, each lost and confused. Before they could catch their collective breath, another order was issued.

"Get in alphabetical order."

VENGEANCE

Since the candidates didn't know each other's names, bedlam again descended on the group until they were back in a loose formation. Paillou moved front and center again.

"That was pitiful! That was UNSAT! You will un-screw yourselves, and you will start now! Is that clear?"

Silence fell over the harried individuals.

"I can't hear you. Sound off like you've got a set. I say again: is that understood?"

Again, nothing emanated from the terror-stricken group. Immediately the piranhas were back in their faces.

"You will respond: Sir, yes sir!"

"One more time, ladies; is that clear?"

An apprehensive reply came from the group in individual voices.

"I can't hear you!" Paillou repeated.

"Sir, yes sir," came forth, louder this time.

"You maggots sound like a bunch of nurses. I said I can't hear you!"

"Sir, yes sir!"

"Again."

"Sir, yes sir!" echoed off the brick buildings.

"Again."

Sweat poured from the candidates as they held their bags straight out from their sides.

"Keep those arms up, you weak maggots—ninety degrees perpendicular from my parade deck."

One of the candidates collapsed in the back.

"Get that piece of shit off my parade deck," Paillou calmly ordered. Two DIs dragged him off, never to be seen again.

Meanwhile, an eternity passed.

"Do you maggots want to get rid of that disgusting civilian trash?"

"Sir, yes sir," came the strained but enthusiastic response.

A grey, flatbed truck pulled up behind the first sergeant.

"Stow that trash on my truck. Do it now!"

The piranhas were back in action.

"Move it, move it, move it! Double time, you maggots!"

They ran into and over each other as they scrambled to put their suitcases on the truck and get back into formation. Finally, they stood at attention once again. Paillou paced back and forth in front of them. He had remained in place while they had bounced off each other, stowing their gear. No one dared to approach him closely, let alone run into him.

"I am a first sergeant of United States Marines. I will be back upon the field of battle. Once I am there, I will depend on naval aviators to sweep the skies of my enemy and provide close air support on the islands in the Pacific theater. If you think I will let screw-ups or weaklings through this program to drop bombs on my head, you are hallucinating."

He continued to pace in military cadence.

"Before you get those coveted wings of gold you will have to come through me. Is that clear, maggots?"

"Sir, yes sir," rang out into the night.

"If you do not have the intestinal fortitude, then quit right now and save me the time. Who wants to quit? Who made a mistake?"

A tall, thin young man took a step forward, fear in his wide eyes. Paillou descended on him with a fury.

"You have got to be shitting me?! Get off this field of honor, you coward. GET OFF!"

Again, two of his DIs sprang into action, jerking the offender out of line and physically throwing him onto the truck with the discarded baggage.

For the first time that evening, First Sergeant Paillou showed emotion, spittle flying as he leveled his inquisition.

"Anyone else? Any more cowards on my field of honor? Take off those civilian rags, strip to your skivvies—now!"

Even stripped of their civilian clothes, the candidates did not present a uniform appearance. Some wore T-shirts, some not, and there were various types: v-necked, crew-necked and sleeveless.

"T-shirts too, gather it all up and put it in my fire pit—move!"

They scurried to comply. This time very few collisions took place, and they were back in formation rapidly. And for the first time, they had a uniform appearance.

"Retrieve your wallets, you idiots!"

Candidates ran for their lives to the fire pit and back as the piranhas struck from all sides. Even with that added distraction they were back in formation quickly.

"Are you standing in my formation with a foreign object in your hands?"

The question unleashed the piranhas yet again. Confusion, nearing panic, filled the ranks. When silence returned, all the candidates stood with wallets firmly clenched between their teeth.

Talbot shook a can of diesel fuel over the pile of clothes. Paillou popped a road flare and walked toward the pit. Its magnesium light blinded the candidates. He tossed it into the middle of the ring. Orange, oily flames licked into the air, releasing black smoke in a thick billow. Turning to the formation, he spoke as the flames crackled and grew behind him.

"The boys have fled, only men have stayed. And by God, I will transform you into warriors or I will kill you. Is that clear?"

Their mumbled, "Sir, yes sir," was drowned out by the roar of the fire.

As they stood with the fire blazing, a column of upper classmen rounded the corner marching as one. They were resplendent in their dress whites, the reflection from the fire highlighting them. Even in the oppressive heat, their long sleeves and choker collars were stiff and uniform. They moved as one and sang as one, marching past the new rabble.

"Avert your vision! You are not worthy to look upon a graduating class."

Once they had passed, the newest class of aviation officer candidates was marched to the barber shop where each head was shaved to the scalp. Next, they were herded through gear issue. With arms so full they were hardly able to hold everything, they were run to the barracks with orders to don fatigues and re-form out front of BAT I.

First Sergeant Paillou was waiting, now in highly starched fatigues, his trousers and tunic dressed: tucked in at the boot and waist. The candidates were not allowed this military courtesy; it would mark them instantly as the new class.

"You maggots are now knobs. You will not be allowed to dress your tunics and trousers like a warrior, because you are slimy disgusting knobs. Issue the head gear."

Silver-painted helmets were issued to each man. If the undressed fatigues left any doubt of their status, the highly visible helmets did not. Re-formed, they were marched to the seaplane ramp four blocks away. For the next four hours, they were instructed and drilled in marching and formation. They were repeatedly marched into the cool water of Pensacola bay. Young enlisted sailors working on the seaplanes were, as always, highly amused. The practice, however, did serve a purpose: the candidates' brand new boots would break in much easier after being doused in salt water.

After drill they marched back to the rear of BAT I where the first sergeant waited, pouring water from a hose into a rectangular mud pit. The candidates were marched directly into the mud. Ankle deep, they began calisthenics as the piranhas barked from the edges. By the time one hour had elapsed, they were covered with the orange mud of the south. Paillou hosed each one clean and stood with his hands on his hips, looking at all of the candidates.

"I love a night run. How about you knobs?"

A less than enthusiastic, "Sir, yes sir," was shouted out.

"I can't hear you." He cupped his hand to his ear.

"Sir, yes sir!"

"Outstanding. Let's do an easy three miles."

After the three-mile run, the exhausted candidates were allowed three minutes to eat in the mess hall, then marched back to the barracks at BAT I. Once there, they were instructed on how to make their beds in a proper military fashion and how to police the area to make everything shipshape.

At 01:00 they were allowed to man up their racks for sleep. A few minutes after lights out, Bement's distinctive voice reverberated through the bay, just loud enough for all to hear.

"Well that was pleasant. I can't wait for tomorrow."

Worn out and frazzled, they buried their faces into pillows, not daring to laugh out loud.

Talbot was the last DI to leave BAT I. Paillou was waiting for him.

"Gunny T, a word," he called to Talbot.

"Yes, First Sergeant."

"Don't ever strike one of my candidates again." He delivered the order with menace.

Talbot began to protest until he caught Paillou's eyes, illuminated by a distant streetlight. There would be no discussion.

CHAPTER 22

12:03 Local, 15AUG (12:03 GMT, 15AUG)
London, England

Kate sat reading a book in the Chief's cramped quarters. She had cleaned it top to bottom over the last two days and had nothing left to do. Still uneasy over having a house dropped on her head, she wasn't ready to venture out on the town alone.

Back in Washington, C.R. Smith had heard about Kate's first night in London. For two days he put the war on a back burner and devoted his attention to finding Kate a proper home and safe haven. He succeeded, cutting a deal with a viscount, who was on the British embassy staff in DC, for his country manor.

It was perfect, close to J.T.'s future base and far away from any targeted areas. Besides, it was supposed to be spectacular. C.R. used his personal funds to gain full access to the manor and grounds.

Midday, there was a ring at the door. Kate went down to answer it and was surprised to find a man holding a telegram for her. C.R. had sent it, detailing the new home and a scheduled pickup from the manor's car and driver. Kate quickly checked her watch. *Two hours—I have to hustle.*

She quickly scribbled a note to J.T., Irish, and the Chief, put it on the refrigerator door, and packed her bags. A second knock came at the precise time C.R. had said it would. Answering it, she found a uniformed chauffer standing on the doorstep.

"Mrs. Dobbs?"

"Yes, I'm Kate Dobbs."

"My name is James, ma'am. I'm to take you to Beckwith Manor."

"Do call me Kate. I need to grab my bags, and I'll be right down."

"Allow me, Mrs. Dobbs. Where shall I find them?"

"Kate, please. They are at the top of the stairs."

"Very well, Miss Kate. Please let me show you to the carriage."

A large Rolls Royce glistened at the curb, rear door ajar, awaiting an occupant. Kate was speechless as James led her to the spacious back cabin and secured the door. She sank into the luxurious leather seat. James was up and down the steps with her bags in an instant and had them tucked in the boot, locking it in place, in no time.

As they left the confines of London, she felt the suffocating stress she had been under lift. The drive was beautiful and Kate sat back, enjoying the countryside rolling by. She knew it might be days before J.T., Irish, and the Chief joined her, due to their duties in London. Kate didn't care; she had been through enough nights of air raids and sirens. Not hesitating for an instant, she had decided to go as the advance party.

After an hour of rolling green hills and farmland, they pulled up to an ornate gate. She got an inkling of what lay ahead as she studied the intricate, heavy iron gate, the stone archway holding it and the gatehouse that stood sentry over it. No doubt, they cost more than any house she had ever lived in. As the Rolls passed, the gateman bowed deeply.

Kate struggled to peer around the driver to see what lay ahead. Meticulously manicured lawns stretched for acres in every direction. She finally got a look at what could best be described a palace at the end of the long, straight driveway made of stone. The sight actually took her breath away, almost as effectively as the concussion of the bomb that had destroyed her last home.

04:45 Local, 16AUG (10:45 GMT, 16AUG)
Naval Air Station, Pensacola, Florida

An empty trash can crashed down the passageway of BAT I at exactly 04:45. It was feeding time for the piranhas. Any slow-moving candidates were flipped in their racks.

First Sergeant Paillou strutted the length of the passageway.

"Reveille, reveille, reveille; you have fifteen minutes to shit, shower, and shave, now reveille! Muster in front of BAT I, in formation."

His directive unloosed a flurry of activity and abuse, finally culminating in the harassed group standing at attention in front of the first sergeant.

"You maggots look like shit! I can't believe my eyes. The US Navy has hit rock bottom with this class; I shall call you the bottom feeders. If you do not get squared away ASAP, I will attrite all of you."

"Attrite" was Navy parlance for washout, and spoken with aggression—emphasis on the third 't'—to give it bite. Used as a noun or verb, to attrite was to be kicked out, to be an attrite was to be labeled for life a failure. Attrite would hang over these candidates' heads like Damocles' sword, long after they left BAT I.

Even after receiving their wings, they would have to prove themselves in an operational squadron and their final destination, the fleet. Mythical and mysterious, the fleet lay at the end of their yellow-winged road. Once there, the blade would fall often, as the cruelty of war proved to be the ultimate arbiter of attrition.

But first, they must make it through the next four weeks of hell, designed to weed out the weak of body, mind, or spirit. They must be culled before precious time and money was wasted on them.

Each day was exactly the same. A 04:45 wake-up. Immediately into the pit. It was normally dry now, unless some heinous crime like a dirty uniform or untied shoe was committed. Next, a three-minute breakfast, followed by hours of drill. Then lunch, more drill, a five-mile run ending again at the chow hall. After chow, more PT, physical training, and general harassment followed by policing of the barracks and uniforms. The day finally ended in the rack at 22:00. They would repeat the entire ordeal the next day, week, and month.

Talbot had developed a particular dislike for Bement, whom he had nicknamed Cue Ball due to his shaved and rather round blond head. Cue Ball let it roll off him like water off a duck's back, which infuriated Talbot, causing a constant escalation of harassment.

Near the end of the fourth week the candidates were cut loose after evening PT to ready their sea lockers for inspection. Each uniform item—sock, shoelace, everything—had to be cleaned, pressed, folded properly, and arranged in an exact order. The BAT I candidates rushed up the ladder (stairs) to ensure their lockers were shipshape.

Cue Ball quickly spun the combination on his lock; he knew Talbot would inspect his gear and give it extra special attention. He pulled the bolt of the lock through the eyelet of the clasp and released the tongue. As the tongue cleared the eyelet, the locker's lid sprang open, banging loudly off the metal frame of Cue Ball's rack. Talbot erupted from within the small floor locker, unfolding like the arms of a praying mantis striking its prey.

"This is the worst locker I have ever seen, Cue Ball! You are a piece of shit! You are as screwed up as a soup sandwich! I want your DOR!"

DOR, or Drop On Request, was a self-inflicted attrite. Naval aviation was an all-volunteer force due to the inherent danger, even in peace time. At any time, a naval aviator could turn in his wings and be done. For a student, uttering the term DOR was enough.

"I want your D-O-R!"

Cue Ball was frozen in place, leaning back from Talbot, his chin drawn in, still in shock. Slowly his face morphed from surprise to fury, his normally pale complexion took on a red hue.

"NEGATIVE!" he shrieked at the top of his lungs.

BAT I's dormitory froze in place, except for David. He had been front row for all of Talbot's abuse because both of their last names started with "B." He saw Bement's hands balled tightly in a fist and moved to put his hand on Cue Ball's forearm.

Talbot's voice grew tight with forced control, his eyes narrowed, and he smiled like a snake.

"Are you defying me, Cue Ball?"

David tightened his grip. The pressure forced a return of Bement's composure.

"This candidate will not DOR."

Talbot looked down, seeing the clenched fist and David's hand squeezing the forearm. He violently pushed David, sending him sprawling onto the floor.

Cue Ball's arm flinched as David yelled, "No!" He caught himself and froze again.

"Do you want to fight me, boy?"

Cue Ball stood silently, neither threatening nor backing down. Talbot turned to his accomplice, who had been watching from the door.

"Get the gloves."

The corporal hesitated, eyes flickering rapidly, revealing his apprehension: he knew Talbot was a former Golden Gloves boxer.

"Get the damn gloves!"

He ran off as Talbot turned back to Cue Ball.

"You, on the fan tail."

Many personal grudges were settled on the fan tails of naval vessels. Out of view of the bridge and the prying eyes of the officers standing the watch, the aft deck provided privacy for the squaring away of problem children as well as personal beefs. At BAT I, the loading dock behind the building was the fan tail.

A small group assembled on the loading dock. Talbot's accomplice handed gloves and protective headgear to Bement.

"No headgear," snapped Talbot.

"Gunny, I don't think that's a good idea. The first sergeant—"

"Screw the first sergeant; I got promoted today. I don't have to take shit from Paillou anymore."

Cue Ball brought his gloves forward to touch them before starting the match. Talbot immediately slammed him in the face with a cheap shot, shattering his nose. He pummeled Cue Ball to the deck within seconds.

"DOR!"

"No!" Cue Ball yelled in response, struggling back to his feet.

Talbot smashed a fist into his jaw before he got fully to his feet. Blood splattered onto David as Cue Ball went down again.

"DOR!"

"Never! You will have to kill me," screamed Cue Ball, tears mixing with blood on his face.

"Then I will," hissed Talbot, striking him in the temple.

Cue Ball crumpled to the concrete, unconscious. Talbot began to kick him while he lay unable to defend himself. David could not stand by any longer; he rushed Talbot. The sadist saw him out of the corner of his eye, slashing out with a brutal right hook, impacting his nose like a sledgehammer.

Bright lights flashed in his eyes as he clawed at consciousness. Flat on his back, the metallic taste of his own blood filled his mouth, and the warm fluid trickled down his throat. Thoughts spun out of control; he was going to throw up. His ears began to function, hearing the heavy thud of Talbot's kicking, as his mind fought for order. Only one salient thought would form. Rolling onto his side, he spit a mouthful of blood.

"First Sergeant Paillou!" he screamed with the force of the Sirens of ancient Greece.

Michael L. Paillou, First Sergeant USMC, materialized on a porch at the end of the BAT I building. Hands on hips, he instantly surveyed the situation then barked an order.

"Clear the fan tail."

The small group began to scurry like roaches caught in the light.

"Assist the downed men!" Paillou commanded with obvious irritation. "Talbot, stand fast."

Scooping up David and Cue Ball, the group disappeared.

Paillou marched down the porch steps with his normal parade field discipline. He closed the distance between porch and fan tail at a measured, yet incredibly quick rate, as if levitating toward Talbot. Never leaving a proper military cadence, he climbed the five steps of the loading dock, his campaign cover remaining in perfect position, parallel to the Earth.

Stopping in front of Talbot, he spoke without emotion.

"I gave you a standing order, Talbot. It was both clear and lawful."

Talbot smirked dismissively at the much smaller Paillou.

"I don't have to take your—"

So quick was the first strike, the only indication of it was the sound of Talbot's nose breaking. Immediately, Paillou unleashed a second blow that shattered Talbot's right jaw as he simultaneously side-kicked the inside of his left knee, tearing tendons and ligaments. Talbot's body succumbed to gravity, but before he could reach the sanctuary of the concrete, Paillou snatched his right arm, twisting it and slamming his right elbow down onto the humerus, fracturing it. Holding the arm, he twisted it until he produced a high-pitched squeal, then allowed Talbot to collapse to the concrete deck.

"Welcome to combat, you piece of shit."

Hundreds of eyes watched from darkened windows.

10:00 Local, 15SEP (23:00 GMT, 14SEP)
Guadalcanal

Major Sean "Thumper" McDonald sat at his desk made from two crates and a wide board. Disgruntled, he was shuffling through intelligence reports, parts requisitions, and award nominations. Colonel Miguel "El Toro" Rojas walked in and sat on a crate across from McDonald.

"Well, Thumper, it looks like you will get your wish."

"How's that, sir?"

"Us old bastards are on the flight schedule. Half of our pilots are sick.

Time for the greybeards to get into the fight."

"Outstanding!" exclaimed Thumper.

19:52 Local, 14SEP (23:52 GMT, 14SEP)
Naval Air Station, Pensacola, Florida

Paillou sat at his desk with two personnel files opened on top of it. Paul Vincent Bement was typed on one, David Blane Brennan on the other. He kept tapping a pencil on Brennan's file. *Who is this kid? There is something about him I recognize. And he has balls, real balls.* After debriefing the corporal, who had been Talbot's accomplice, Paillou had broken his nose and sent him on his way without another word spoken.

He continued to tap on the file. There was a sharp rap on his door frame. Paillou looked up to see Lieutenant Stutzman standing in the jamb. *Oh shit, this isn't good.*

"Interesting night, eh, First Sergeant?"

"Aye, aye, sir."

"Are we going to have to do any damage control?"

"Negative, sir. Everything is squared away."

"Outstanding. Let me know if you need anything."

"I will, sir."

"By the way, I had to calm down the flight surgeon. Have a little smoker here tonight?"

"Yes sir, there was some unauthorized training. But I took care of that, and it won't happen again."

"Yes, I saw that in sick bay. And the candidates?"

"I had the corpsman check them out, sir; a couple of broken noses, but otherwise okay."

"Roger that." The lieutenant glanced down at the names on the file. "Congratulations on promotion to Sergeant Major."

"Thank you, sir. I'll have a wetting down at the Top Club this Friday. Of course, you are invited."

"Excellent, I can always use a free beer. Good night, Sergeant Major."

Paillou sat mulling over his options. Deciding, he yelled to his outer office.

"Corporal, get me Bement and Brennan."

08:11 Local, 15SEP (00:11 GMT, 15SEP)
Sierra Madre Mountains, The Philippines

Butler leapt from the cover of the bush with the speed of a lion, sinking his KA-BAR fighting knife into the wild boar's neck. He pulled it close while it struggled in its final death throes, spurts of blood pulsating across his face. His Negrito companions jumped for joy as the boar squealed its last breath.

Quickly hoisting it up into a tree by its hind legs, they field dressed it. Once lightened by gutting, it was tied to a long stick and marched triumphantly into camp. Kowalski looked up at his blood-splattered captain and elbowed Donnelly.

"Hey, has the captain gone native on us?" he whispered.

20:12 Local, 14SEP (02:12 GMT, 15SEP)
Naval Air Station, Pensacola, Florida

Flipping on the lights as he burst into the dormitory, the corporal went directly to their racks.

"Bement, Brennan, on your feet. Sergeant Major Paillou wants you front and center."

They were on their feet and dressing in an instant. Cue Ball looked over at David.

"I'm sorry, David, I—"

"Shut up, Candidate, and move."

David and Cue Ball stood at attention in front of Sergeant Major Paillou's desk. Bement broke military etiquette by speaking without being spoken to.

"Sir, Candidate Brennan had nothing to do with this. He should not be punished. I am at fault and take full responsibility—"

"Silence," Paillou snapped without looking up. He returned his attention to the files on his desk as he spoke.

"First Sergeant Talbot was out of line. That little chapter in our journey to manhood is closed. He will not be back; there will be no retribution. Do not mistake this for an excuse to be weak or worthless."

Both stood rigidly as Paillou began to tap David's file again.

"Why do I know you, Brennan?"

"Sir, this candidate is from Texas—"

"I goddamned know where you are from Brennan; why do I know your name? Why do you look familiar to me? Is your father in the corps?"

"My father and brother are dead, sir."

It hit Paillou like a tsunami, all at once: *Holy shit, this is the kid of that guy that died trying to save my ass.* He sat quietly, stunned by the revelation.

"In China?" he finally asked.

David's eyes awoke from their trained stare on the wall above Paillou's head, dropping to meet his.

"How did you know that?"

He shifted uncomfortably in his wooden chair then cleared his throat.

"I was there."

Cue Ball had no idea what they were talking about and began to blink nervously.

"What happened?" demanded David.

Paillou looked down at his desk, closed both files and met David's glare.

"I was in a Raider unit. We were pinned down and running out of ammo. The Japs were ripping us up. Our asses were in a deep crack. A DC-3 tried to get in with some supplies and got the shit shot out of it. While it pulled off, the Japs kept hammering it as it egressed. Your father and brother used the distraction to try and get in."

He paused clearing his throat and trying to gather himself.

"As they dived in, a triple-A gunner got a bead on them and blew off a wing. They crashed. There were no survivors. It was a very heroic act."

The sound of cicadas' rubbing legs filled the thick, humid air as David's blackened eyes surrendered tears.

"Candidate Bement," said Paillou, "you are dismissed."

Cue Ball touched David's arm as he did an about-face and left the room. Paillou rose from his desk and moved next to David.

"You are brave, like your kin," he said quietly. "You show them honor. Continue to. Dismissed."

CHAPTER 23

15:45 Local, 12OCT (04:45 GMT, 12OCT)
Cape Esperance, Solomon Islands

The battle of Cape Esperance was in its second day as the strike package pushed from altitude. Colonel Rojas stood his Dauntless dive bomber on its nose as he dove on the Japanese surface action group below. Leading his air wing, he had the option of picking any target. He settled on the biggest ship, a heavy cruiser.

As he accelerated almost straight down toward the target, the morning sky filled with smoke and hot steel fragments. At 3,000 feet, he released his thousand-pound bomb, and just as it fell free, a five-inch, triple-A shell vaporized his aircraft.

"El Toro is down, El Toro is down!" rang out over the UHF frequency.

McDonald rolled his Corsair on a wing, looking down just in time to see the flaming mass hit the calm, turquoise water. But El Toro's bomb fell true. Before he rolled back wings level, Thumper saw it hit the cruiser amid ship.

"Bastards!" he yelled out loud as he rolled in on the same ship, charged his guns, and began to hammer the bridge with .50-caliber fire. Screaming in rage, Thumper made multiple strafing passes until he was Winchester, or out of ammunition.

Before the Cactus Air Force was done, two Japanese warships had joined El Toro on the bottom. McDonald pulled off target for the last time as triple-A chased him. He suddenly realized, *Shit. I'm in charge.*

16:01 Local, 12OCT (22:01 GMT, 12OCT)
The Tank , Naval Air Station, Pensacola, Florida

A steel tube contraption clanged down steel rails with an ear-splitting noise. Strapped inside what appeared to be the skeleton of an aircraft cockpit was a horrified officer candidate. It slammed into the water of the pool with a terrific force, flipping forward until it was upside down, and quickly sank.

Inside the submerged training device, the panicking student flailed helplessly, trying to get the harness unlatched so he could escape. Bubbles swirled around him; his sinuses had filled with jets of pool water on impact. He was disoriented; he was drowning. His mouth and eyes opened in stark terror as a Navy diver made his way toward him, quickly releasing the harness and pulling him from the cockpit.

Breaking the surface, spitting pool water and snot, the young man screamed over and over.

"D-O-R, D-O-R—I'm not going again!" He ran from the pool deck, still in full flight gear after being pulled out of the water.

Next in line was a lanky Georgia boy who shook his head and refused to man up the Dilbert Dunker. He was immediately escorted from the pool deck. Both young men were gone when the class returned that evening to change uniforms for dinner. The unmade racks were testimony enough. They were not mentioned again out of fear that whatever had caused them to quit might be catching.

The candidates were in the last phase of training before the flight side. Their previous four weeks had been aerodynamics, engines, and navigation; this was swim week. They had already done the survival swimming, the high-obstacle jump into water, and the mile swim in flight suit. Now they were completing the last event, the Dilbert Dunker.

Countless naval aviators had already been dragged under to Davy Jones' Locker, the bottom of the ocean, after surviving the ditching of a crippled aircraft at sea. Crews watched helplessly from the decks of ships as these pilots struggled with the straps of their harnesses and parachutes, only to be pulled under with the aircraft as it sank.

The Dilbert Dunker had been developed to try and minimize the losses. Students would get into the training device in full flight gear, ride the rails into the pool, let it sink, and then practice their escape. Four attempts were all they got. If they couldn't do it successfully they would be attrited.

Andy walked up to David and Cue Ball after dinner. "What am I going to do? If I can't do it tomorrow they will attrite me."

"Wiggle your toes," said David.

"David I'm serious. I'm about to be sent home."

"I'm serious too. An old friend, famous fighter pilot, and airline captain extraordinaire once told me. When things get all jammed up and you think you are going to lose it, just wiggle your toes. It releases the stress."

"Wiggle my toes?"

"Wiggle your damn toes," agreed Bement.

The next morning, Andy looked at David and Cue Ball as he sat in the metal beast. They smiled and wiggled their finger tips at him. He returned the smile and passed a thumbs-up to the instructor, who released the contraption upon the signal. Freed from its perch, it fell toward the water, picking up speed quickly as it crashed into the surface of the pool. Flipping with a splash, it quickly sank.

Andy sat calmly in the cockpit, waiting for the bubbles to clear and wiggling his toes. His hands were still on the reference points of the fake stick and throttle, just as he had been instructed. As the bubbles cleared, he methodically slid his right hand from the stick and up his belly until he found the metal release. With his right hand on the release, he moved his left hand from the throttle to the canopy frame of the cockpit. Simultaneously, he released the latch and pulled with his left hand hard down, deeper into the tank. Resisting the disorientation, he swam sideways away from the training device and up to the light.

David and Cue Ball watched intently as he broke the surface, glancing back immediately to where they knew the diver would surface. Only letting his mask appear out of the water, the diver raised a thumbs-up after what seemed an eternity, and re-submerged.

Two days later, four battalions moved as one, in lockstep, toward the parade field at Naval Aviation Schools Command. They marched like Marines because they had been trained by Marines. Sergeant Major Paillou led the procession. Behind him was the honor battalion: his own BAT I, bottom feeders no more.

Today, they would move from candidate to student naval aviator, from the parade deck to the cockpit. Their glory, however, would be fleeting. Very soon, they would be starting all over again.

But not right now, not here, not today. Today was theirs, and they would revel in it. Today was a rite of passage. Today was a party at the Pensacola officers' club. Every single young lady with a dream of seeing the world also knew what day it was. P-cola, as the young men called it, also had another nickname: Mother-in-Law of Naval Aviation.

Mustin Beach Officers' Club was located on the beach overlooking Pensacola Bay, only a short distance from the brick building that housed the tank containing the Dilbert Dunker. To David, the chasm seemed like a thousand miles as he stared at the facility. It didn't matter; it was behind him. His focus remained on what was in front of him, what lay ahead in the South Pacific.

Even the nubile virgins flooding into the O' Club didn't distract him from his thoughts, but a sharp tug on his dress white sleeve finally did.

"Come on, David, let's get a move on! I saw one that looks like Jean Harlow." Cue Ball was literally dancing on the balls of his feet. The sight of the large young man squirming like a two-year-old who had to go to the bathroom caused David to laugh out loud.

"My gawd, you are just like Irish."

Undeterred, Cue Ball dragged him under the canvas awning that stretched over the sidewalk leading to the front entrance. He continued to tug him through the door. Newly constructed of red brick with wood accents, the club matched the tank, which matched the BAT buildings, the exchange, and new chapel as well.

They swept through the white pine doors into the foyer. On the right was the entrance to the "dirty shirt" bar. Flying coveralls and work uniforms were only permitted in the "dirty shirt."

All of the club's walls were gaily painted in soft pastels with borders of white pine woodwork at the top. Foot-long golden wings, inlaid in the crown molding, beckoned to David as he looked around the room.

Suddenly, the door to the "dirty shirt" kicked open and banged off the foyer wall. Five drunken flight instructors pushed through. Behind them, the dimly lit room, with dark walls and furniture, formed a black hole that contrasted sharply with the light of the foyer.

"Look, new meat for the grinder!" an especially mean-looking pilot shouted.

David glanced at the squadron patches sown on the men's flight suits; they were in the advanced squadron. That meant they were combat veterans. They looked much older than their years, and scary. Young damsels instinctively moved away, positioning themselves behind their white knights.

David stared at the mean one, wondering if his meat grinder comment referred to training or the fleet. Lieutenant Stutzman came through the door, laughing at the other men's antics, ushered them all back into the bar and closed the door. Cue Ball leaned toward David's ear.

"Don't worry about them. It can't possibly be worse on flight side, we are almost officers now."

David wasn't so sure, but Cue Ball had already sprung into action. He made a beeline toward the starlet look-alike, whisking her up on his arm and putting her securely under expert escort.

"Don't worry, sweetheart," he murmured. "I'll protect you."

At the rear of the O' Club was a series of rooms, each with a wall of glass that overlooked the lawn, beach, and bay beyond. To the right was the formal dining room, elegant yet not pretentious. A seafood buffet was being served. The young maidens peeked into the dining room, craving glamour and excitement, seeing themselves dining every Friday night at O' Clubs around the world, living the adventure of a naval aviator's wife.

They weren't contemplating the hardship of long separations or the sting of loss that came in waves with the world's most dangerous profession. Many of these innocent girls would learn through the harsh reality of experience.

Today, however, it was all fairy tales and dreams, with Paul Vincent Bement their personal guide through Wonderland and into their private reception.

CHAPTER 24

05:45 Local, 17OCT (11:45 GMT, 17OCT)
Naval Air Station, St. Louis, Missouri

The flight line of Lambert Field, NAS St. Louis, was still. Silent N2-S2 Stearman aircraft stretched for what seemed like miles in the early dawn light, their bright yellow color just coming to life as the first soft rays of sunlight caressed them.

Student naval aviator David B. Brennan stood in his new khaki flight coveralls holding a leather flight helmet, goggles, and gloves. He was nervous. It had been weeks since he had last flown with Irish; he hoped he had not forgotten how. Checking his brand-new, Navy-issued aviator's watch, he decided to go look for his instructor.

David found him engaged in close-quarter battle with a large, Navy-issue coffeemaker. An unintelligible string of insults, laced with profanity, filled the air and mixed with the acrid smell of burnt coffee.

A short, squat lieutenant commander turned to face David. His complexion was rough and pockmarked from severe acne as a youth. With his closely cropped hair and intense stare, he was intimidating.

"You Brennan?"

"Yes, sir."

"Good, you're early. Let's brief. I'm Lieutenant Commander Flannigan. I'm the boss around here. You know anything about coffeemakers?"

The brief was very familiar. It could have been J.T. or Irish sitting across the little wooden table. It was a good review; David nailed every question about the N2-S2. Lieutenant Commander Flannigan looked at him suspiciously and asked more, in rapid-fire order. Again, David handled the questions with ease.

"Okay, let's go fly," said Flannigan.

They headed straight to the maintenance shack, checked the logbook quickly, and went to the aircraft that had the same number painted on its side that was on the maintenance log. Flannigan demonstrated a preflight, told David to get in, and watched him climb expertly into the cockpit. As he strapped in, David felt a thump on his leather helmet. He looked up to see his instructor glaring down at him.

"You got prior flight time?"

David nodded. Flannigan rubbed his freshly shaved chin in contemplation, then manned up the rear cockpit. His bark reverberated through the voice tubes.

"Start us up, taxi to the duty, and take off."

David thought to himself, *Great. My first flight and I've already made the commanding officer angry. I better do this right.* He didn't pause to realize this was supposed to be a demonstration flight.

He taxied down to the end of the runway, did the engine run-ups, positioned near the threshold, received a green aldis lamp—two-colored light: red for stop, green for take off—from the tower and began a takeoff roll. David eased the tail up and rotated so smoothly in the still, morning air that Flannigan couldn't feel the transition to flight.

On climb out, he began shallow, clearing turns, looking for traffic. Throughout the maneuvers the aircraft stayed balanced and exactly on climb speed. Flannigan's voice seemed to change; he actually sounded happy.

"It's a great day! Fly northeast to the Missouri. Isn't it a glorious day?"

David nodded in agreement, flying toward the Missouri River. Glancing over his right shoulder, he could see where it met the Mississippi, and just to the north, where the Illinois River ran into the confluence as well. Passing through 5,000 feet, Flannigan's joyous voice sang out.

"Do a squirrel cage!"

David immediately complied. Aggressively but smoothly, he overbanked, letting the nose fall through the horizon, building speed as he simultaneously aligned on a farmer's field heading south. Leveling the wings as he hit maneuvering speed, he pulled four Gs, initiating a squirrel cage. He looped, did a Cuban 8, an Immelman, and then finished up with a split S, arriving back on the starting altitude, airspeed and heading exactly.

Suddenly, the mixture control went to idle cutoff and the Continental engine sputtered to a stop.

"Engine failure—land," came over the tubes.

David set up a high key over a farmer's pasture and spiraled down, landing smoothly and stopping mid-field.

"Start it." The instructor's gruffness was back. "Let's get back into the air."

Flannigan and David traded off control as they flew back to Lambert, doing nonstop aerobatics all the way to the field. Since they were the only ones in the pattern, they did a split S into the break and then flew seven touch-and-go landings, finishing with a full stop.

David kicked the tail and goosed the Continental to get the Stearman back in line without a tow. He started to get out, but Flannigan pushed him back into the seat.

"Solo," he said. "Be back in an hour. Have fun, don't crash."

The young aviator took off with the biggest smile he had ever worn, clearly visible to the diners in the Chase Park Plaza's top floor, glass-walled dining room, as he soared by level with the windows.

Lieutenant Commander Flannigan went directly to his office and called his counterpart at the formation and instrument, TA-6 Texan squadron.

"Cowboy, Crater here. I got a kid wasting my time and gas."

"That bad, huh?"

"No, that good. Flies the Stearman better than me."

"How many flights has he had?"

"Counting the one he's currently on, two."

Cowboy whistled.

"Send him over. We will fly him and see what all the boy really knows."

Again, David was up bright and early, waiting outside Lieutenant Commander Cerne's office when he arrived. Cowboy looked over at him as he walked in.

"You Brennan?"

"Yes, sir."

"Enter."

David stood at attention in front of Cerne's desk.

"Okay, Mister, let's see your wallet."

"Sir?"

Cerne didn't respond; instead, he held out his hand. David complied. Cerne pulled out David's commercial license and instrument card and studied the American Airlines ID card intently.

"Well, I guess we don't need to waste gas on teaching you instruments. You want to tell me why you are here when you could be on deferment, flying airliners and getting rich?"

David shifted uneasily. He knew this question would repeatedly come up, and he was uncomfortable answering it.

"I'm here to become a naval aviator, sir."

"I know what you are here for, Mister. I want to know the why."

David resisted the answer, more from a lack of ability than defiance.

"That's an order, son!"

As David looked at the salty Navy lieutenant commander, a flicker of hatred flashed in his eyes. "Japs shot down my father and brother."

He let the statement hang. Cerne's brow furrowed, trying to figure out how that could have happened and decided it didn't matter.

"We've all lost a lot, and we will lose more. The Navy isn't in the vengeance business, son."

David glared back at Cerne, tempted to ask how many family members he had lost, but said nothing. Instead, he reset his stare on the wall above and behind the lieutenant commander's head.

"We don't need any lone wolves out there," said Cerne. "You start chasing your own agenda and you will put your own wingman in danger. We are here to win a war, Mister, not get personal retribution. You read me?"

"Loud and clear, sir."

"Outstanding. Well then, we are going to go up on a little four-plane formation check ride in the TA-6 Texan after lunch, to solve the mystery of how it is that Naval Aviation Cadet First Class David B. Brennan seems to have already been trained as a naval aviator."

Cerne shoved a TA-6 Texan manual across the table, told David he had four hours to get familiar with it, and dismissed him.

03:00 Local, 19OCT (19:00 GMT, 18OCT)
The Jungle, The Philippines

Ominously, the jungle had changed, evolved for the occupying Japanese. It had hidden their crimes, but now it hid the avengers who sought justice. Butler's letter had infuriated the Japanese high command. They had taken it as a personal affront to their collective honor. An order was put out to be even more aggressive, and a bounty was put on Butler's head.

However, the effect on the troops in the field was much more profound. Nogushi's reputation had been one of a warrior, a Samurai of the Rising Sun. For his unit to be wiped out, and then for him to be humiliated by being hung as a common criminal, sent reverberations through the ranks.

If it could happen to Nogushi, then they were all accountable, they were all vulnerable. This was a huge psychological shift for the Japanese; they had always been the aggressor.s Their army had operated with impunity for years. Now platoons, entire companies, were disappearing in the dense, tropical rain forest. They began to fear the looming jungle. When they entered it, their concern was watching their backs—which kept their wanton slaughter and pillaging in check.

Hiding deep within the jungle's concealing layers, Kowalski quietly observed his captain interact with a Negrito tribesman.

"Hey, Sarge, you ever read *The Heart of Darkness*?"

Donnelley looked up, grasping what Kowalski really meant. "Yep, haven't we all?"

"I think the captain needs a copy."

"Sometimes combat does bad things to good people," said Donnelly. "We'll get him back. We just need to get out of this damn bush."

Despite his own reassuring words, Donnelley looked on Butler with worry.

13:10 Local, 18OCT (19:10 GMT, 18OCT)
Naval Air Station, St. Louis, Missouri

With three of his most experienced flight instructors crammed in his stuffy office, Cerne came to the point quickly. He looked up at the combat-tested aviators and spoke rapidly.

"Okay, gents, we have a ringer here. I want to know just what this little shit is capable of. I suspect we may be surprised; he's pretty damn intense."

Sitting at his desk, he poured himself a glass of water from a tall glass pitcher.

"We will start with four-plane formation, then move on to a little dogfighting. Jimmy, you are in his backseat. Don't say a word or do anything unless—"

"Yeah, I know: unless he's gonna kill someone."

"Okay, good. He's never flown the Texan, this being a first flight in type and a formation hop to boot. It should overload him, and we can see what we really have."

A division of four TA-6 Texans rumbled and snorted on the main runway of NAS St. Louis. They were in finger four formation and ready for takeoff. David was in dash four, at the far right end of the flight. Cowboy looked left and right for a thumbs-up from each cockpit. Satisfied, he ran up the power and kissed off the second section. He released the brakes and began to accelerate with his individual wingman locked in place on his left wing.

Ten seconds later, David's section followed. It had been a while, and he was in an unfamiliar aircraft with a lot better performance than the Stearman. It was also more responsive. He initially over-controlled it on rotation, then settled down into a tight, parade wing position.

His section lead made a cranking motion with his hand and nodded his head backward, signaling he was raising the gear. David searched for the handle, getting out of position momentarily before finally retracting the landing gear. He bobbled around again as he got the feel of the Texan at cruise speed, and then assumed a perfect parade position again. Monitoring his progress through mirrors, the section lead loosened him into cruise formation as he closed in on Cowboy's flight of two and rendezvoused.

After a series of break-ups and rendezvous, they split up into flights of two again for some formation aerobatics. The puffy clouds of Indian summer began to build in the afternoon sky, joining together in small ranges that looked like strung popcorn. Steep walls and valleys formed an aerial playground. David stayed welded in place for the basic maneuvers through the valleys of the gods.

The section lead grew bored finally, snapping over the common frequency.

"Take trail position, 1000 to 1,500 interval, stand by to maneuver."

Tail-chasing through valleys of clouds is the most joyful expression of powered flight. Speed is relative; the rush of clouds past the canopy at close range provides the reference the brain needs to sense speed.

The 1000 to 1,500 interval was not an arbitrary distance; it was the kill zone. A Navy fighter's normal armament was six .50-caliber machine guns. Squadrons' ordnance men would sight in each gun so they all converged at 1,500 feet. By converging the guns' aim points, it concentrated the aircraft's fire into a deadly mass, the center of which was aligned with the piper of the electric gun sight.

David took position in the heart of the gun's lethality envelope.

"Set combat power."

He pushed the mixture to full rich and cycled the prop lever to max pitch, then slowly matched the lead's power addition until the throttle was all the way forward.

Slowly, the lead aircraft rolled left, not stopping until it was inverted. The Texan's nose plunged toward the Earth, pushing the airspeed to the red line. Aggressively, it rolled wings level and pulled four Gs up the face of one of the puffy clouds. A valley revealed itself to the right, and the lead Texan rolled toward it, then pulled deeply down into it. The valley began to close off, forcing the lead to pull steeply, straight up the face of a cloud. David was in hot pursuit as they crested the clouds, and the lead Texan rolled inverted again, pulling down the backside of the cloud. Their canopies skimmed the wisps of cloud that clipped by at incredible speed. With their noses now pointed down, the first Texan twisted in a left turn, pulling out below a cloud overhang.

The lead Texan pulled tightly to hold the cloud face close and prevent David from pulling lead pursuit and thus get his nose in a position for a shot. As the overhanGs edge flashed by, the lead snap rolled inverted, pulling into a split S and continuing to hold the cloud tight. David held on even through the rough ride of the wingtip vortices. The lead pulled under the bottom and back up the opposite side until the cloud fell away. At the apex of the climb, David noticed he was closing on the lead rapidly. He saw the flicker of the propeller in the afternoon sun change. He went to idle power!

The lead aircraft grew rapidly in David's front windscreen, showing only its plan form (view of the aircraft's top) as it turned left. That visual cue told him that the lead Texan's pilot had pulled on a maximum performance break turn. He was trying to force David into an in-close overshoot so he could reverse their positions and shoot David as he floated out in front of him. David didn't bite. Knowing he had an airspeed advantage, he pulled up and did a pirouette roll in the opposite direction. This gave him the nose-to-tail separation he needed, and he pulled for a shot.

Looking over his left shoulder at David, the lead pilot knew he had sold the ranch and didn't get a cent for it. He was in serious jeopardy and tried the same last-ditch maneuver in the opposite direction. Again, David matched it with a rudder roll the other way. As the airspeed dropped away to almost zero, he let the nose fall through to regain it and his 1,000 to 1,500 feet of separation. With the speed he had built, he used that energy to pull for a shot.

Out of airspeed and ideas, the lead faked another break turn and split S-ed under David, attempting to run away behind him. Still with an airspeed advantage, David didn't let him get away. He matched the move and pulled for the kill as they fell to the Earth together.

Clearly defeated, the lead transmitted, "Knock it off," over the radio, irritation apparent in his voice to everyone on the frequency.

Cowboy had watched the entire dogfight from overhead. "Okay, let's RTB. Bells, you've got the lead."

They flew back to NAS St. Louis in echelon right formation. All four aircraft were perfectly spaced on a forty-five-degree line of bearing. David was in dash two with Cowboy watching from his right wing as dash three.

They entered the traffic pattern for an aircraft carrier-type break-up, peeling off one at a time and landing in order. David only bounced once. Considering it was his first landing-in-type ever, his instructor was impressed.

All four aircraft taxied in order, parking together on the flight line. Before they had even unstrapped, Lieutenant Bellman, the pilot they had fought, was on their wing yelling to David's flight instructor in the rear cockpit.

"You were supposed to let him fly!"

"I did."

"My ass! I'm not blind. No kid off the street knows how to dogfight like that, even if he does have a commercial license."

"Bells, I never touched the stick or said a damn word—"

"Bullshit! Next time you want to fight, we'll start neutral and I'll wax your tail." Bellman stormed off toward the hangar.

Cowboy was leaning on the other wing, listening. "You telling the truth, or just screwing with Bells?"

"Skipper, I never said a word or touched a control."

He nodded and turned to David, who had wisely remained silent throughout the conflict.

"Okay, Mister Brennan, let's go debrief so you can tell us just who the hell you are."

CHAPTER 25

08:00 Local, 21OCT (14:00 GMT, 21OCT)
Union Station, St. Louis, Missouri

A Missouri Pacific Streamliner locomotive eased out of the train shed attached to Union Station. The train shed had the largest roof span in the world when built in 1894. It also was the world's biggest and busiest train station, still handling 100,000 passengers a day. David marveled at the bustling activity.

Slowly, the diesel engines powered the train to speed as it pulled onto the open track. Its whistle blew as the Streamliner's locomotive pulled the train toward the river. It had been a whirlwind stay in St. Louis, and he had quickly fallen in love with the city. He wanted to stay and explore more but for now, his journey led back south, to Pensacola yet again.

Cowboy had flown him four more times, on four-plane formation hops to get him used to operating in a division, and then assigned him to advanced Fighter Operational Training Squadron Four (VOT-4). In VOT-4, he would be flying the F2-A3 Brewster Buffalo.

The Buff had proven itself woefully inadequate as a combat aircraft. Slow, underpowered, and a handling nightmare, it was no match for the Zero. In fact, the Grumman F-4F Wildcat was no match for the Zero, and it could fly circles around a Buff.

Its performance, and the tendency of its landing gear to collapse when trapping on board the carrier, got it transferred to the training command. Navy brass figured if you could teach a student to fly as a fighter pilot in the Buff, he'd be a tiger in the Wildcat or the new F-6F Hellcat.

David didn't care. To him it was a fighter and would propel him to his wings and the fleet. His dream to fly fighters was coming true, and he was happy. But he also knew that his little advantage was now gone. He would be even now with the other students in the most competitive training program in the world. Plus, he would have to do something he'd never done: land on an aircraft carrier. Only after he carrier-qualified would he receive the coveted wings of gold.

They said the carrier looked like a tombstone from the air, but he'd worry about that when the time came. For now he intended to sit back, relax, and watch the Mississippi River roll by. As the Streamliner meandered down the great river valley, he marveled at the difference in perspective from the eagle's eye view that he and Irish had enjoyed a few short weeks ago. He also understood what Irish had said as the beautiful, bustling river towns zipped by one after another. The risk of living on the river's edge was indeed worth it, both economically and aesthetically.

David thought about how much his life had changed in just four short months. He felt transformed and profoundly tied to his father and brother Trey. They had shared not just blood but experience. It was an experience that resulted in being accepted into a cloistered community, one with a cultish loyalty among members and the most severe consequence possible for failure.

He knew that what lay ahead was still the biggest challenge, and it wasn't carrier qualification. CQ was a hurdle and no more, though significant and certainly dangerous. Combat, however, was the true test he faced. It had already claimed a portion of his mind, even threatening to consume his very soul. Yet he had not fired or even witnessed a single shot; he had not even been within 2,000 miles of it.

10:05 Local, 22OCT (23:05 GMT, 21OCT)
Guadalcanal

Thumper sat in the back of a green canvas tent. Less than three months old, it was already moldy, sun-bleached, and rotting on its poles. Stifling heat and oppressive humidity necessitated that the sides be rolled up, allowing bugs to pass freely and feast on the human inhabitants.

He held three separate messages from USMC Pacific Fleet HQ. The first, dated two weeks earlier, promoted him to lieutenant colonel. The second, dated one week earlier, assigned him as the air wing commander and promoted him to full colonel. The third was a message to the wing commander.

Sitting with the three squadron commanders, now officially Thumper's commanders, he passed all three messages to them. No one spoke; congratulations were not appropriate. El Toro lay at the bottom of the Pacific. Besides, each man took it for what it really was: an extension in hell. A hell that was about to get worse.

07:16 Local, 23OCT (13:15 GMT, 23OCT)
Chevalier Field, Naval Air Station, Pensacola, Florida

David stood looking at the line of F2-A3 Brewster Buffalos. Despite their reputation, they were combat-tested fighters and in their dark blue fleet paint, they looked the part. He had only been back two days, and he was going on his first flight. The need for new aviators had become critical. The big push was on.

His first flight, and every flight from now on, would be solo. The Buff had only one seat. But he would not be lonely, because they had told him he would not fly with less than one wingman for the rest of his training. They were being trained as fighter pilots, and fighter pilots never flew alone.

Easing the blunt-nosed fighter off Chevalier Field's longest runway, David quickly raised the gear handle and established best climb speed. He snuck a peek in the mirror attached to his canopy bow at the instructor's Buff that was chasing him. A large smile appeared on his face as he turned toward the practice area.

06:15 Local, 24OCT (22:16 GMT, 23OCT)
The Jungle, The Philippines

Sergeant Donnelly sliced through the jungle toward the small pond that had become their water supply and base camp. He found Captain Butler sitting peacefully on a rock, weaving a rope out of shredded frond leaves. The rope was good, too good. Donnelly looked at it as he spoke.

"Hey, Captain, when are we going to head down and get some supplies?"

Butler didn't look up, his attention fixated on his task. "We got all we need here." His hands continued to expertly weave the split fronds into a stout rope.

"Yes, sir. Still, we should at least gather some intel."

"Okay, you and Kowalski take Rubio."

"Sir, I'd like you to come. We may need an officer."

It was a totally bullshit response; Donnelley's concern was not having an officer with him. It was the fact that his commanding officer had most definitely gone native on him. He was a student of war; he had read about the last conflict in the Philippines forty years earlier. He knew he had to get Butler out of the bush, and quickly.

Butler set down the rope and glared at his sergeant, seeing through the ruse. Subconsciously, he rubbed the silver crucifix.

"Okay, Sergeant Donnelly, let's take a trip to civilization."

CHAPTER 26

A frantic pace had been set and kept over the past few weeks. Before, each student naval aviator was an insignificant generic cog in a very large machine. Their previous pace had seemed erratic. They would have a lot of down time, then spurts of activity. Now, they were a specific piece of the machine—and it needed more of that piece: fighter pilots.

Had they consciously considered why so many more fighter pilots were needed, it may have given them pause. However, they were too busy studying and flying. Each day, they checked the posted scores of the previous day's flights. Competition was keen. Everyone wanted to be number one so they could get their first choice of aircraft.

David was in the hunt, but his head start had evaporated. He was one of many now, just another student headed to war. The attrition rate had decreased but still circled overhead like a vulture, patiently waiting. Death, however, was not as patient. Its specter had become a constant presence as the accident rate reached a horrendous level.

Not a week went by without a fatal accident at one of the many airfields surrounding Pensacola. Baron Field had already been nicknamed Bloody Baron, and for good reason: a nonstop string of fatal accidents.

Flying twice a day, they were clicking through the syllabus: familiarization, formation, night flight, and tactics. In tactics, they learned the Thatch Weave. The Japanese Zero could outmatch anything the American Navy could put in the air. To compensate, a fleet lieutenant named Jimmy Thatch had developed a weaving maneuver that revised fighter tactics.

Established fighter doctrine of the day put the lead fighter in an attacking role, and the less experienced wing man would cover his six. Thatch's tactic involved mutual support, where both fighters were shooters. Starting 3,000 to 5,000 feet apart, the fighters would turn toward each other, cross paths, reverse and turn back toward each other again.

By using this tactic, either fighter could shoot a Zero at the merge. If the engaged fighter was pushing a Zero, unable to get into a firing solution, the free wingman could take a high deflection shot as their flight paths crossed. Japanese fighters were very lightly armored, so a short burst at the merge point was more than enough to blow them out of the sky.

Defensively, it worked even better. The engaged fighter would simply drag the Zero in front of his wingman, who was free to maneuver into the firing envelope and blast him off his tail. The positions of flight lead and wingman were equal and interchangeable in this new aerial combat, dictated more by circumstance than rank or experience. He had flown his last tactics flight that morning.

This was unthinkable to the rigidly hierarchical Japanese, thus they never comprehended, let alone adjusted, to the weaving tactic. The result was devastating to the Japanese naval aviators. Their experience level had been the highest in the world for carrier warfare. Now, with each engagement, the Japanese air wings were depleted of experience while the US Navy's increased.

A pivotal policy cemented the diverging experience levels. The US Naval Aviation Training Command had demanded and received combat-experienced aviators to teach students the harsh lessons of war in the friendly skies of Florida and Texas. Lessons were learned well. The young aviators went to the fleet proficient in tactics, gunnery—and more importantly, they were confident and aggressive. The Americans showed up knowing how to fight and eager to do it. Their Japanese counterparts showed up knowing how to fly and not much more. By the end of the war, the Japanese could do little more than deliberately run their aircraft into US ships.

All this would come to David and his classmates in due time. At the moment, they were engaged in battle with a non-maneuvering flapping piece of material that seemed as wily as a Zero. Revealing its shortcomings in a glaring manner, the Brewster Buffalo's numerous problems were becoming all too apparent. Chief of its many design flaws was an inadequate vertical empennage and rudder. The total surface area of the vertical stabilizer was insufficient to keep the short, coupled F2-A3 stable in the yaw axis when accelerated from the neutral position.

In other words, the tail was too small and too close to the nose to keep the airplane from wobbling in maneuvers. Thus, when rolling in and then reversing the turn to shoot the target banner, the unstable nose would scatter bullets everywhere.

The gun pattern involved six aircraft. First, the chase plane would take off and orbit the field while the tractor aircraft would taxi out, with banner attached. Once ready, the tractor would take off, holding its nose down to maximize the acceleration rate. After it achieved maneuver speed, it would pitch violently up and the attaching line would play out during acceleration. With the aircraft zooming skyward in the pitch-up, the banner would get yanked from the runway cleanly.

When the banner was off the runway, the tractor would lower its nose but continue to climb out steeply. At this point, the chase plane would join on the tractor and visually check that all had gone as planned.

Next, the four shooters, call sign: Duck Flight, would position on the runway and take off, following the tractor over the Gulf of Mexico. They would proceed out to sea into the appropriately named warning area. Ships and aircraft had been notified that this area was a gunnery range, clearly marked on navigation charts. They would give wide berth, knowing students were doing the shooting.

As they reached their pre-determined position, the chase would call on station and report the banner's orientation. Twelve and six meant it was straight up and down. After calling the position, the chase aircraft would climb overhead to be the airborne referee. At eighty knots, the tractor set a straight and wings-level course.

Closing with a 150-knot advantage, the shooters, led by an instructor pilot, aligned with the tractor to pass just off its right wing. David's BAT I officer, Lieutenant Stutzman, was leading the shooters.

"Duck one, at the initial," he transmitted as they lined up in trail. "Ducks, the banner flies one and seven, you are cleared in hot."

They flipped on their gun sights as they continued to close on the banner. In echelon right, they were in tight parade position as they hurled toward the tractor at 230 knots indicated airspeed. David was in dash two, fighting to maintain a perfect position as they bounced toward the target in the unstable Gulf air.

He concentrated on keeping his stick movements to a minimum so he wouldn't mess up his fellow wingmen. Suddenly, the tractor and target banner came into his peripheral vision. It was closing at an incredible rate. They were going to pass close, very close. *Are we going to hit the tractor?* The excitement was building to a crescendo when they flashed by the tractor with a mere 30 feet of wingtip separation.

Lieutenant Stutzman yanked off his wing and out of view as he pulled toward the high reversal and perch.

"Ducks in the pitch."

David was now temporarily in the lead and counted to five, then yanked on his own four-G pitch-up turn, pulling 2,000 feet higher and abeam the tractor-banner. As he began to reverse his turn, he saw the lead roll in toward the tractor-banner.

"Duck one is in hot."

Fully reversed he was aligned again in the same direction, 2,000 feet higher than the tractor-banner and offset laterally. David quickly flipped on his master armament switch, picked up his interval (Lieutenant Stutzman's aircraft), now at the low reversal. With the lead aircraft in sight, David rolled in, pulling down and toward the tractor-banner.

"Duck two is in hot," he transmitted.

David pulled aft of the tractor and put his piper on the target as he saw the lead pull off target, flying past the tractor again.

"Duck one is off, switches safe."

"Duck three is in hot," was transmitted by the aircraft behind him.

David reversed his turn, rolling 180 degrees to the left to hold the piper on the banner. He flipped the switch that charged his guns. The banner seemed to be gyrating wildly. As it passed through his piper, he squeezed the trigger. Fifty-caliber bullets exploded out of the four machine guns, shaking the F2-A3 with surprising force.

The cacophony of the shells erupting from their guns shocked him into releasing the trigger. It was a fortunate reaction, because the rounds were literally being scattered to the ocean below. He didn't have a second to react to the closing banner except to duck under it by pushing the stick forward. It flashed over his head as he wrestled on a four-G turn, pulling past the tractor and transmitting.

"Duck two is off, switches safe," he strained into his microphone.

"Duck four is in hot."

David was all screwed up and he knew it. He had to get his act together, and quick, or he'd get a flight down. He snatched on six Gs, thrashing the unruly Buff back into position. He couldn't take a time-out, not even a breath. This dynamic event was in motion and could not be stopped; it could not even be slowed down. The G-stressed voices continued over the radio.

"Duck three is off, switches safe."

"Duck one is in hot." The lead was back in for his second run already.

He yanked on a high reversal turn, flipped on the master, and pulled for the tractor-banner again.

"Duck two is in hot."

"Duck four is off, switches safe."

David saw the lead reverse at the low reversal point and the smoke from his firing guns.

He was starting to see the entire pattern. Stutzman was at the low reversal, Duck four was past the tractor and pulling back up to the high reversal. Duck three was ahead of four, reversing to get set for his roll in. Fluid was too rigid a term to describe what was going on.

An irrepressible smile cracked on his face as he got it. Jon's voice rang in his memory: At high G, rudder is king; at low G, aileron is. He continued to pull, centering the piper on the target banner, and instantly recognized that the rudder was the problem. Rather than wrestle the rudder to get the Buff to reverse, he unloaded to zero G and used only the ailerons. The Buff effortlessly snapped from right wing down to left wing down, without pulling the piper from the banner.

"Duck one is off, switches safe."

He squeezed the trigger.

"Duck three is in hot."

A steady stream of fifty-cal made its way to the banner as he held the piper on the target by increasing the pull. One thousand, two thousand, three thousand. At the same time, he released the trigger, relaxed the G, and switched off the master arm. Passing easily behind and aft of the banner, he jerked on four Gs to pass next to the tractor again.

"Duck two is off, switches safe."

"Duck four is in hot."

David made three more hot runs before his guns would spit no more. He had to stay in the pattern, so he used the extra passes to practice the flying mechanics of it. Both he and Stutzman were out of ammo and announced it at roll in by transmitting "Winchester" instead of "hot."

Three and four were not as successful getting into a firing solution each time, not daring to shoot if the alignment wasn't correct. His buddy Robbie, in dash four, was called off twice by the chase aircraft. Finally, all four aircraft had expended their ammunition. Lieutenant Stutzman made a final run announcing last pass, and then began a lefthand orbit instead of reversing after the pitch up. Each of his ducklings followed suit and rendezvoused, RTB-ing after reformulating.

Waiting for the banner to be scored, the chase debriefed the pattern work when they were back on deck. David received an above average for being able to shoot on the first pass. Unfortunately, he balanced that out with a below average in head work for flying under the banner. Billy Ray seemed happy with a single below average for pattern work in dash three. Robbie was obviously worried about a below for pattern and another in airmanship for being called off target by the chase.

Lieutenant Stutzman was talking and flying with his hands, the way fighter pilots do, when the tractor pilot came in with the scores. He looked directly at Robbie.

"You point at me again with hot guns and I'll attrite you on the spot. Do you read me, Mister?"

"Aye, aye, sir."

He unfolded the ordies' score sheet. It contained the score for each shooter. The bullets for each were color-coded in different dyes. When they passed through the banner, they left a colored ring on it. The ordnance men would count the differently colored rings for the score.

"Black?"

Robbie showed his color-coordinated ordie card.

"Zero hits; absolutely pathetic!"

"Purple?"

Billy Ray held up his purple card.

"Three hits; sad."

"Blue?"

Lieutenant Stutzman instantly looked at David as he held up his own blue card. He knew the order was inverse to hits, and this little shit just outscored him.

"Twenty-seven out of eighty, exceptional for the Brewster."

"Red?"

Even though it was obvious who had red, David held up his card.

"Thirty-two. Damn lucky, son. We will see how long that lasts."

All in all, it was a better-than-average Gun-1. No mid-airs, no simo runs, and no errant bullets.

"Okay, gents, no grades for hits on Gun-1. You're dismissed. Mister Brennan, stand fast."

David stood at attention as the others filed out.

"Relax, Brennan." Stutzman was tapping the score sheet with his pencil.

"I don't believe in luck, Mister Brennan. I know all about your background, but it still doesn't explain this."

Lieutenant Stutzman was a natural leader, soft spoken and confident. His look demanded an explanation, very loudly and very clearly.

"My father's friends taught me how to shoot skeet from the back of a moving pick-up," replied David.

Stutzman nodded, trying not to smile in appreciation of the obviously exceptional training this kid had already received from who-knows-who.

"Okay, you're a good shot, but that still doesn't explain being able to shoot in the Brewster."

David thought about it, trying to gather an acceptable explanation in his head that he could verbalize. Stutzman patiently waited.

"Sir, normally the rudder is king at high-G. However, in the F2-A3, when you try to turn with the rudder, it uncouples the nose in yaw, moving it all over the sky, which makes tracking the banner impossible. So I decided to reverse by unloading the G and using aileron only."

Stutzman smiled slightly, stood up and patted David on the back as he left.

"Don't tell any of the other instructors about our little secret."

"Aye, aye, sir."

He left David in the briefing room and walked from the wooden hangar to the parking lot. He had to look for his old Ford, having forgotten where he had parked it. Two, sometimes three, flights a day were wearing him down; he was tired. He drove the short distance to BAT I and parked out front.

Stiffly, he walked up the cement steps into the brick colonial building and down the hall. Candidates locked up into the position of attention as he wearily passed by. Their starched uniforms and the highly polished tile floor contrasted sharply with his rumpled, sweaty appearance.

Stutzman's flying coveralls had a large salt stain on its back; his face wore a mask of oil from the Brewster's leaking engine. His matted hair had no chance of dragging a comb through it until he washed it thoroughly in the shower.

He was sitting in a daze when a sharp knock on the door snapped him out of it. He looked up, still slumped in his chair, and waved Sergeant Major Paillou into his sterile office. Paillou closed the door behind him.

"Problem, Sergeant Major?"

"No, sir. A favor."

"Ask away."

"Sir, I heard the Brennan kid is in your squadron, and I was just wondering—"

Lieutenant Stutzman cut him off with a raised hand and a chuckle. He opened the bottom drawer of his desk and pulled out a bottle of Scotch and two glasses. Pouring a healthy dose into both glasses, he passed one to the sergeant major.

"I just flew with him on a gun hop. You don't have to worry about that little bastard. He outshot me on his first attempt."

Paillou whistled under his breath. "I thought you were the top gun over there at Training Four?"

"So did I," the lieutenant replied as they clinked glasses.

CHAPTER 27

Irish sat in the great room of Kate's Manor, as they called it now. The beamed cathedral ceiling was thirty feet overhead. Suits of armor stood guard in each corner. Heraldry of various clans, emblazoned on shields, hung high on the grey stone walls. A fire crackled in the oversized fireplace.

Having been an involuntary subject of the British Empire, Irish sat uncomfortably in the lair of the lion, feeling very much like his name should be Daniel. He heard the uneven gait of heels on the slate floor and knew it was J.T. approaching down the long entrance hall.

A heavy oak door creaked open and J.T. entered with a bottle of single malt scotch, two glasses, and two very large Cuban cigars.

"Well, well, made ourselves rather comfortable, haven't we?"

"Irish, you of all people know that life does not have to be unpleasant."

"Yeah, yeah, sure. So when are you going to tell me why we are really here?"

"To enjoy a fine scotch and a Cuban, of course."

"That's not what I meant and you know it."

J.T. walked the twenty paces to Irish's end of the table, smiling, and poured two glasses of scotch, adding an equal amount of water to release the flavor. He lit a cigar with infuriating precision and care, rolling it through the flame from a large sterling silver lighter. Satisfied, he handed it to Irish and repeated the process. After taking a long draw off the Cuban, he exhaled a billowing cloud of smoke with a contented grunt.

"We are going to plan the air invasion of Europe."

Irish shrugged, downed the scotch, and shook the empty crystal glass at J.T. for a refill. With a freshly charged glass, he leaned back in the oversized chair, looped his leg over an armrest, and took a long draw from his fine cigar, exhaling in the same manner as J.T.

"Sounds easy."

J.T. nodded and they clinked glasses.

14:21 Local, 07NOV (20:21 GMT, 07NOV)
Warning Area South of Naval Air Station, Pensacola

Yanking off the high perch, the F2-A3 Buffalo pulled in a hard turn, descending toward the tractor below. All 1,300 horsepower of the Wright Cyclone, straining through the propeller, accelerated the heavy aircraft with the aid of gravity, toward the banner at an exhilarating rate. The banner appeared to grow in the windscreen. Fifteen hundred feet before reaching the banner's altitude, the F2-A3 unloaded slightly and reversed its turn, centering the piper on the target as the four-fifties spit blue-tinted rounds.

David held the trigger for a full three-count and released it, flying behind and to the right of the tractor aircraft. The 150-knot advantage as he ripped by so closely was eye-watering.

"Two is off, switches safe."

He looked up over his left shoulder as he pulled four Gs to get back to the high perch. Something was wrong. Billy Ray was way out of position as dash three. He was late and long. Robbie was rolling in from the proper position. Billy Ray had way too much distance to cover for the sequence.

"Three, come—"

Static instead of a transmission filled their earphones. Overhead, the chase was desperately trying to call off dash three. Lieutenant Stutzman heard the attempted transmission. He whipped his Buff around with all his might at the top of the high perch and was horrified to see both three and four closing on the banner—neither aware of the other's position.

Stutzman screamed over the radio, "SIMO RUN, SIMO RUN!"

It was the emergency radio call that meant two aircraft were on a simultaneous hot run at the banner. But it was too late. Robbie had already squeezed the trigger. When the call registered he released immediately, but Billy Ray was pulling hard to get into position and flew into the one-second burst as he came out from underneath Robbie's nose. At such close range, five of the twenty rounds hit the cockpit, killing Billy Ray instantly. His Brewster, now an unguided missile, spiraled out of control until it slammed into the tractor aircraft at over 150 knots of speed advantage.

David reversed just in time to see the flaming debris falling to the ocean below. There were no parachutes.

"KNOCK IT OFF, KNOCK IT OFF, KNOCK IT OFF!" shrieked over the radio. "Dash two, you have the lead. Take four and the chase bird back to base; chase's radio is out. Duck one has the on-scene command, RTB now."

David wanted to cry out in anguish; he wanted to make it all stop. He wanted to get off the merry-go-round but couldn't. He willed himself to set cruise power and head back for Pensacola. Robbie joined on his left wing, and with the chase on his right wing, they flew silently back to Chevalier Field.

05:22 Local, 08NOV (20:21 GMT, 07NOV)
The Jungle, The Philippines

A full moon hung over the islands, its illumination reaching everywhere but the deepest jungle. Rubio waited on the edge of a clearing around a Japanese-occupied village. Butler and two of the Negrito Indians had slipped into the settlement, and Rubio nervously scanned the well-lit clearing for them. They should have been back by now. In fact, they shouldn't have gone at all. It was too bright for a reconnaissance mission.

A hand reached out of the darkness of the jungle and tapped him. Rubio nearly jumped out of his skin. Captain Butler held a finger to his lips, eyes shining brightly in the moonlight. His skin was darkened with a mixture of berries and clay. Were it not for his blue eyes, he could have been one of the Negrito tribesmen who rose from the jungle floor on either side of him. Butler motioned Rubio toward the jungle where they rendezvoused with Donnelly and Kowalski and moved deeper, under cover of darkness.

At sunrise, Donnelly found Butler in a stream, washing off the berry and clay mixture. As he emerged from the water, Donnelley handed him a khaki uniform shirt and trousers.

"How are you feeling, Captain?"

"Good, Sergeant, real good."

"Did you find anything out?"

Butler nodded slowly, spreading out a Tagolog newspaper on a large rock.

"You are not going to like it." Tapping the yellowed paper, he added, "I'm no expert on the language but from what I gather, Corregidor fell, and it happened months ago."

Donnelly, who could read Tagalog, took the paper and studied it intently, shaking his head slowly.

"Worse than that, sir: they never got reinforced. Looks like MacArthur escaped to Australia and everyone else was left behind. Poor bastards, they didn't have a chance."

Butler pulled on his pistol belt and squatted down to tie his boots.

"Our plan to wait for reinforcements just went out the window. We need to hook up with someone who has a link to the outside world."

"What do you suggest, Captain?"

Butler pulled a well-worn map of the Philippines out of his ruck and studied it.

"Well, we know they landed in Lingayen Bay and moved south on Bataan. A second thrust landed somewhere south of Legazpi, because they chased us up the number one highway toward Manila."

He pointed to the chart with his KA-BAR knife, lost in thought, then continued.

"Now, we haven't seen a US aircraft since week one, so we have to assume the Japanese consolidated their position and overran the fighter base at Clark. Luzon is the big prize, and it appears they have it wrapped up. That leaves the islands to the south as our best bet for an unoccupied or lightly occupied area."

He rubbed the crucifix against his lower lip as he thought. Donnelly smiled, happy to have his captain back.

"We will march down the Sierra Madre range until we are south of Santa Cruz, cut across to Batangas, and try to slip across the strait to Mindoro Island. Let's saddle up."

"Yes, sir." Donnelly saluted and went to muster the troops.

08:01 Local, 08NOV (14:01 GMT, 08NOV)
Naval Aviation Schools Command, Naval Air Station, Pensacola

David stood at rigid attention in front of a long, green, felt-topped table. Three senior naval aviators in dress khaki uniforms were seated on the opposite side. Each had a cool glass of water in front of him. David did not.

Out of his peripheral vision, he could see the glasses sweat, drops running down the length of the glasses. They seemed perfectly coordinated with the droplets of sweat sliding down his back, picking up speed until reaching the waistband of his boxers.

Looking up from a stack of papers, the senior officer who sat in the middle stared at David. He was a large man, with a barrel chest and a nose that clearly had been broken more than once. His grey, flattop crew cut was professional and perfect. Overall, his physical appearance demanded he not be trifled with.

"Son, do you understand that this is a FENAB?"

"Yes, sir."

"And that a FENAB stands for Field Evaluation of a Naval Aviator Board?"

"Yes, sir."

"In short, we are here to determine if Lieutenant Stutzman should lose his wings and whether Candidate Robinson should be terminated or continue training."

David was astounded. He had anticipated Robbie being on trial but not Lieutenant Stutzman. His bearing broke, and he met Commander Caulfield's fixed gaze.

"But, sir, Lieutenant Stutzman was not at fault. He attempted to—"

"We will be the judges of that, young man!"

"Son," added another commander seated at the table, "in this man's Navy, you don't come back as a flight lead from a simple training mission short two aircraft and two aviators without getting asked why."

David snapped back to attention in an attempt to regain his military bearing, but inside, his mind spun out of control.

"Now, if you don't mind, Candidate," Commander Caulfield snorted, "we will ask the questions."

It had only been a day and already the accident had been investigated, adjudicated, signed, sealed, and delivered. The accident boards were getting a lot of experience lately and had streamlined the process. All that was left would be a memorial service at the chapel and the shattered lives of those left behind.

No accident comes without a chain of events and findings of fact. In this case, it was judged that the chain consisted of:

a. Billy Ray being out of position,

b. Robbie seeing David coming off target and assuming it was Billy Ray,

c. the untimely failure of the chase's radio, and

d. both Robbie and Billy Ray failing to recognize a simo run.

Lieutenant Stutzman was absolved. However, he would carry the guilt of losing a friend and a student under his command. Robbie was given a flight down but returned to training status. David's role had been as a witness, but he carried his own guilt. He knew if he had been more proactive and made the radio call for a simo run immediately, it might have broken the chain of events. This shaped him as an aviator; he would never again follow protocol just for the sake of protocol. He would never be just along for the ride, no matter how junior or new he was.

Robbie sat on the concrete steps of the NAS Pensacola bachelor officers' quarters. The red brick building towered over him, its square columns rising into the air, framing him, confining him. Cyprus trees, with Spanish moss hanging from outstretched limbs, added to the macabre scene. He sat, shrinking inside, wishing he could fade into oblivion. He had killed his friend, shot him dead, and that had led directly to the death of Lieutenant Junior Grade Ford. My God, Lieutenant Ford survived a combat cruise, and I killed him.

Robbie's father, Rear Admiral T.J. Robinson, had sent him a telegram of encouragement, but it had the opposite effect. Now his father knew of his failure and would be humiliated by it.

Walking through the lobby, David saw Robbie and went out to sit next to him on the steps.

"Hey, Robbie, how are you doing?"

"Are you kidding, David? I just killed two guys, remember?"

David patted him on the shoulder. "Billy Ray was out of position, the chase's radio failed. Hell, if I had made the call when I pulled off, it wouldn't have happened."

"That wasn't your job, David. But it was damn sure my job not to shoot down my friend. Besides, it really doesn't matter. I can't hit the broadside of a barn from the inside. They'll put me back in the air because of my old man, then quietly attrite me for performance."

They sat silently as the cypress trees swayed in the hot breeze. Robbie began to weep.

David sat by his side until he was done. "Let's get a beer."

"Okay."

They entered the BOQ bar, a small, dark room off the main lobby. The other students looked at them as if they had the plague. Robbie started to leave, but David caught his arm and pushed him to the bar.

"Don't worry about these guys," he murmured. "They are just scared. And don't worry about your check ride either."

They bellied up to the bar and ordered two Budweisers.

CHAPTER 28

07:00 Local, 10NOV (20:00 GMT, 09NOV)
Guadalcanal, Solomon Islands

Colonel Thumper McDonald sat at the same crate desk with the same rotting tent overhead in the same stifling, motionless air. What was different was that his body was joining the systemic rot.

He held a compress against his ear, which was oozing blood and puss in a continual flow. The flight surgeon had just lanced it an hour ago. His executive officer entered with his normal smile.

"How's the ear?"

"Oh, I had a very pleasant visit from the doc. Cripes, first dysentery and now diphtheria. How's everyone else holding up?"

"We are at forty percent strength with you off the schedule."

"I'm not off the schedule."

The XO looked up from his ledger, his smile gone. "Colonel, we can't afford to lose another wing commander."

"What we can't afford to lose, Paul, is this island. Keep me on. That is an order."

"Aye, aye, sir. I'll put you on a milk run, at least for today."

Thumper sat at the end of the PSP, Perforated Steel Plate, makeshift runway made of sections of steel joined together. The steel matt did prevent potholes from forming from the constant rain, but that was about it. The metal runway conformed to the ground beneath it, so the ride was often a wild one. All considered, the Navy Seabees did an incredible job just keeping it open, but it was still a roller-coaster ride.

He was most definitely not in the mood for a roller-coaster ride. Warm blood mixed with puss trickled down his neck. He didn't bother to wipe it off, knowing it would only get worse at altitude. He was lightheaded, and his sinuses hurt whenever he turned his head too rapidly. Thumper was in no shape to fight, and he knew it. He also knew his men were watching.

Finally, he was ready and looking to his wingman, Captain Paul Lady, for a thumbs-up. Receiving it, he flashed a return and shoved the throttle forward. Two thousand horses began to be fed. All eighteen cylinders of the Pratt and Whitney R-2800-8 Double Wasp engine were hitting and providing power to the three-bladed Hamilton Standard prop. Even sick, Thumper found the power impressive. He continued to feed the engine its high-octane diet and looked for his favorite little mogul, using it as a ski jump to launch him into the air. Airborne, he quickly raised the gear and held the nose down as he pushed the throttle all the way to combat power.

The R-2800 was so powerful, it could not take off at full throttle; the aircraft simply could not control the torque. At slow speeds, it would actually torque roll with the wheels still on the runway. That would result in the Corsair flipping on its head, normally burning furiously.

Once the rudder got enough airspeed over it to counter the torque, you could let the horses loose. Thumper shot over the Japanese lines at treetop level, accelerating like a bat out of hell. A few undirected, small arms rounds rose out of the jungle, harmlessly searching the sky for him. He pushed the long nose down a tight valley that ran to the ocean, using the gravity to help him accelerate to a speed of 340 knots indicated.

Feet wet (over the ocean), he pulled the nose up thirty degrees with a three-G pull. The added gravity pulled mucous from his sinuses; he let it swirl away in the wind caused by the open canopy. Zooming to 5,000 feet, he lowered the nose and started a steady-state, 250-knot climb. He left the canopy open as the temperature dropped, using it to battle his fever. At 15,000 feet, he began to chill and closed it, continuing to climb to 23,000 feet.

Leveling off, he eased back the throttle and prop levers to cruise power, closed the cowl flaps, and leaned out the mixture to save fuel. Their milk run was a simple search and destroy mission. They would fly up the slot, and if they came across any Japanese shipping or aircraft, destroy it. Simple.

The Japanese had wised up and only came down the slot at night now. So these were normally long, boring missions—exactly what Thumper needed right now. Just the thought of yanking and banking turned his stomach.

Armed only with .50-caliber, his Corsair trimmed up nicely. The runway was so rough, they only liked to load bombs if they knew they would drop them so they wouldn't bounce off their attachment points on landing.

He looked right to see Paul in perfect position. Thumper had not even thought of his wingman since take off roll. *Shit, I'm definitely not on my game.* Minutes stretched to hours; time expanded. Seconds were his enemy, coinciding with the drips from his ear. No matter how hard he willed it, time would not go faster.

Thumper's eyes were drawn to movement in his right mirror, momentarily suspending his pain as he reacted to it. Paul was rocking his wings and pointing to his eyes, then the ocean; he saw something. Obviously unable to function as an effective lead, Thumper passed it to Paul with a simple hand signal.

Paul immediately stood his Corsair on its right wing and rolled over on his back, pulling for the turquoise water below. Thumper gingerly followed, letting a wide space build between them so he could look for whatever they were diving on. At 15,000 feet, he couldn't believe what he saw: a large freighter under tow. *Geez, how the hell did I miss that?*

It had gone dead in the water the night before and was now a very fat target. An oceangoing tug strained to pull it to safety. Methodically, Thumper flipped on his master armament switch and charged his six fifties with the toggle. He twisted in the millimeter setting for strafe into his gun sight as he saw Paul's guns begin to smoke. His pain was gone, his focus back. Glowing balls of lead began to fly up to and past him. He was on government time now. He noticed a line of spent shell cases, ejected from Paul's guns, tumble by his canopy. *Focus!*

The freighter's bridge began to sparkle as Paul's rounds impacted. Thumper put his piper on the waterline of the ship. He wanted to sink it quickly with secondary explosions and go home. Paul pulled off target. Thumper snapped on the trigger. His Corsair vibrated and shook as the six machine guns spit pounds of incendiary rounds with each second. He held the piper on the waterline until the last second, released the trigger and began a four-G pullout. The ammunition-filled freighter metastasized into a large orange ball of flame and debris. Thumper flew through the middle of it at 420 knots. As the debris fell like hail against his Corsair he closed his eyes, certain he was witnessing death: his own.

15:05 Local, 9NOV (21:05 GMT, 09NOV)
Naval Air Station, Pensacola, Florida

Pea-sized ice pellets crashed against the metal roof of the briefing shack in waves. Lightning struck the field, followed by a succession of thunderclaps that shook the shack, threatening to toss it across the tarmac.

Lieutenant Stutzman sat calmly briefing as if in a quiet classroom on a cool, spring day. The three students flinched with each thunder report. Finally, David couldn't take it.

"Sir, shouldn't we seek shelter?"

"It will be gone soon. Focus! Soon you will be briefing with bombs and triple-A exploding in the background."

The storm swept out with the same speed and vigor with which it had swept in, and the sudden silence seemed strange, foreboding, nearly as distracting as the fury of the storm.

"Brennan!"

"Yes, sir?" David refocused.

"You get your average amount of hits today and you are top gun. That means your first choice of aircraft."

A vision of the brand new Hellcat flashed through David's mind but was gone in an instant, forced out by consequence. Robbie squirmed in his seat, knowing what was next.

"Candidate Robinson, if you don't get some damn hits today, fifteen minimum, you are done."

Deflated, Robbie just nodded.

"Okay, let's get our ordnance cards and man up."

David yanked Robbie out of his chair, dragging him immediately to the ordie shack to beat the others.

"Hi, Chief."

"Hi-ya, Candy-date. Fine Navy day."

"Yes, it is, Chief. Yes, it is."

David quickly signed his log and slid Robbie his. As he did, he performed a sleight of hand, switching the color cards that were matched to the dyed, .50-caliber rounds in each aircraft. But he was no magician; both the chief and Robbie noticed. The two candidates stood uncomfortably until the chief smiled a large, all-knowing smile.

"Have a nice flight, gentlemen."

Lieutenant Stutzman and the third student walked up to the counter as David and Robbie scurried off. Stutzman kept glancing up at the chief, who still held that large smile.

"Anything I need to know, Chief?"

"Oh, no, sir. You have a delightful flight."

Stutzman didn't like the sparkle in his chief's eye. That was normally a danger sign.

David coaxed the Brewster off the high perch. He was beginning to develop a distaste for the F2-A3. It seemed to spend an inordinate amount of time flying sideways.

"Duck one off switches safe, guns jammed."

Funny, I swear I saw smoke and ejecting cartridges. Focus!

He flipped on his master armament switch, electrically charged a round in each gun with the toggle, and executed his unloaded reversal. Centering the piper of the gunsight, David pulled the trigger. He concentrated so intently on each run that he was surprised when his guns emptied.

"Two is off, Winchester."

They quickly rendezvoused, then flew back in finger four. David was on the left wing, Robbie and the new guy on the right. David passed a thumbs-up to Robbie, but he either didn't see or ignored him.

On deck, before David had unstrapped, Robbie appeared on his wing.

"David this isn't right, I'm coming clean."

"Hang on, Robbie, let's think about that."

"No, I didn't earn it."

"You will have plenty of time to earn it, in the fleet."

He shook off the response. "I'm no good to the fleet if I can't shoot. I'm already a screw-up, David. Don't make me a cheat." He turned to walk away.

"If you come clean," said David, "we are both in the wringer."

Robbie stopped and turned around. "Then I'll DOR."

"Robbie, please. Let's talk about it tonight," David said to his back as he walked to the debrief alone.

Behind them, the tractor dropped the banner and the chief's crew chased it down in an old battleship-grey Ford pickup.

After debriefing the basic airmanship of each student by Lieutenant Stutzman, the group fell into an uneasy silence. Everyone except the new guy seemed to be on edge. Finally the chief strolled in, whistling a merry tune. His presence was unusual. Normally, he sent in a third class petty officer with the totals. He also still had the silly grin on his face.

"Lieutenant Stutzman, sorry about the jammed guns: no hits."

"Number four: twelve hits."

"Mister Brennan, you were off a bit: seventeen hits."

Robbie instantly snapped out of his funk; those were his hits!

"Cadet Robinson," continued the chief, "I don't know what to say. We must have double loaded you: 92 hits."

I knew it, thought David. *The lieutenant was shooting; that's why the chief kept grinning. He knew we were both shooting for Robbie.*

The awkward silence gave way to relief as they all realized that Robbie had gotten his own hits—seventeen, in fact, two more than he needed. The new guy, still clue minus to what was going on, was just happy to be done with the guns syllabus, although the thought of the final stage of training took the dumb grin off his face.

08:05 Local, 10NOV (21:05 GMT, 09NOV)
Guadalcanal

Acrid, poisonous smoke filled the cockpit. Thumper coughed and choked on the toxic fumes. *I must be alive.* Blinded by the smoke, he forced his eyes open long enough to pull for the bright spot he hoped was the sun and not the burning ship. Putting the glowing orb in the center of his windscreen, he held it there with the stick and closed his eyes again.

Wind noise getting quieter, I've got to be going up. Knowing by the noise level that he had slowed, he grasped the emergency handle and blew open the canopy by releasing a charge of compressed air. It slammed against the stops with terrific force. The noise was as deafening as it was welcome; he knew it would suck out the poisonous gases.

Thumper fought to orient himself and his aircraft. His internal gyro was tumbling. He forced himself to scan the instruments. His inner ear told him he was rolling left, the instruments claimed right; his intellect voted with the instruments. Stopping the roll, he forced his weeping eyes to scan the rest of the instruments.

Shit, 100 knots and I'm pointed straight up. I have got to get the nose down; I won't survive a spin. He yanked the stick into his lap, pulling the big nose down to the horizon, ending up inverted on his back yet still in control. Before he could right his air machine, the first wave of nausea swept through his body. Thumper struggled with his oxygen mask, releasing it just as he projectile-vomited into the swirling tornado of the cockpit.

Feeling the nose fall through the horizon, he struggled to roll upright as wave after wave of nausea enveloped him like an incoming tide. Even after he had nothing left in his stomach, the retching would not abate.

When it finally stopped, he unzipped his flight coveralls and ripped off a piece of his threadbare T-shirt, using it to clean his goggles. Next, he pulled a water bottle out of his map case and flushed his eyes, bending low to get out of the worst of the turbulent cockpit air. Thumper rinsed his mouth but dared not drink even though he was dehydrated. With his aircraft and body finally under control, it was time to assess the situation.

His engine had a miss but was running suitably enough to get him back to the 'Canal if it didn't get worse. Scanning the engine instruments, he realized he was still at full military power. He reached for the throttle quadrant and set 24 inches of MAP and 2,200 RPM on the prop. Satisfied with the power plant, he trimmed for cruise flight. He noticed the controls were sluggish. Looking at his left wing, he understood why. His flight controls had holes and tears, as did his wing and, obviously, his oxygen system.

Most disturbing was the fuel escaping through holes in the wing. Deciding that the leaking fuel was the most critical threat, he pushed the power to military again to burn as much as he could before it was gone. He knew in his current state he wouldn't last long in the water. Even if he did, the puke all over him would draw sharks as if he had been chumming.

Thumper looked around his cockpit, panicking when he realized his map was gone, sucked out with the smoke. He was disoriented and had no idea where he was. Sitting back defeated, he glanced to the right wing to see if it too was losing fuel; it was. Then, a large smile grew on his face as he beheld the most beautiful sight he'd ever seen: a dark blue F4-U1 Corsair, in perfect parade formation.

Paul gave him the hand signal for climb and pointed the way. Thumper eased to the right forty-five degrees and climbed for home.

05:47 Local, 10NOV (21:47 GMT, 09NOV)
The Jungle, The Philippines

Captain Butler kept his men climbing. He knew there was safety in the mountains. They marched for two days, dawn until dusk, not stopping at all. Their provisions were nearly gone anyway, and they didn't have time to scrounge or hunt.

Early on the third day, they reached a small plateau that allowed a panoramic view of the valley below, including the town of Santa Cruz. Columns of troops were clearly visible in Butler's binoculars. He could also see that shipping was being offloaded in Lamon Bay to the east. Putting away the binoculars, he pulled out his map.

"We need to get off this island now. It is fixing to get most unfriendly."

"You still want to go through Batangas?" asked Sergeant Donnelly.

"No, it is too big. We will have to find a smaller fishing village, and steal a bonka boat. We will have to move nonstop. Let's go."

The worn-out band could sense Butler's urgency and got quickly to their feet, disappearing into the jungle within seconds.

09:02 Local, 10NOV (22:02 GMT, 09NOV)
Guadalcanal

Thumper nursed the crippled Corsair above a thunderstorm cell. Paul continued to stick to his wing in silent support. A twitch caught Thumper's attention, and he glanced at the instrument panel in time to see his hydraulic pressure gauge flicker twice, then drop to zero. Great. No landing gear, no flaps; a belly landing on that roller coaster of a runway.

He turned to Paul, held up three fingers and gave a thumbs-down, signaling that his hydraulics were gone. Paul nodded acknowledgment, knowing he'd have to land first. From his position on the wing, he could see that the vapor coming out of Thumper's wing was decreasing. He goosed his engine to get Thumper's attention and asked his fuel state by making a Hawaiian hang-loose signal, sipping from the thumb. Thumper checked his fuel gauge and calmly passed a zero to Paul.

Six minutes later, the big R-2800 sputtered to a stop. Thumper feathered the prop and set his best glide speed of 120 knots. There were three positives in his cornucopia of negativity: One, he had cleared the line of storms. Two, he could see the canal. And finally, he should have enough altitude to make it. He trimmed the tattered controls as best he could and pointed straight at Henderson Field.

Adrenaline and dopamine coursed through his veins, dulling his pain and focusing him intently on his approach. He would not get a redo—it was literally do or die. As he crossed the northern beach line, the Japanese began to fire small arms and triple-A, the intensity increasing when they realized he was not maneuvering. Thumper was still at 7,500 feet, well out of range of everything except the triple-A. Even so, he didn't maneuver. He couldn't afford to; the wind was at his back. He would have to turn around and land the opposite direction at Henderson Field. To do this, he had to hit the abeam at 1,500 feet or more.

Paul wouldn't leave his wing, even as the triple-A thickened. Thumper finally tapped his glare shield, signaling, "Land now," to Paul, then kissed him off. Paul reluctantly complied, snapping off a perfect salute as he rolled away and accelerated for Henderson.

At 4,000 feet, the ground fire dramatically increased. At 3,500, a few rounds began to find their mark. At 3,000 feet he was being peppered, watching in amusement as holes appeared in the top of his wings. He didn't care; there was no fuel in them.

"Shoot away, you pointy-headed bastards!" he shouted into the rushing air.

Confident that his armor plating would protect him, he focused on the approach. Tracers chased him across the forward edge of the battle area. He arrived abeam the runway at 1,300 feet, low for a dead-stick approach. However, with no gear or flaps producing drag, he knew he had more than enough airspeed.

Scanning the field to check his distance abeam, he saw Paul clear the runway. Thumper nosed over in a steep descent, calling on every scintilla of experience he had to help save him. His brain was alive, running a constant update of distance, altitude, and airspeed. As the riddled Corsair descended, it gained twenty knots of precious speed. He would need it for the tight turn to final. Thumper used an aim point 1,000 feet short of the runway.

Passing through the ninety-degree point, just a quarter-turn to go, he recognized he was tight and steep. He dropped the nose further and pulled the stricken Corsair to centerline, using forty-five degrees angle of bank. It protested, buffeting as he yanked on the heavy nose to get around the corner. At 500 feet, he was lined up on centerline but still pointed very nose low and descending at 1,800 feet per minute. *I just might make this.*

He dropped the airspeed out of his scan; he had all he could get and was committed now to the landing. At 150 feet, he began a slow transition to the landing attitude by easing the nose up and bleeding off the airspeed.

At 50 feet, he put the nose on the far end of the runway as airspeed decayed rapidly…140…130…120…110. The Corsair was close to stalling! Flashing across the threshold, Thumper used the last speed he had to break the rate of descent in the flare.

The Corsair touched down lightly on the PSP runway at ninety-three knots, on its belly. Sparks flew and the Corsair bucked, preferring the hostile air to the rough ground. He slid for what seemed an eternity. *Don't roll, don't roll, don't roll,* he chanted while he fought with the stick and rudder to keep the aircraft from flipping and balling up. The gull wing design, with wingtips raised, helped. Finally the metal-on-metal screeching stopped, and the Corsair lay dead on the far end of the runway.

Thumper sat staring straight ahead. The spike of adrenaline and dopamine in his blood was rapidly being consumed. Guns fell quiet, no engines turned in the eerie silence. For a second, he wondered if he had made it.

A light tap on his right shoulder seemed to instantly activate his pain and fatigue. He struggled to look to his right—the sun was high and behind the tapper—he squinted but could only make out a figure in the white glare.

"You okay, Colonel? That was one hell of a landing, sir! Damndest thing I've ever seen."

Thumper recognized the voice of his wingman, Paul. He slowly pushed up his goggles and awkwardly pulled off the canvas flight helmet.

"Thanks for the milk run, Paul."

06:38 Local, 10NOV (06:38 GMT, 10NOV)
Kate's Manor, Bowdown House, Greenham Common, England

Kate walked into the dining room, already dressed. She crinkled her nose at the smell of stale cigars and spilled scotch. Neither man noticed her presence. Exasperated, she went straight to one of the large windows and threw open the heavy tapestry drapes. Sunlight instantly filled the room as if a flashbulb had popped off. J.T. and Irish flinched at the intrusion.

"Geez, Kate, a little warning would be nice!" snapped J.T.

"Okay, here is your warning," she retorted. "Neither of you two old goats will be of any use to the war effort if you get sick. You are not taking care of yourselves. Three all-nighters in a row—this isn't college, and you damn sure aren't college boys. Now get something to eat and go to bed!"

"Okay, okay." J.T. set down the stack of papers he was holding and turned to Irish. "I just don't see how it can be done, anyway. We just don't have the production to get enough C-47s in time."

He walked toward the bright window and looked across the vast lawn. At the far end, he saw the gardener working in his lorry. It resembled a small tractor but had a flatbed full of peat moss, and it was pulling a small trailer so the gardener could double the peat load. J.T.'s jaw dropped as he comprehended through bloodshot eyes.

"Son of a—"

"Language!" Kate snapped this time.

"Oh, sorry, Kate." J.T. turned to face Irish with a smile. "Gliders."

Irish smacked himself in the forehead with the palm of his hand.

"Son of a—"

"Irish!"

"Sorry, Kate," Irish apologized, and turned back to J.T. "Of course, with gliders we can double the amount of troops per C-47. That should do it."

They both delved into the reams of papers on the table.

"Oh, I give up." Kate exited, headed for the kitchen.

By the time she returned, wheeling in a large silver and glass serving cart loaded down with breakfast and coffee, the two men were slapping themselves on the back excitedly.

J.T. looked up. "Kate, we just won the war!"

"How nice, now sit down and eat."

CHAPTER 29

A tall, thin man wearing coveralls, parka, and cowboy boots stood at the front of a standard issue Navy briefing room. He held two paddles that looked like solid tennis rackets, painted orange. The student naval aviators stared at him, wondering who he was.

"I'm Lieutenant Roach. Most people call me Bug, but you will call me Paddles. I'm your landing signal officer—LSO for short, Paddles by tradition. But I like to think of myself as more of a, how should I put it…" He put his hand to his chin in deep contemplation.

"…a god."

He glared down at the fledgling Tail Hookers as they squirmed, not knowing if he was serious.

"Gents, this is where the rubber meets the road. This is where we put the naval in naval aviator. You maggots haven't done crap yet! You are no better than Air Corps pukes or damned airline pilots. If I catch you flaring your landing like one, I'll stomp it out of you. Flare to land, squat to pee! Naval aviators don't ease our landings on the deck; we crash it on. You will do exactly as I tell you. I will fly your aircraft, and I will decide when you can land. If you do not respond, I will get rid of you."

He walked slowly in front of them, shaking a paddle in a threatening manner at each candidate.

"You have to go through me to get those wings of gold. When you roll into the groove of the USS Wolverine and look down at that postage stamp,

I guarantee you will shit your brains right out the exhaust pipes. If you want to stay alive, if you want your wings, you will do exactly what I signal. Any questions so far?"

None of the youngsters moved or spoke.

"Good. One more thing: we don't fly the Brewster up here anymore. We kept collapsing the gear. We fly the Wildcat. Go get a manual and be ready to fly this afternoon by 14:00. Dismissed."

04:48 Local, 12NOV (20:48 GMT, 11NOV)
The Jungle, The Philippines

The jungle was unsettled, hostile. It craved blood to absorb into its floor and nourish its foliage and heart. Butler's subconscious registered the unease. He knew the bloodlust of the deepest and darkest jungle was unquenchable.

They had to get off this island. Luzon wanted their blood; he felt it. He was certain it was their sacrifice that was being demanded now. Butler drove his men south relentlessly, twenty hours a day, until they reached the foothills overlooking the Sulu Strait.

"Rubio, we need some local intel. I still think Mindoro is where we need to go, but I don't want to jump off the fox's back into his mouth."

Rubio didn't get the reference to The Gingerbread Man, but he comprehended the meaning.

"I'll go after sunset, Captain."

"Okay, let's get some sleep until then."

15:00, Local, 11NOV (21:00 GMT, 11NOV)
Naval Air Station, Glenview, Chicago, Illinois

David cranked the landing gear furiously, trying to retract it before he oversped it. He couldn't believe the Navy's frontline fighter relied on a chain and crank system. Even the lowly Brewster had hydraulically actuated gear. Of course, it also tended to collapse when trapping, carrier landing, aboard the ship, which explained why he was cranking. Twenty-six-and-a-half rotations later, he locked the handle and made a glorious discovery.

The Wildcat was a true high-performance fighter. His VSI was pegged at a full climb, *My God, this is a rocket ship*. Snapping on a sixty-degree angle of bank turn, he headed for Lake Michigan.

With a renewal of his youthful enthusiasm, David bent the little Wildcat every way he knew possible. He actually giggled to himself as he performed a squirrel cage. Its power-to-weight ratio was like nothing he had ever experienced. He could only imagine what the new Hellcat or Corsair was like.

Diving at a freighter steaming toward Chicago, he made a simulated strafing attack. At full throttle, he reached a redline speed of 275 knots very quickly as he squeezed the trigger. Pulling four Gs in a zoom climb back to 10,000 feet, he was giddy at the little aircraft's performance.

To the south, he spotted a small line of thunderstorms. Giant popcorn hung like balloons in the air, bathed in the brilliant afternoon sun. He dove on them, investigating every nook and cranny, dancing across the faces of clouds with the sun as his partner.

All too soon, his fuel approached landing weight, and he forced himself to break away from the clouds and head back to Glenview. The Wildcat eagerly entered the carrier pattern, inviting an aggressive, carrier-style break turn. As he eased the G in the turn, he unlocked the gear and learned an important lesson. The gear handle jerked out of his hand, rotating so quickly that it came all the way around and struck him hard on the arm before he could move it. A large bruise began to form, the mark of a Wildcat pilot.

Literally slapped back to reality, David settled into the field carrier landing practice circuit, known as the FCLP. A carrier deck was painted on the runway so the students could practice landing on it. After eight touch-and-goes, he made a full stop landing. An LSO had been on station, and David had found it surprisingly difficult to follow his direction and fly his machine.

When the paddles went down, showing he was low, he added power. When high, he would ease it off, always making the pre-briefed three-part corrections. He tried to comply immediately when the cut signal was given, by pulling the throttle to idle on his R-1820 engine. The resulting impact was jolting. No wonder the Brewster's gear broke!

This was new and very different from any flying he had ever done. And as always, just as he got comfortable with a stage, they moved on. He was beginning to suspect it was by design.

Taxiing clear of the runway, he turned onto the ramp. His plane captain stood ready, directing him into a spot and giving him the hand signal to shut down the engine. As the RPM of the prop decayed, it seemed to spin backwards in the afternoon sun. David sat transfixed by the optical illusion, lost in thought. He replayed in his mind each pass, each correction. The plane captain stood at ease, waiting; he'd seen this many times before and knew better than to break a naval aviator's post-flight meditation.

David felt a tap on his left shoulder.

"Hey, snap out of it."

He was startled to see Bug Roach squatting on the wing of his Wildcat. "Not bad for a CQ-1."

That's not right, David thought. *He'd only been on a familiarization flight #1, not a carrier qualification flight #1.*

"Sir," replied the young pilot, "I'm on FAM-1. I still have two more FAMs before CQ-1."

Bug shook his head, which was topped with a large, well-worn cowboy hat. "Not anymore, shipmate. That was good enough for a CQ-1. Your plane captain is fueling you with a pattern load. CQ-2 is in twenty minutes."

"But, sir—" David protested.

Bug ripped into him. "In case you haven't noticed, Dilbert, we are at war! My job is to get naval aviators to the fleet yesterday. You just moved up a class, so turn to!"

"Aye, aye, sir."

"Outstanding. Attention to debrief."

Bug debriefed David on each pass individually, from approach to landing. He read from a small blue notebook that contained a strange shorthand. Each pass was graded on a 4.0 scale. The shorthand for a top grade was "OK." Next was a fair, written in shorthand as "(OK)" and valued at a 3.0; then a no grade, or gash, because it was entered as a simple horizontal line. It was valued at 2.0. A wave-off, "WO," was an unsafe approach that caused the LSO to wave the paddles to send the pilot around for another try; it had a value of 1.0. For the rest of their naval aviation careers, each pass at the ship would be graded and de-briefed. For further motivation, the grades were published on the ready room wall, color-coordinated to stand out for all to see.

Naval aviators in general were aggressive and very competitive. An ongoing competition raged throughout every CAG (Carrier Air Group) in the fleet. Whenever a naval aviator went into another squadron's ready room, the first thing he did was glance at the greenie board (so named because the top grade, an OK, was colored green) and size up the competition.

After Bug read the passes and grades, his persona became more conciliatory, switching from evaluator to teacher and coach.

David launched back into the pattern and flew CQ-2. By the time his plane captain (PC) helped pull him out of the aircraft, he was exhausted.

"Man, that was hard," he said, more to himself than the PC.

CHAPTER 30

08:15 Local 12NOV (21:15 GMT, 11NOV)
Guadalcanal

Every aircraft in his air group was turning its props, with the notable exception of a well-holed Corsair that had been unceremoniously dragged off the PSP runway by a Navy Seabee bulldozer. Stripped of any usable part, it looked like a rotting corpse as it lay in the mud.

Somehow, his maintenance troops had gotten every other aircraft up and loaded overnight. Colonel Thumper McDonald looked over his shoulders; each aircraft was loaded with a 500-pound bomb, even the fighters. Each bomb's fuse was set with a time delay to allow it to penetrate deep within a ship before detonating.

All eyes were on him. He checked his watch for the tenth time. As it struck 06:00 on the second, he pushed up the throttle to takeoff power. His wingman rolled with him, launching into the air alongside him, off Thumper's favorite ski-jump mogul. At ten-second intervals, sections of Corsairs, followed by Dauntless dive bombers, rolled until the entire air wing was airborne.

No doubt, the Japanese troops across the FEBA were on the radio reporting the launch of the strike package, so Thumper initially turned the flight south. He rendezvoused the air group south of Cape Henslow at 2,000 feet. The strike package separated into two groups. All the Corsairs with him, and the SBD Dauntless dive bombers, stepped up in trail.

Thumper switched up the Navy's strike control frequency and received the targeting info for a surface action group. Translating the coded numbers, he carefully plotted the latitude and longitude of the surface action group

(SAG), and its course and speed, on his mo-board with a grease pencil.

The course and speed of the targets would put them southwest of Rendova Island, of the New Georgia group, when his air group would be in a position to attack. *Perfect. I'll hide behind the island and have bombs on target before they know what hit them.*

After plotting a few intermediate checkpoints and a timeline, he descended the flight to wave-top height and headed north, up the slot. The sixteen Corsairs and eight SBD Dauntless dive bombers skimmed their way toward the SAG.

His plan was simple. He hoped to sneak up the slot, the nickname they had given the New Georgian Sound which ran up the middle of the Solomons, split his group high and low, and draw down the Zeros to chase his Corsairs as they dropped. That would clear the way for the slower SBDs.

The F-4U Corsair was almost twice as fast as the Dauntless; this would provide the separation he needed. At fifty miles out, he clicked his transmit button twice. The dive bombers began their climb to 15,000 feet. Crossing the island of Rendova, he clicked three times and pushed the throttle all the way up. Each Corsair division offset to get time separation for their bomb runs. It was critical, so they wouldn't frag each other. Getting blown out of the sky by your buddy's bomb would not be good.

Thumper pressed straight ahead at 350 knots, barely ten feet off the wave tops. Each of his wingmen was stepped up slightly; even so, the entire flight didn't get higher than twenty feet above the waves. He knew they were close and scanned the horizon for the sign of warships. After less than thirty seconds, he saw a wisp of black smoke and turned toward it. After a few minutes, he saw the telltale humps on the horizon. Thumper eased his division to starboard twenty degrees, putting the largest hump on the nose.

Closing at 350 knots, the superstructure of the battleship Hiei grew out of the mist. Checking it against his target photo, he continued to close the distance to the Japanese warship. They were still unseen; the Japanese guns were quiet. He was gambling that the Japanese fighter CAP, the combat air patrol, was at high altitude, overhead.

At two miles, he jammed on emergency combat power and pulled four Gs straight up. Reaching sixty degrees nose high, approximately 5,000 feet above the ocean, he rolled the F-4U on its back and pulled four Gs again. This time, Thumper pulled toward the water, placing his gun sight on the Hiei amidships.

The sky erupted in black puffs. Glowing orange globs the size of golf balls whisked by his canopy. The SAG was shooting every gun they had. Thumper knew the Zeros would be diving on them now; it was exactly what he wanted. Hiei quickly filled his windscreen as he dove on it. Again, he was on government time. He held steady, keeping the piper in place as the AAA increased in intensity and accuracy.

At 1,500 feet, he pickled his bomb and yanked on six Gs. He had to roll up on a wing as his Corsair flashed between the smokestacks of the battleship. Pushing back for the deck, Thumper tried to get small by showing only his tail to the gunners. Behind him, his bomb fell true, impacting just above the waterline. The armor-piercing MK-82, 500-pound bomb penetrated three more decks before exploding in the engine room.

Paul Lady, flying as section lead, put his bomb on the bridge. Dash 2s went short and dash 4s went long. It didn't matter; the Hiei was dead in the water and doomed, but still she drew blood. First Lieutenant Bob Jameson, in dash 2, was flamed pulling off target. Thumper saw the burning Corsair careen into the water in his rearview mirror.

He couldn't think of the young man in it; there would be time for that later, whether he wanted to or not. Phase one of his plan had worked. They had gotten their bombs on target. Time for phase two. The Corsair strike package would drag the Zeros to the deck, and they would give chase. Corsairs were faster; he needed to use that advantage to pull them as far away as possible from the target.

Thumper knew the Zeros were diving on him. Even as low as he was, he had to force himself to glance over his shoulders. He saw what he expected: fifteen to twenty black dots, getting bigger. When he could make out their wings he called, "Action," over the radio.

Captain Lady hard-turned to the right, and Thumper went left. Each pulled an easy three Gs, baiting the Zeros to come down and play. They took the bait, splitting their flight and committing to a low-turning fight. Thumper continued to drag them until he saw his second division come off the water.

As briefed, they turned toward their strike leader on the action call. Thumper dragged five tasty targets in front of his hungry boys. They pounced; two of the pursuing Zeros immediately fireballed as the leathernecks opened up. Thumper snatched on a six-G break turn, causing the lead Zero to bend his aircraft around as hard as he could pull. His wingman, who was flying lower and on the inside of his turn, was concentrating on maintaining position and keeping the Zero lead in sight. Suddenly, he impacted the water halfway through the turn. A tremendous plume of water shot up as he hit the ocean.

Desperately trying to get a shot, the lead Zero continued to pull, only to overshoot Thumper in close. Unloading and rapidly reversing his turn, Thumper also reversed rolls. Out-maneuvered, the Zero tried to climb away. Thumper let loose a two-second burst, disintegrating the aircraft.

Rolling in from 15,000 feet, the SBDs were now attacking from high while the Zero CAP was engaged on the surface with the Corsairs: phase three. Third and fourth divisions continued to push the Zeros, while Thumper's lead division and the second division zoom climbed, reversing course in an Immelman, returning to cover the SBDs egress.

Thumper marveled at the scene. The Japanese battle group put up a hail of gunfire and triple-A. Red tracers intermingled with the black puffs of smoke as shells exploded. The turquoise sea was the backdrop. Suddenly an orange slash, trailed by billowing smoke, punctuated the scene as triple-A found its mark, destroying one of his SBDs.

Colors seemed magnified, almost artificial, as the scene continued to play out. Aesthetic beauty was juxtaposed with the brutal violence of action and intent. For those who had never witnessed or experienced the duality, it seemed wickedly ironic. To a warrior, especially an experienced one, it was in balance: the yin and yang of life and death, intensified by combat. Visual was contradicted by aural as the battle raged. Voices, stressed by G-load and circumstance, violated the beauty as they rang out over the frequency.

"Bandits, right five o-clock."

"Bomber three is hit; they're going in!"

"Watch for parachutes."

"No chance, it's a fireball."

Off target, the SBDs were headed out to sea. Bombs exploded on two Imperial Japanese destroyers as the scene built to a crescendo. Four Zeros dove on the slow SBDs.

Thumper's division, now down to three, attacked. Offset to the north of the SBDs, they needed help with the geometry.

"Bomber flight, check north sixty degrees," he transmitted over the strike frequency. "Bandits six o-clock and closing."

The Zeros turned hard to the north to cut off the fleeing SBDs. Three Corsairs flashed over the SBDs, just clearing them, and immediately opened fire on the pursuing Zeros. They were so close, the SBD leader flinched as the Corsair guns barked to life, passing just over his canopy. Shot in the face, the Zero lead exploded in synchronicity with the Battleship Hiei as fire reached a magazine. Violence now tipped the scale of balance and consumed ocean and air.

Reefing on seven Gs, Thumper pulled into the vertical after flying through the Zeros' debris field. His plan was to do a half-Cuban eight and fall in behind the SBDs, covering their withdrawal. Nearing the top of the looping maneuver, tracers streaked toward his canopy. He returned fire as he desperately looked for the source of the tracers. Just prior to the merge, he got sight and directed his fire by easing in left rudder.

His redirected rounds stitched across the Zero's wing, blowing it off at the root as they merged. Totally out of control, it nearly hit Thumper's Corsair as it tumbled past. Continuing his pull, he was on his back pulling toward the water and his egressing dive bombers. Rolling upright, thirty degrees nose low, he gained sight of his SBDs—and watched in futility as a Zero flamed the tail-end aircraft. The dying SBDs tail gunner continued to fight ferociously as they fell to the sea, getting a revenge kill just before splashing at full speed into the ocean.

Giving up the chase as the tail gunners of the six surviving SBDs began to converge on him, the last Zero turned back toward the sinking ships. Guns and radios fell silent as survivors fled the death and destruction in their wake.

Turning south, down the western side of the New Georgia group, they began a climb to altitude. Thumper took station behind the dive bombers. It was then that he noticed his own flight had been whittled down to just two. Looking up and to the right, he saw second division was down to three, then looked left, relieved to see both third and fourth divisions were at full strength. He counted the crewmen in his mind. Nine letters home tonight.

He looked down at the dark navy blue dive bombers floating above the turquoise water, the afternoon sun sparkling across its pure surface.

Circling overhead until the SBDs landed on Henderson field, Thumper rolled over on a wing and entered the pattern through a steep, oblique turn. Even after all that had happened, he still felt thrilled by the performance of the Corsair. Gear and flaps extending, he pulled the F-4U around a tight pattern, rolling wings level on final, less than five seconds before touching down on the familiar PSP runway.

Braking hard to clear the runway for the rest of the Corsairs following in order, he looked over his shoulder just in time to see a Corsair on final shed a flap panel. It rolled uncontrollably, crashing into the jungle, happening so fast that not a word was transmitted. Corsairs continued to recover, flying through the billowing smoke of the burning aircraft. Thumper shook his head.

"A damn landing accident, after all we just went through! Life is not fair, just not fair."

Colonel Sean "Thumper" McDonald was emotionally depleted. He had seen enough. He was too old to watch young men die. It was taking a toll on him. He sat, head down, his thoughts as out of control as the condemned Corsair. He wanted to go home. He wanted someone else to write the letters and then order more men into the violent skies.

"Colonel, are you all right?"

Thumper looked up into the blue eyes of his nineteen-year-old plane captain. Bloodshot and glassy, they reflected back the pain of a much older man. He felt ashamed. This young corporal dodged shells and bombs all day, then counted the planes as they returned. He would spend all of this night readying them for tomorrow, and he was doing it without feeling sorry for himself.

Thumper patted him on the back.

"I'm okay, Billy. Get me Captain Lady, would you please?"

Billy's face contracted in pain, and he nodded toward the smoke.

"Sir, that was Captain Lady."

23:00 Local, 12NOV (15:00 GMT, 12NOV)
Mindoro Island, The Philippines

Rubio shook Butler and Donnelley awake at 23:00. "Sir, we must leave Luzon now, tonight. I have arranged for a bonka boat to take us to Mindoro. We must hurry. The Japanese are everywhere and grow in numbers by the day."

Butler was instantly awake and whispering orders. "Gather everything. Leave no sign we have been here."

The gaunt warriors double-timed through the night. They were running away from the jungle of Luzon more than they were running to the sanctuary of Mindoro.

At 03:00, they set sail. Butler turned and watched as they moved silently away from the rain forest. In the bright moonlight, it rose up the steep hills as if in righteous outrage that its sacrifice was denied. He turned away, facing the soft ocean ahead, rubbing the crucifix. He didn't look back.

The moon gave way to the sun as the celestial cycle continued unabated, unaffected by the catastrophic events on the surface of planet Earth. Morning colors lit the jungle floor and warmed it from millions of miles away. Butler watched the light waves refract through the sparse foliage, stopping to let them bathe his face. Sergeant Donnelley touched his elbow.

"Captain, we have to keep moving. It is getting light."

Butler turned and smiled at his sergeant.

"Yes, it is getting light, Paul. This place has a different feel to it, don't you think?"

Donnelley nodded in agreement as they continued to move through the bush.

Arriving at their ultimate destination, the village of Paluan, they could see that it was not an average one. Young men came forward in various pieces of uniforms. What they lacked in uniformity, they more than made up for in esprit de corps. Captain Butler and Sergeant Donnelley moved toward the center of the village. As they did, the Filipinos raised their weapons in silent salute. Rubio whispered into Butler's ear.

"These are your men now."

"They are yours, Rubio."

"No. Maybe someday, but now they look to you. They look to an American officer for leadership. That is just the way it is."

CHAPTER 31

12:08 Local, 22NOV (18:08 GMT, 22NOV)
USS Wolverine, Lake Michigan

Unseasonably warm, the day was still chilly and the water was icy. It would render a pilot's hands useless in five minutes and kill him in less than forty-five. In spite of the danger, four Wildcats headed for the middle of Lake Michigan. From their low altitude, the huge lake stretched before them like an ocean. David was dash three in the formation, heading out to the USS Wolverine. His mouth stayed dry, no matter how many times he drank from his water bottle.

The Wolverine had started out its career as a ferry until the Navy converted it to an aircraft carrier. Here on Lake Michigan, there was no threat from German or Japanese submarines. She could operate unmolested, turned into the wind all day, as student naval aviators landed on and took off from her deck.

David noticed they were circling. He stole a glance at the water below, but all he could see was a small fishing boat. He continued to sneak glances at the lake but could not find any other ships or boats. On their third circuit, he realized that the shape of the fishing boat was unusual. Easing out from dash two, he took a hard look. *Holy cow, that isn't a fishing boat; it is the damn Wolverine. It doesn't look like a postage stamp, it looks like a tombstone!*

18:20 Local, 22Nov (18:20 GMT, 22NOV)
Kate's Manor, Bowdown House, Greenham Common, England

J.T. and Kate sat at a small table in the cavernous dining room, two solo candles flickering between their plates. Kate had rejected the fifty-service table as too impersonal; she wanted a more intimate setting.

She had come to comprehend pilots' zest for life. This exuberance that she had witnessed so often, and occasionally detested, she now realized was generated by proximity to death. After experiencing the bombing and collapse of their apartment, she understood how fragile and fleeting life could be. Most people, especially in America, had no exposure to this on a large scale. Pearl Harbor had changed things, and yet it was still far away from Main Street, USA. Here in England, the bombs fell every night. There were shortages of everything, so it was important to revel in even the smallest niceties.

Pilots inherently knew this. She had thought J.T. and his buddies were a bunch of overgrown boys, but Kate was taken aback to realize that their childlike behavior was due to a deeper understanding of life. They did not stop to smell the roses just for the scent; they stopped because each time could be their last. She had seen their behavior as excessive but now understood it as exuberance, a celebration of life and everything in it.

They were adventurers in the true sense of the word. Even the mundane, in their world, was never the same—and could turn deadly at any time. She had also seen the dark side: the twitches, the hard drinking, and the nightmares. Secretly, Kate had coveted being close to the danger; it was exciting. But now, she was living it and could understand life's seductive duality. The closer you stood to the edge, the better the view.

Kate gazed across the table at her fellow traveler in life. He held her eyes with his.

"What are you thinking, J.T.?"

He sat back in his chair, carefully placing his fork next to the china plate and picking up the silk napkin from his lap. His brow was furled in deep contemplation as he dabbed his mouth. He began to speak but paused to sip at the wine in the crystal goblet. Finally, he formulated his thoughts.

"I was thinking of taking you upstairs and getting you out of that dress."

Kate let out a howl of laughter. "Well, just because you're deep doesn't mean you are not simple."

"Excuse me, dear lady?"

The candles glinted off her eyes as she held out her hand.

13:20 Local, 22NOV (19:10 GMT, 22NOV)
USS Wolverine, Lake Michigan

David flew up the wake, forcing himself to ignore the ship and reference only his lineup and the LSO. Bug stood on a platform near the stern of the flight deck, port side. His arms were stretched straight out like a child playing airplane. David matched his wings to BuGs paddles, following him when he leaned, adding power when he moved them lower, and pulling it when he held them higher.

Suddenly, Bug pulled a paddle across his throat. David immediately yanked the throttle to idle and held his aircraft's attitude constant. He watched Bug go by but before he could look forward, he was jerked to a landing on the flight deck with such force that his head banged off the gun sight, cracking it. He had forgotten to lock his shoulder harness.

Momentarily stunned, he spotted a sailor in a yellow flight deck jersey, literally hopping mad—jumping up and down trying to get David's attention—giving him the signal to raise his tail hook and flaps. Once the hook was raised, David followed the handler's hand signals, taxiing over the lowered barricade and goosing the power as he crossed it. The aviation boswain's mate passed him off to another handler, tossing him a hurried salute.

The next handler stopped him and passed him off to yet another sailor with a white skullcap and jersey. He was wearing khaki pants and whipping a small, checkered flag over his head. What is going on? Finally, he realized the sailor was the launch officer. He quickly ran the power up.

As his Wildcat's engine strained against the brakes, the barricade went up behind him while another F-4F rolled out on final approach. Confusion reigned in his mind when the launch officer dropped the flag, touching the deck with it. David released the brakes, the three blades of the Curtis propeller dug into the wind, and he looked toward the bow just a few hundred feet away. It will never fly—the deck is too short!

In an instant, he was over the bow and airborne, his head still swimming. He flew straight for a while, until he heard the voice of the air boss over the radio.

"The pattern is all yours, son. No need to go to Canada."

David re-calibrated his brain, looked for his interval, and turned downwind as he dropped his hook and flaps. This time, he remembered to lock his harness for another trap on board the Wolverine.

All four traps were a blur. Following his last one, he was refueled and shown a small chalkboard that had RTB, return to base, written on it. After he was launched, he stayed low, cranked up the gear, and let the Wildcat run. When it hit its maximum speed of 300 knots, he snatched on four Gs until the nose was straight up. Zooming through 4,500 feet, he pulled the Wildcat onto its back, leveling at 5,000 feet, the pre-briefed rendezvous altitude, and rolled upright. He returned overhead the ship and looked for his lead safe, which was flown by an instructor. Getting a tally on his lead, he maneuvered his F-4F to affect a rendezvous and slid up the bearing line, joining in formation.

The lead pilot signaled David to take a relaxed cruise position and he settled in to wait for the rest of his flight to finish. He glanced at the ship and saw Robbie come off the deck as Donaldson trapped aboard. *Good. We will RTB soon.*

As he watched the next flight of four enter for a carrier break, the silence over the radio was shattered.

"Engine failure, engine failure off the bow!"

He looked down just in time to see the Wildcat splash in front of the ship. Wolverine's officer of the deck tried to veer the sluggish ship away from the floating aircraft, to no avail. The ship's hull crushed the little F-4F and swept it under her keel before Donaldson could escape. Nothing surfaced in the wake.

David was shocked at how fast it had happened. They had been engaged in a beautiful, technological ballet that had turned fatal in the blink of an eye. Silence returned to the radio frequency. The Wolverine turned back into the wind. The only sign that anything was out of the ordinary was a whaleboat (scow) circling the area of impact. Robbie joined the flight and they RTB-ed to NAS Glenview, one aircraft short.

A radio played softly in the background. Tommy Dorsey's band filled in for conversation as the two student naval aviators awaited their qualification status—and more importantly, the fate of Donaldson. David's only concern for the last few days had been whether he would qualify. Now that seemed incredibly shallow as they awaited word on their fellow pilot.

Lieutenant Bug Roach swept into the room, as always, cutting a wide swath. He walked over to the radio and flipped it off.

"Congratulations, gentlemen, you are the only two who carrier-qualified out of your class. The other two flights got pretty rattled after the accident."

"Sir, what about—"

Bug cut David off. "He's gone. I'm sorry, but it's part of the deal, gents.

Not everyone gets to go home a hero. Remember, everybody and everything out there is trying to kill you. The ship, aircraft, enemy, even your own lead sometimes. Stay on your toes. Expect it. It will be less of a surprise when it happens."

Bug debriefed them on their carrier landings and handed each a set of orders.

"You two are short-fused out of here. Pack your sea bag and be back here in an hour. Your butts will be on a train to P-cola, tonight. You graduate in four days; call anyone you want to be there now. You will be in a squadron by the end of the week. Welcome to the fleet, gentlemen. Check six!"

CHAPTER 32

17:45 Local, 22NOV (23:45 GMT, 22NOV)
Union Station, Chicago, Illinois

David stood in one of a row of phone booths in the corner of the main terminal. He had fed the better part of a roll of nickels into the coin slot. Robbie continuously banged on the wood-and-glass door.

"Come on, David! We are going to miss our train!"

"Okay, okay," David yelled through the glass. Into the phone, he said, "I'll see you guys in P-cola in four days. Love you, Mom. Bye."

Before he could hang up the receiver, Robbie pushed open the door and pulled him from the booth. "Run!"

David grabbed his bag and ran after Robbie. Their train was already pulling out as the two sprinted down the platform and jumped onto the last car, nudging past the conductor.

"See?" David said. "Plenty of time." The portly conductor shook his head, laughing, as the young naval candidates moved down the aisle.

"Where do you want to sit, David?"

"I'm hungry, what about you?"

"Yeah, I haven't eaten since breakfast."

"Me neither. Let's go to the dining car."

David took a seat and across the dining table from Robbie, and studied the train schedule. Below the City of New Orleans, the tracks clicked by, covering a mile a minute. Thus far the trip had been subdued, almost morbid. They both quietly mourned the loss of their friend. David put down the schedule and spoke.

"I've got an idea."

"Oh, no you don't," Robbie said as he finished off his bottle of Coke. "Your ideas are always dangerous."

Ignoring him, David tapped on the schedule. "We need an Irish wake."

"I don't like the sound of this, David."

"Hey, secure the sweat pumps, will you?"

"David, we just finished. We are naval aviators. Please, let's not screw it up the first night."

"It's okay. I've worked it all out. We get off the train in St. Louis, hit the town and get a room in the Union Station Hotel. Get up the next day and catch the southbound, early. We'll get to P-cola Sunday morning, instead of Saturday night, It'll still be the weekend, and nobody will notice or care."

Robbie shook his head nervously. "I still don't like it."

"Trust me. Have I ever led you astray?"

"Yes. Yes, you have! In fact, I can't count the number of times."

"Oh, come on, you are sounding like a pantywaist." David flagged down the nearest waiter. "Sir, may we please have two of your coldest beers?"

18:00 Local, 23NOV (07:00 GMT, 23NOV)
Guadalcanal

Colonel Thumper McDonald sat watching the sun set over the Pacific, enjoying his dinner of captured Japanese rice and fresh fish. Captain Johnson, his new operations officer, found Thumper's hiding spot and regretfully interrupted.

"What kind of fish is that, Colonel?"

"Grenade."

"Grenade fish?"

"Affirmative, young captain. An enterprising corporal realized that if you toss a grenade into the lagoon you get a tasty treat."

"I'm not much on fish. What is it seasoned with?"

"Ocean salt and gun powder."

"Yum, yum," quipped Captain Johnson.

"Indeed, you had better hurry, Johnny. All the identifiable species are almost gone."

The captain hurried off, returning ten minutes later with an ammo can lid heaped with fish and rice. He sat down next to Thumper to watch the sun set.

"I don't suppose you came out here just to join me in the senior officer's mess," said the colonel.

Captain Johnson tried to speak with a mouthful of hot fish.

"No … no, sir."

He gave up trying to speak and handed a message to Thumper, who quickly read it and turned to his captain.

"You read this?"

"All available assets. Doesn't sound like much fun does it?"

"Nope, not a bit."

09:00 Local, 23NOV (15:00 GMT, 23NOV)
Union Station Hotel, St. Louis, Missouri

A clock in the Gothic stone tower began to chime. The sound, reverberating off the large red clay tiles of the roof, made its way to David and Robbie's room. Awakened by the first chime, Robbie counted eight more.

He bounded out of bed, grabbed the alarm clock, looked at it and threw it against the wall next to David's bed.

"Damn it—we forgot to set the alarm!"

David rolled over, talking toward the wall.

"So what time does our train leave?"

"Right now!" Panic edged Robbie's voice.

"Hmm, I see. Well, let's not get our panties in a bunch."

"Too late, mine are in a definite bunch!"

David sat up, holding his head, and swung his feet out of bed. "Okay, I'll get a shower."

"Shower?"

"Yeah, I think better in the shower. Secure the sweat pumps, shipmate. We'll figure something out."

Robbie scurried about, packing their bags and calling the front desk to request their bill be readied for checkout. After hanging up, he heard the distinctive sound of a single snap of the fingers. David had emerged from the bath room, hair slicked back, perfectly in place, wearing a towel and a confident grin.

"Pack your trash, Robbie, we will be in P-cola in a heartbeat and in style."

"Either that or the brig."

"Oh ye of little faith! Have I ever let you down?"

"We have already discussed that, and we can add one more to the list."

David laughed it off and dressed calmly, way too methodically for Robbie.

He snapped the clasp on his sea bag, stopping one last time in front of the mirror.

"I look good in a uniform, don't I?"

"David!"

"Admit it."

"Okay, okay, you look good. Let's go."

"Damn right I do."

Running down to the desk, they hurriedly paid for the room and headed down the grand staircase. David stopped Robbie, pushing him against the wall under the stone arch by the main doors.

"Stop here."

"Why? What now?"

David ran to the other side of the arch and faced it, then spoke: "Relax, I have the plan."

Robbie shrieked back at the wall, his voice traveling along the smooth arch as David's had.

"Come on!"

He was infuriated. Then he clearly heard David softly chuckle. Running across the entranceway, he grabbed David and his bag, and pushed him out the brass and glass doors. A long yellow cab pulled forward and they jumped in.

"Lambert Field, my good man, and step on it, please."

"You got it, Mac," replied the gruff cabbie.

As they sped away from the curb, Robbie protested. "NAS St. Louis—you are going to have us turn ourselves in. That's the plan?"

David ignored him. "Civilian side, good sir; American Airlines terminal, to be exact."

He settled back in the large seat for the forty-minute ride to the airport.

David had the door to the cab open before it came to a full stop at the curb of the main terminal of Lambert field. "Wait here with the bags, Robbie," he said, and quickly disappeared inside the terminal as Robbie sat nervously in the cab. Confidently striding out of the terminal fifteen minutes later, David went straight to the front passenger window and paid the cabbie, adding a large tip.

"Come on, we are flying to New Orleans—where, by the way, we will catch our original train with time to spare."

Robbie shook his head in disbelief, grabbed their sea bags off the cab floor, and followed David into the building. They bypassed the counter and went directly to a gate, not stopping there, either. They proceeded out an open door to a waiting DC-3 that already had engines turning.

Captain Jon Gaus stood next to the door and shouted over the exhaust noise generated by the R-1820s. "Is this the other wayward sailor?" Robbie stopped to shake hands, but Jon jerked his head toward the cabin door. "You knuckleheads already have me ten minutes behind schedule. Get aboard."

The DC-3 was packed with wartime travelers. David and Robbie tried not to bang their sea bags off the passengers as they moved forward. Storing their bags under the radio operator's table, David pointed to a small seat behind it. "We only use the radio operator on long, international flights," he told Robbie. "You sit there. I'll be up front on the jump seat."

Robbie dutifully flopped in the seat as the DC-3 began to taxi. Take-off was smooth as silk and he was sound asleep before they had reached cruising altitude. Several hours later, the sudden silence stirred him; the absence of the comforting drone of pistons brought him to consciousness and only added to his disorientation. David kicked his shoe.

"Come on, we have to move."

"Now what?" Robbie asked as he struggled with the bags.

"Cab to the New Orleans train station. This time, you pay. We might even have time for a trip to Bourbon Street."

"No, I can't take it. Straight to the train station!"

David laughed his easy laugh. "Okay, Robbie. Let's go."

Arriving at the Pensacola Station, the two bone-weary voyagers made their way to the cab stand. Even with the two hours of sleep they got on the DC-3, they'd still had less than five total in the previous thirty-six. They collapsed into an old checkered cab.

"Where to, candidates?" asked the driver.

"Base," replied Robbie wearily.

"Are you kidding?" said David. "We still have twenty-four hours of freedom, and it's Saturday night. The San Carlos Hotel, my good man."

Robbie groaned in agony as the taxi eased away from the curb.

Entering the bar of the San Carlos, David dropped his bag and raised his arms in triumph.

"All hail the conquering heroes and newest carrier-qualified aviators in the fleet," he shouted.

Packed with student naval aviators now anticipating free drinks, the bar erupted in cheers. David and Robbie were flooded with questions and received a generous amount of slaps on the back. They held court into the wee hours.

CHAPTER 33

10:00 Local, 26NOV (16:00 GMT, 26NOV)
Naval Air Station, Pensacola, Florida

Ringing clearly in the pleasant November air, the NAS chapel's bell announced the hour. The stifling humidity that had ruled the training grounds and obstacle courses had finally relented to autumn. In northern Florida, the fall was the best time of year. Longtime residents moved to their porches and verandas to enjoy the weather. Screened porches, in the red brick houses of officer's country, held dining tables and chairs as they became the focal point of everyday life.

Here in the genteel South, the war seemed so far away, its pace of life unchanged, refusing to surrender the Southern lifestyle for a mere war. Laura remembered it well, having lived happily in the south with Charles-Henry all those years ago.

She looked away from the officers' housing toward the sea of starched white in front of the grandstands. Out there somewhere was her David. Her little boy was gone. Waiting for her would be a young man, a warrior. She fought back the urge to cry. Her emotions were a jumble of pride, sadness, pity and fear. Laura was very aware of what lay ahead for these boys who seemed to be masquerading as men. They were so young.

Many, maybe even most, would not return. She understood that this group was the first wave of reinforcements, charging to the sound of the drums. They would be rushed into battle where they would face the experienced aviators of the Imperial Japanese fleet.

This group, more than any other, would pay the price of inexperience.

Thinking of her first war, she knew that eventually the superior numbers of the Allies would overwhelm the small island of Japan. Nonetheless, a heavy price would be paid.

Glancing across the brilliantly white-clad sons of America, she let her mind wander, not wanting to factor the cost to the country. Kaitlyn, only sixteen, sat next to Laura. Sensing her mother's trepidation, she gently took her hand while William squirmed, trying to figure out which white knight was his brother.

Laura held a small printed chart that the Navy, being ever-efficient, had provided so they could find David's unit. Experience told her they would be lined up by height; David would be in the middle of his group. Finally, the speeches no one was listening to ended. Laura handed each of her youngest children a brand new, navy blue ensign's shoulder board.

Each shoulder board had a brass button at its pointed end and a wide, single gold stripe at the other. A braided gold star was in the middle; it signified the wearer was an Officer of the Naval Line. A war fighter, not a supply or JAG Officer, the star meant that in a time of conflict this officer would be in harm's way.

In her hand were the golden wings of a naval aviator: spread, feathered wings of a bird with a shield at the center and a fouled anchor behind that. It represented the most dangerous profession in the world—and that was during peacetime. During war, the danger was immeasurable. An entire squadron could be, and had been, wiped out in a single strike.

These wings were well-worn. Sean "Thumper" McDonald, now Colonel USMCR, had sent them to Laura before he had shoved off to play fighter pilot at the ripe old age of forty-three. God only knew where he was, no doubt in the middle of it. She sighed loudly.

"Okay, kids, let's go find your brother."

* * * *

David eased the 1936 Ford sedan to a stop in front of BAT I.

"I'll be right back, gang. I have something I have to do."

Checking the alignment of his wings in the reflection of the windshield, he straightened his cover and marched toward the main entrance of BAT I. Laura watched from the passenger seat.

"He doesn't even walk the same," she said to no one in particular.

Ensign Brennan slapped three times on the bulkhead framing the door. "Enter," rang out from within.

Sergeant Major M.L. Paillou sat at attention, studying the daily muster.

"Speak," he snapped without looking up.

"Sir, I wanted you to be the first."

Paillou looked up and studied Ensign Brennan for a full three-count. "You are the sir now, Ensign."

David came stiffly to attention. "The ensign requests the honor of receiving your salute, Sergeant Major."

Paillou rose to his feet, taking his campaign cover from the desk and meticulously placing it on his head with two hands. Coming to rigid attention, he popped off a perfect salute. David returned the show of mutual respect and handed the sergeant major a silver dollar, a naval tradition. Executing a perfect about-face, Ensign Brennan marched toward the door.

Paillou called out after him, "Ensign Brennan, you don't have to die to be a hero."

David hesitated and proceeded out the door. Candidates braced, standing at attention against the bulkheads as he walked down the hall and out the main entrance. He emerged from BAT I, changed forever.

CHAPTER 34

23:00 Local, 29NOV (07:00 GMT, 30NOV)
Naval Air Station, El Centro, California

Following graduation, David treated his family to four days on the beach in a fishing cottage at Gulf Shores, Alabama. Just across the border from Florida, it was beautiful and empty. The white-sand seclusion was perfect for the family to reconnect. David was more at ease around his mother than he had ever been, but was still antsy to get into the fight before it was over.

Each night, he took them out to dinner so Laura wouldn't have to cook. Each day, they spent on the beach, and every morning he and Laura would go for long walks searching for shells. But it couldn't last; they all knew it. An atmosphere of apprehension hung over them.

On the last morning, they got a ride from one of David's flight school buddies to the Mobile train station and boarded a train for Dallas. After a long, painful good-bye, David got back on the train and continued west.

Arriving in Imperial, California, at 23:00 on a Sunday night, he looked around in disbelief. *This can't possibly be the right place.* A tumbleweed blew past his feet as he stood in disgust. After looking around the empty station, he found a sailor asleep in a jeep behind the building.

"Are you my ride, sailor?"

Startled, the young sailor jerked awake.

"Yes, sir. Anyone with you?"

"No, I'm afraid I'm the only one sentenced to El Centro and the old Wildcat."

"Okay, sir. If you say so. The squadron duty officer asked me to bring you by his quarters when you arrived."

David looked up at the young sailor, who was actually only a year younger than himself.

"Duty officer? Am I in trouble already?"

"I wouldn't know, Ensign."

"Oh well, what are they going to do, send me to El Centro?"

Looking at the young ensign quizzically, the sailor chose not to respond and started the jeep as David jumped in with his gear.

Driving through the pitch-black night toward the air station, David knew they were surrounded by farm fields; he could smell them. Having grown up in Texas, he was familiar with the smell of freshly plowed fields and fertilizer, but he was surprised: the farmers were planting even though it was almost December.

Hardly slowing as they blew through the front gate, David held on for his life as the sailor wheeled the little jeep around a sharp turn to the BOQ, the bachelor officer quarters. Screeching to a halt, the young sailor pushed David's bags to him, then speeding off, yelled through the cloud of dust.

"Good luck, Ensign. He's in room 113."

David dropped his bags louder than needed in front of the door marked 113. Irritated, all he wanted to do was sleep; 23:00 local meant 01:00, body time. The crowded train had not been conducive to sleep. As he raised his hand to knock on the door, it opened, startling him.

"About damn time, Brennan. You've been screwing off for a week."

Lieutenant Stutzman stood in front of the shocked ensign.

"Lieutenant, what are you doing here? I thought you were slated for Hellcats."

"Not after that mid-air. The Navy doesn't reward failure."

"But sir, that wasn't—"

"I was flight lead. I was accountable. End of story."

He motioned David in and walked to the icebox where he retrieved two Budweisers and popped the tops with a wall-mounted opener. David accepted the offered beer.

"Is that why I'm here?"

"Nope. You are here because we thought you'd survive, while your classmates would need the advantage of the Hellcat."

A twinge of jealousy rose from David's gut. He washed it back down with a hard swallow of cold beer.

"Of course, had you got more hits on your guns check ride and got top gun, they would have had to give you your first choice."

David shrugged and said nothing.

"Well, the good news is, this is the General Motors FM-1 Wildcat, a better breed of cat."

Lieutenant Stutzman tossed an operating manual to David.

"They pulled two guns and some excess armor, so it is a lot lighter. It's not an F-4F; it is an FM-1."

Not convinced, David thumbed idly through the manual, then set it down.

"Do I still have to crank the damn gear?"

Stutzman laughed and showed a fresh bruise on his forearm.

Intense training was the rule for the next two weeks—two or three flights a day, every day. Air-to-air dogfighting, strafe runs, bombing practice, and every single flight was a two-plane, at least. In fact, most were four-plane formations. David was getting very comfortable maneuvering in a group.

Assigned to Lieutenant Stutzman's division as dash two, David flew every flight on his wing. He had always felt Stutzman was a good stick, but the more he flew with him, the more he realized just how good. As a lead he was smooth as silk; it didn't matter if they were descending through clouds or pulling five Gs on a strafing run. David found maintaining a proper wing position was effortless.

Stutzman was also right about the FM-1: it was a much better fighter than the F-4F, and Ensign David Brennan began to love it. He even began to love flying in the Imperial Valley. Chocolate Mountains to the east and the San Jacinto Mountains to the west, in the middle of the valley was the Salton Sea. Actually a 15-by-35-mile lake created by a flood from the Colorado River in the early 1900s, the Salton Sea had formed on the ancient bed of the inland sea, so it had no ability to run off. In fact, the basin in which it had formed was below sea level by 220 feet. The aviators loved running in on a target with the altimeter reading negative numbers.

It also presented the perfect environment for training. Brackish and secluded, there were no fishing or pleasure boats on its surface. The Navy built wooden target silhouettes of Japanese warships and floated them on the Salton Sea. Large practice strikes flew out of NAS El Centro daily, rehearsing coordinated attacks.

David thought the Chocolate Mountains were captivating. And indeed, they did look like chunks of chocolate floating in chocolate-flavored milk.

But still, he couldn't figure out what made the mountains look so much like their name.

It came to him on a live-fire mission. They were in a racetrack pattern, dropping 500-pound bombs in the twilight sky. The beauty of the blue-white flash of the bombs detonating was in sharp contrast to their purpose, but no less captivating. Even so, his eyes were drawn back to the Chocolate Mountains. No strata, no trees, or variation of color. The mountains and desert floor were pure colors, unlike most mountain ranges. That's why they looked like chocolate.

CHAPTER 35

18:08 Local, 13DEC (02:08 GMT, 14DEC)
Naval Air Station, El Centro, California

Already feeling like a veteran fighter pilot after two-and-a-half weeks in the FM-1 Wildcat, David strutted into the ready room of VF-27. Lieutenant Stutzman was waiting for him.

"Brennan, time to get used to this thing at high altitude and at night. Plan a mission to CAP over San Clemente Island at 32,000 feet, maintaining station for two hours, then RTB here. Do not run out of gas. Do not come spinning out of altitude and crash. The air is different up there, thinner and thus faster. It makes the aircraft very touchy and causes it to do weird stuff. Questions?"

David stared back at Stutzman.

"Yes, sir. To start with, what do you mean thinner and faster?"

Stutzman sighed, betraying concern over the coming flight.

"Look, the wing and the airspeed indicator only know one thing: how many molecules of air are coming over it or through it. Up high, the air is thinner, thus fewer molecules. So, to get the molecules, the wing needs to fly and the air speed indicator needs to show a given airspeed—they have to go faster. That accelerated speed will still indicate on your airspeed indicator as what the wing needs, but will actually be much faster. Your indicator will show 200, but the true airspeed could be 350 or higher."

David rubbed his chin and thought about the information he had just received.

"Okay, but how does that affect the airplane?"

"No one really knows, to be honest. It involves flow dynamics that are way above my pay grade. What it means to us is the airplane doesn't act in the way we are used to, so be careful!"

* * * *

David cranked the gear handle furiously, and the brand new R-1830-86 Twin Wasp engine pulled strongly as the FM-1 climbed to altitude. Passing 10,000 feet, he shifted the engine's supercharger to high stage and put on his oxygen mask. They allowed both the engine and aviator to continue to breathe deeply as they propelled higher into the evening sky.

Night light starts on the ground, an inverse constellation that illuminates its stars from beneath. As the sun fades below the horizon, its remaining energy is preoccupied with lighting the last remnants of clouds, and it gives up on lighting the Earth. As the surface darkens, the manmade light of homes and cities shines brightly.

Heaven's constellations began to reflect back as the sunset became a mere memory. David's oxygen mask felt bulky and uncomfortable. The higher he got, the more the flow of oxygen seemed to be forced down into his lungs. Pressure breathing was unnatural and very difficult to get used to.

Reaching 20,000 feet, higher than he had ever been, David felt the character of the Wildcat change. It was no longer friendly and seemed to be trying to swap ends. With each minute movement, it wanted to uncouple. David tried a couple of easy turns as he continued his climb and was shocked at how quickly it entered pre-stall buffet.

Even with adequate indicated airspeed, his Wildcat was getting unruly. Forces were affecting his aircraft that he didn't understand. He decided to respect them and treat high-altitude flight as a completely different regime. Lieutenant Stutzman's advice to be careful was sage indeed.

David felt compelled to see how high his FM-1 would climb. Reaching the service ceiling of 34,700 feet, he kept going. His Wildcat continued to claw at the thin atmosphere. At 37,000 feet, he didn't think it could go any higher, but it did. Heading west, the horizon of the Earth was a well-defined line. He continued out to sea, flying toward the last vestige of light.

He could see the curvature of the Earth in the dissipating twilight. Planets announced the coming of complete darkness. David turned down his cockpit lights, which suddenly seemed very bright. Reaching to turn up the heater, he realized it was already up all the way. Glancing at the outside air temperature gauge, he was surprised to see minus forty. Subconsciously, he pulled up the woolen collar of his leather flight jacket to fend off the chill.

Crossing the coastline, he could still clearly see San Clemente Island and gingerly turned his Wildcat toward it as he pulled up the zipper on his jacket. A clear night, the coast was sharply defined, meandering into the distance for hundreds of miles. It was entrancing.

Turning down his cockpit lights again, David looked straight up through his canopy at the stars sparkling to life. A powerful serenity fell upon him. Thoughts of his father and brother came to him. David realized it was just a year ago that they had crossed this same coast.

Only a year, and yet it feels like an eternity. He could hardly remember their faces. He could hardly remember his own past self. The ever-present hollowness in his belly turned sour. *When do I get my vengeance?* David raged at the night.

Now at an altitude of 39,280 feet, he flipped on his gun sight. The bright, white piper blinded him. David selected the night setting and rolled the Wildcat inverted, pulling it into a power dive. It buffeted in protest. He ignored it, jamming the throttle forward and wrenching the nose sixty degrees down. He began to jerk the aircraft left and right, looking for a target ship to practice a strafing run on.

Scorching through 37,000 feet, the Wildcat's protestation turned into outright rebellion. Approaching it' redline indicated airspeed of 275 knots, a phenomenon not yet fully understood by aerodynamicists occurred: mach tuck. Part of the airflow on the straight wing actually went supersonic, causing the Wildcat to abruptly pitch even more steeply nose down. The airspeed indicator leaped past the redline limit. The aircraft was now completely out of control.

With the Wildcat over-speeding and shaking violently, David tried to pull the nose up to slow down. Panic crept into the cockpit when nothing happened. A shock wave had attached forward of the elevator, blanking the control surface. Not knowing what else to do, he yanked the throttle to idle and held the stick in his lap.

As he plummeted toward the dark ocean, the air grew denser and the altimeter unwound. The density actually slowed the FM-1. Decelerating, the mach tuck reversed, pitching up so violently that the Wildcat further decelerated, causing the shock wave to detach. David still had the stick in his lap. The pitch control bit into the thicker air. He saw the G-meter spike to nine before he blacked out.

11:20 Local, 14NOV (03:20 GMT, 14NOV)
Mindoro Island, The Philippines

Captain Butler came out of the thatched hut, walking directly to Sergeant Donnelly. In the hut was the only functioning radio on the island, an HF that had enough range to communicate with Pacific Command.

"What's the word, Captain?"

"The word is to sit tight and await orders. Monitor the frequency only, unless large naval or air movement is observed."

"Hey, suits me, sir."

"Yeah, me too, but I have a feeling it will only be temporary."

19:43 Local, 13DEC (03:43 GMT, 14DEC)
Gulf of Santa Catalina

Nine Gs had gotten the nose close to the horizon before the loss of blood to his brain induced unconsciousness. The aircraft was trimmed to fly at its normal cruise speed of 150 knots, which was the airspeed David was at before he began his ill-advised maneuver. The Wildcat continued to raise its nose, seeking 150 knots. Still at idle power, the FM-1 decelerated rapidly as the nose rose into the night sky.

At twenty degrees nose high, David began to revive. His instinctive reaction was to yank back on the stick. Continuing to slow, the unpowered Wildcat, now below 100 knots, went out of control. He countered as the wing rolled off, introducing a yawing momemment, snapping the aircraft into a spin.

Already disoriented, he struggled for clarity as he was thrown around the cockpit. The illuminated coastline spun in the distance as he fought with the angry Wildcat. *If I panic, I will die!*

J.T.'s voice came to him clearly: First, do no harm. David released the stick and rudders, forcing himself to scan inside the cockpit and analyze the instruments. His attention was drawn to the altimeter unwinding like a broken clock. Airspeed, altitude, heading.

They were all out of whack. Only the airspeed held constant, and it showed

60. Sixty knots; I'm in a spin. Grabbing the stick, he thrust it forward. After referencing the turn needle, he matched the stick to it and put in opposite rudder. Coastline, ocean, coastline, ocean. He felt the rotation break and watched the turn needle come off the peg. Instantly, he centered the rudder and stick. The nose dropped, and the airspeed jumped to 100. He glanced at the altimeter and was surprised to see it at 15,000 feet. Satisfied with that, he left the nose down to build up flying speed. Slowly he fed in throttle, careful to counter with rudder and keep the recalcitrant Wildcat in balance.

Indicating 200 knots, David eased on a gentle two-G pull, leveling the nose, and turned for the coast and home. He'd had enough training for one night.

CHAPTER 36

VF-27 pilots stood at attention on the quay side of the USS Suwannee (ACV-27) as their FM-1 Wildcats were craned onto the flight deck. They had flown in the day before, landing on North Island's airfield and taxiing in single file, with police escort, down the street to the docks. Like a family of ducklings, they followed their squadron commander in a perfectly spaced row.

The Suwannee had briefly served in the Atlantic as an oiler before being converted to an auxiliary aircraft carrier on 24 September, 1942. Later designated escort carriers, they were known in Navy slang as jeep carriers, adapted from their initial mission of running lend-lease jeeps and trucks to England. With the critical shortage of aircraft carriers, the Navy converted the ships into smaller carriers and rushed them to the fleet.

VF-27's fighter pilots considered it the minor leagues. They all wanted to be on a big, fast carrier, taking it to the Japanese. It was a blow to their egos, being on the second string.

The skipper was counting heads after a boisterous night in Coronado. Festivities had culminated in VF-27 being asked to leave the Hotel Del Coronado after demonstrating carrier landings on the bar. Now bloodshot and quiet, they were nonetheless resplendent in their aviation greens.

Naval aviators had their own uniform and relished it even though, due to the green color, they were often mistaken for Marines. Starting off with brown shoes that set them apart—all other officers wore black, leading to the derisive term "black shoe," meaning non-aviator—green trousers, khaki blouse, black tie, and a sleek, matching green single-breasted tunic wrapped up the elitist ensemble. No ribbons were worn on the jacket, nothing to distract from the pilot wings. To prevent any confusion if the tunic was on a hanger, wings were also worn on the shirt. It was all topped off with a fore aft, or garrison, cap, tilted rakishly, with rank on one side and, instead of the standard officer crest, a miniature set of wings on the other.

All hands were counted, staterooms for the senior and bunk rooms for the junior were assigned, and they filed up the gangway. At the top of the gangway, each officer turned aft to face the flag on the stern, saluted, and asked the officer of the deck, the OOD, for permission to come aboard. Once on board, they were led to the ready room, then released to find their bunk rooms, known as BK.

David followed Ensign Scott Ryder down the portside passageway. Scott already had the call sign "Rough," but David was still without one and it was beginning to bother him. There were some really bad ones, though, so he kept his mouth shut so as not to bring a wrathful call sign down upon himself.

Rough Ryder tried to decipher the code painted on the bulkhead above each space. Finally, he gave up and followed the crowd.

"You ever been on a ship, Ryder?"

"Not out of a cockpit."

"Then how do you know where we are going?"

"I don't, but the lieutenant said to go down this passageway until it ends, turn to starboard, and it will be right there."

They continued down the passageway, opening hatches, stepping over and through the oval housing that held the hatches, called knee-knockers for the obvious reason that if you weren't careful you knocked your knee. Once through the hatch, they would turn and close and dog, or lock, it. It was a slow process for the newbies, and embarrassing, as young seamen and old commanders alike shuffled by, sneering at the two nuggets for slowing up the flow as they struggled with the heavy hatches. The Navy was different than most services. A Marine was in the Corps, a soldier might identify himself as infantry or artillery, but a sailor identified himself as a member of the crew to a specific ship.

Also, unlike other branches, in the Navy everyone shared the same risk, from admiral to seaman apprentice. Especially in battle—they were all quite literally in the same boat. A general might give an order from hundreds of miles away; a fleet admiral gave it from the flag bridge.

This sense of shared risk bonded the crew to each other and their ship. She would carry them to battle and to safety afterward. She would shelter them in inclement weather and provide refuge in a storm—but only if the crew worked as a team to keep her squared away and repaired her damage. If she could fight no more, she would provide an eternal resting place for those lost.

A sailor's loyalty was given to his ship. He might speak ill of the Navy, but let no man ever speak disparagingly about his ship. Many bars around the world erupted in riot over a slight about a crew's ship. A crew was singular, its members shipmates for life.

Naval aviators were the exception. The air dales had an absolutely horrendous life expectancy in combat. Squadrons would launch and sometimes not a single aircraft returned. They would struggle off the flight deck in overloaded aircraft, seeking the enemy. Once found, they would dive into the Zeros and the triple-A, dropping bombs and torpedoes or engaging in dogfights. Combat mission complete, they would try to find their own ship and land on it.

Many perished after running out of fuel and crashing into the ocean. Many more died attempting to land battle-damaged aircraft on the pitching deck of an aircraft carrier. The rest of the Navy looked upon them with a mixture of ambivalence and reverence. If they wanted their own uniform, let them have it. Chances were they would never wear it out.

Successful in locating their BK, the ensigns banged open the door with their sea bags and flipped on the overhead lights. Cat calls rang out from within the BK.

"Turn off those damn lights!"

"How are we supposed to find our racks?"

"Go red, you idiots!"

"What?"

One of the crusty, second-tour guys, Lieutenant Junior Grade Russ Mitchell pushed aside the curtain to his rack and deftly leapt to the floor. He pointed to the rack under his.

"That's yours, Brennan."

As he pointed out Rough Ryder's rack, he flipped the three position light switch, from white to red. Dark red lights replaced the bright white ones in the overhead fixtures.

"Ten of us live here. We all have different schedules. Check the racks before you go white."

"Okay, okay, we are new, you know."

"No excuse."

He pivoted and hopped into his rack, whooshing the curtain closed. David and Rough tried not to laugh but couldn't stifle their giggles.

"I guess we might as well take a nap too."

David nodded his agreement in the eerie red light.

"Would you two nuggets shut up."

Nugget was a reference to the gold bar on their collars, equivalent to calling them new guys. A naval aviator would lose his nugget status after his first cruise, regardless of his rank.

"Ho, the hell, ho," giggled David.

* * * *

"SHIFT COLORS," boomed over the 1MC, the loudspeaker system, located all over the ship. "NOW SET THE AT SEA WATCH. SECURE THE SEA AND ANCHOR DETAIL." David jerked awake and looked at Rough. He was wide-eyed as well. Before he could whisper, the overhead lights flipped to white.

The squadron duty officer stood next to the switch.

"Reveille, reveille, reveille; all hands on deck. Skipper wants an AOM in thirty minutes, nooowww, reveille." He did his best to impersonate the boatswain mate on the 1MC. Nothing but groans and pillows came from within the BK.

"What's an AOM?" asked Rough.

"It is a boring, all-officer meeting, where we get lectured or bitched at," snapped Mitchell.

David and Rough got up, grabbed their towels and went in search of a head, or bathroom. Finding one, they ran into the OOD they had saluted when coming on board. He held a child's pink sand pail with all his toiletries inside of it.

Both aviators snickered.

"Black shoe," Rough whispered to David.

Bright light and shiny stainless steel assaulted their eyes. The head reeked. It really reeked. And it was hot, humid, and cramped. The black shoe was already in a stall. David picked another one, hung his towel on the hook outside of it, pulled the curtain, and stared at the shower apparatus.

"How does this work?" he mumbled out loud.

"Set the rotary dial to desired temperature and push the button on the nozzle that is located on the end of the hose," came from the black shoe's stall.

David pressed the button, singeing himself with very hot water. He reset it to full cold, with the same result. The ship's lieutenant smiled in his stall at the yelps.

"Spray it off the overhead ceiling. It will cool as it drops."

David did as instructed. It was like showering in a light rain: slow but workable. Both nuggets had just gotten all soaped up when the water dribbled to a stop. "Now what?"

"Engineers are shifting freshwater tanks; it will be awhile, boys."

As they stood soaped and drying from head to toe, they heard the repeated sound of water splashing to the floor, accompanied by a loud, "Aaaahhhhh…" Then came the distinctive sound of toiletries being put into an empty bucket.

Late for the AOM, they ran down the passageway. Reaching Ready Room 6, they squeezed through the door together.

"Nice of you to join us, gentlemen," Lieutenant Commander Jasper commented as they rushed in.

"Sorry, sir," the two ensigns replied in unison.

"As I was saying, we are headed to the Pacific and war. I know some of you are disappointed that we were assigned an escort carrier. You think we won't see action. Well, all I can tell you is that you are wrong, flat wrong. We are steaming directly to the Solomons as fast as this ship will go. Once there, we will join the fight for Guadalcanal. No ports of call. We will unrep, underway replenish supplies, all the way."

With its hatches battened down and all aircraft securely chained to the deck, the USS Suwannee steamed at its flank speed of eighteen knots for the better part of four weeks. The aviators fell into a routine of doing their ground jobs and studying flash cards of Allied and Japanese shipping and aircraft. Charts were studied and tactics lectured as the temperature continued to rise.

07:50 Local, 25DEC (23:50 GMT, 24DEC)
Mindoro Island, The Philippines

Butler and Donnelley continued to drill and train their volunteers for the inevitable day the radio gave them a mission. They had lain low, trying to prevent any outsiders, Filipino or not, from seeing them. If the Japanese caught wind of Americans on Mindoro, they would tear the island apart to find them.

So they fell into a routine of training and gathering any intelligence they could. Each day they monitored the radio and listened to the updates. Along with generic instructions to everyone on the network, they occasionally heard reports of ships' movements. By the accents, Butler guessed the coast watchers were Australian.

Compared to being chased around the jungle on Luzon, this was pretty easy duty. Donnelley had even scrounged up some beer.

CHAPTER 37

1943
09:00 Local, 29JAN (22:00 GMT, 28JAN)
Task Force 18, Solomon Sea, South Pacific

Task Force Eighteen (TF-18) steamed toward Guadalcanal: six cruisers, eight destroyers, and two escort carriers. All hands were on edge because Rear Admiral Ike Giffen had the task force in the wrong tactical formation.

The US Navy was, in reality, two separate services: East Coast and West Coast, Sixth Fleet and Seventh. Their threats, tactics, formations, even the culture were vastly different. The East Coast was by-the-book and rigid; the West was more flexible in tactics and culture.

Probably because of the vast distances of the Pacific, the line officers were forced to operate on their own for long periods of time. By contrast, the East Coast was never more than a few days from a friendly port. Washington, DC and the bureaucratic Navy were always in close proximity.

While the East Coasters were buttoned down, the West Coast boys were open-collar. Heat forced a relaxation of the uniform code. This disregard for uniform regulations drove the East Coast senior officers mad. Rear Admiral Giffen, a favorite of Admiral King CINCUS, Commander in Chief United States, the top admiral in the Navy, took personal affront to the policy. He even refused to step foot on Vice Admiral Halsey's flagship because of it. Halsey was his superior.

Giffen was as inflexible in tactics as he was with petty regulations. An Atlantic sailor, his experience was battling the German Wolf Packs of U-boats. Try as they might, his Pacific staff could not convince him that the main threat here was air attack.

VENGEANCE

So they continued to cruise with the destroyer screen out in front of them in an anti-submarine warfare (ASW) formation. The capital ships were completely exposed to a torpedo or dive-bombing attack.

Even worse, Giffen's primary concern was arriving on time. He became enraged each time the task force had to turn into the wind to launch and recover aircraft because it took them off course. He vented openly and loudly that his best defensive weapon was a ball and chain.

His staff suggested sortieing the carriers first to give them a head start, then catching them later. He chastised his staff as if they were idiots, unable to even consider anything but the convoy tactics of the Atlantic.

10:50 Local, 29JAN (23:50 GMT, 28JAN)
Rabaul, Papua New Guinea

Lieutenant Commander Joji Higai, one of the top torpedo aircraft commanders in the Imperial Japanese Navy, sat excitedly as targeting information was passed. His fifteen-aircraft unit from the 701 Air Group had been moved to Rabaul. Once there, an additional sixteen G-4M Betty Torpedo bombers were put under his command. Their mission was clear: engage and sink Allied ships trying to support Guadalcanal.

He quickly plotted the latitude and longitude and measured the distance to Task Force Eighteen: 700 miles. Glancing at his watch, he did the math quickly in his head. We can be in position and use the coming darkness to cover our attack. Higai was a bold planner, a veteran of the Pearl Harbor attack. He was as decisive as he was insightful.

Abruptly, he stood and turned to his operations officer.

"I shall lead all torpedo bombers in a glorious strike. Fuel to maximum range."

"And fighter cover, Commander-san?"

"None. Our target is beyond their range. We shall use twilight and the divine wind to cover our attack."

Hours later, Giffen's Task Force Eighteen, still in formation to fend off German U-boats, steamed fifty miles north of Rennel. Late in the afternoon, the picket ships made radar contact with a group of unknown aircraft.

Lieutenant Commander Robert Pittman, flight director, ran half the length of the USS Chicago's main passageway and climbed the eight ladders to CIC, combat information center. His chief met him at the door.

228

"Sir, we hold bogeys, bearing 3-5-0, range 1-8-0, angels (altitude) medium."

"Roger that, Chief. Signal the flattops to turn into the wind and launch the alert five, snap vector for the fighters 3-5-0 for 1-8-0."

"Aye, aye, sir."

"Petty Officer, signal the flagship requesting to break radio silence."

"Aye, aye."

15:50 Local, 29JAN (04:50 GMT, 29JAN)
USS Suwannee, Task Force 18, Solomon Sea

Ensign David Brennan sat in the cockpit of his FM-1 Wildcat, sweltering in the South Pacific heat. Soaking wet in his own sweat, he was also nearly bored to tears.

"TURN TO PORT, HEEL TO STARBOARD! LAUNCH THE ALERT FIVE FIGHTERS."

His ears still ringing from the 5MC, the flight deck PA, David was startled when the Suwannee began an aggressive turn to the left. Top-heavy and lumbering as the bow came around to port, the flight deck lurched, leaning to starboard so far David thought his Wildcat would slide off into the ocean.

"SNAP VECTOR, THREE-FIVE-ZERO, FOR ONE-EIGHT-ZERO. WEAPONS RED AND FREE," echoed over the flight deck as the lead Wildcat's R-1830-86 engine barked to life. David fumbled with his engine controls before finally bringing the 1,200 horses on line. Looking up, he saw his plane captain holding his tie-down chains, which meant he was loose from the deck.

Stutzman's Twin Wasp engine roared at full power as he launched down the steeply listing deck. Suwannee was not yet into the wind as a second aircraft rolled. David signaled to pull chocks and ran his power up. He was behind. He should have been second. A third Wildcat rolled; now he was really late. Finally ready, the flight deck officer ran over to his aircraft, frantically waving a small white flag as David saluted. The flight deck officer touched the deck and David let go of the brakes, going to full power.

Never having taken off from a ship in a fully-loaded Wildcat, he grew concerned over the slow acceleration. He noticed the heaving bow was pitching up into the Pacific sky. *I'm not even moving!* Dropping into an ocean trough with a bang, the ship's bow slammed to a stop. Now running downhill, he was quickly approaching flying speed. *I'm going to hit the water!* The bow pitched back up just as he reached the end, and he was propelled into the sky.

Initially over-controlling the flight controls, David settled down and cranked the gear handle as he turned right to 350 degrees on his compass. Gaining sight of his flight, he kept his nose down to accelerate and catch them. Trimming the Wildcat as it reached redline speed, he looked up in time to realize he was closing on his flight at an incredible rate. *Shit, we briefed 140-knot rendezvous. I'm doing 275!*

He chopped the power; it was too late. His closure rate was 135 knots and he was in close. J.T.'s maneuver in Texas flashed into his conscious. Sidestepping the flight, he yanked on four Gs, pulling nose high to use gravity to slow him. Reaching forty degrees in his pitch up, he began a slow roll to the left. He kept the flight in sight and 1000 feet below him. At the apex, he was inverted and looking up through the canopy, which was pointed down at the ocean. His airspeed decayed to 120 knots rapidly, and he eased some power back on, continuing the roll. Finishing the roll, he dropped onto the left wing of Stutzman gracefully, at 140 knots.

Lieutenant Stutzman was not impressed, clearly shaking his head in the lead aircraft. With all his chicks on board, he bumped up the speed to 180 and began a long climb to 25,000 feet.

15:52 Local, 29JAN (04:52 GMT, 29JAN)
USS Chicago Combat Information Center (CIC), Solomon Sea

Lieutenant Commander Pittman looked up as his petty officer clamored through the door. The look of disbelief on his face told the story.

"Please tell me radio silence is lifted."

"Negative sir, not, repeat not lifted."

Pittman leaned back in his chair, incredulous, trying to control his emotions as his plotters and radiomen looked at him. Radios were humming in query, waiting to carry the guiding voices of his men to the combat air patrol. Pittman cleared his throat and calmly spoke.

"Send the following message: All due respect, we must address the known threat. I say again the known threat. Request radio silence lifted."

Visibly uneasy being placed in the middle of a fight between officers, the young petty officer dutifully returned to the signal bridge.

15:54 Local, 29JAN (04:54 GMT, 29JAN)
Task Force 18 Flagship, USS Wichita, Solomon Sea

Rear Admiral Giffen flew into a rage as he read the Chicago's signal from the Flag Bridge.

"Flag Admin!"

"Aye, aye, sir," responded the flag administrative officer.

"I want a punitive letter of reprimand in that man's officer service record by eight bells."

"Punitive, sir?"

"Do not question me, Lieutenant Commander, or I shall have you write one for yourself. And straighten that tie!"

His chief of staff, Captain Dean Fournier, had seen and heard enough.

"Rear Admiral Giffen, Pittman is merely trying to do his job—"

Giffen cut him off, seething.

"I realize you are West Coast, Captain. However, I would remind you that even here, a rear admiral outranks a captain."

"And it is my duty to remind you, Admiral, that we are indeed in the western Pacific and not the Atlantic, and we have an airborne threat inbound."

"Leave my bridge, Captain!"

17:55 Local, 29JAN (06:55 GMT, 29JAN)
120 Nautical Miles North of Task Force Eighteen, Solomon Sea

Lieutenant Stutzman strained to see from horizon to horizon. He had split his BARCAP, barrier combat air patrol, division, but without vectors from fighter control, it was futile. They circled until finally, with fuel exhausted, he picked up his microphone and transmitted, "Bingo."

It was a simple one word message that told everyone monitoring the frequency that the BARCAP was returning due to low fuel state. At 18:50, the last Wildcat trapped back on board the Suwannee. Her CAG, Commander Air Group, immediately signaled the Wichita, requesting another CAP be launched. Giffen refused.

On the captain's bridge, one level below the flaGs, Captain Fournier read the semaphore signal from Suwannee's CAG, again requesting a CAP be launched in the remaining sunlight. He knew what the answer would be.

A Navy chief quietly entered the bridge, walking straight to Captain

Fournier, and whispered into his ear.

"Sir, radar holds a group of bogeys, unidentified aircraft, to the east. The admiral has chosen to ignore them."

Captain Fournier nodded and walked over to the Wichita's skipper. Captain Bill Dinella was slumped in his command chair, watching his crew maintain station in the task force formation.

"Bill."

Dinella swiveled his chair to face Fournier.

"What the hell is going on, Dean-O?"

Fournier shrugged and pointed up to the flag bridge.

"I'd go to general quarters if I were you; air attack."

Dinella locked Fournier's intense brown eyes. They had known each other since the Naval Academy. Dinella was a no-bullshit Philly-boy. He had grown up fast and tough. Without dropping his glance, Dinella called out in a loud command voice.

"Officer of the Deck, OOD, I have the CON, control of the ship."

"Skipper has the CON," was the immediate and loud response.

"Sound general quarters. Standby to repel an air attack. Signal the task force to do the same."

An excruciatingly loud claxon rang out followed immediately by the 1MC.

"General quarters, general quarters, all hands man your air defense battle stations. General quarters, general quarters."

"Secure the 1MC," Dinella ordered to his OOD.

The noise from the 1MC was replaced by Rear Admiral Giffen's shrieking.

"Who ordered GQ?"

"I suggested the task force go to GQ," Fournier spoke up immediately.

"You? Belay that order! Captain Fournier, you are hereby placed in HAC, arrest in quarters. Leave the bridge!"

"Stand fast, Captain Fournier."

Dinella swiveled in his chair, facing the admiral with cold eyes.

"This is my bridge, Admiral Giffen. Captain Fournier is here at my behest."

Ike Giffen was absolutely furious.

"Sedition, is it? Mutiny!"

19:01 Local, 29Jan (08:01 GMT, 29JAN)
50 Nautical Miles East of Task Force 18, Solomon Sea

Lieutenant Commander Higai had circled Task Force Eighteen with his thirty-two aircraft, ready to attack out of the darkened eastern sky. Turning toward the task force, he descended his aircraft and split his wing into two groups.

19:19 Local, 29JAN (08:19 GMT, 29JAN)
Task Force 18 Flagship, USS Wichita, Solomon Sea

All hands were quiet on the bridge of the Wichita. When the elephants battled, it was best to stay out of the way so as not to be stomped. Captain Dinella broke the tension.

"Yeoman, enter into the ship's log that Captains Dinella and Fournier ordered the fleet to GQ against the Task Force Commander's orders."

"Do you think logging your sedition will lessen the charge—"

Before Giffen could finish his accusation the night sky erupted in fire and steel.

"Radar?" Dinella yelled over the din.

"Sir, radar reports a hornets' nest of attackers, all descending to the surface."

"Very well, pass the word: torpedo attack, orient all gun azimuths to the surface."

"Aye, aye, Captain."

A G4M Betty emerged from the darkness, its twin Kasei 25 radial engines pounding out 1,850 horsepower, propelling the land-based bomber to 250 knots as it lined up on the USS Waller.

"Torpedo in the water; starboard bow Waller!" a lookout passed from the external flying bridge.

"Call torpedoes targeting this vessel only; pass the word!" commanded Dinella.

"Aye, aye."

As the Betty pressed the attack strafing the Waller, she executed an emergency full rudder starboard turn. Seeing the Wichita, the Betty's pilots turned tightly to engage her.

"Bandit, starboard bow, 5,000 yards closing; constant bearing decreasing range."

"Right full rudder! Gunner orient port guns to threat axis 0 3 0 degrees."

Wichita heeled hard on Dinella's order; the superstructure leaned the opposite direction of the emergency turn.

"Incoming!" Tracers were in the air.

"Starboard guns 2 1 0, prepare to fire on egressing bandit; seek shelter!"

Heavy, red, 20-millimeter cannon fire tore into the superstructure as the crew ducked for cover below the exploding glass windows. Rounds ricocheted throughout the steel bridge, finding soft flesh. Starboard side guns added to the mayhem, chasing the fleeing Betty. Wichita and Chicago's guns converged on it, bringing it down just off Chicago's port bow.

Blood began to mix with the glass fragments as the wounded writhed on the deck.

"Medical corpsmen to the bridge; damage control report." Dinella sat calmly back in his command chair.

"Damage minor."

"Very well."

"Bandit, starboard beam!"

"Right full rudder; let's put our bow on him, Helmsman."

Aye, aye, sir," came the answer in a weak voice.

Dinella looked up. In the red light, he could see his young helmsman valiantly struggling with one arm to spin the ship's wheel, the other dangling limply at his side.

"Officer of the Deck, relieve the Helmsman. Gunner, starboard bow, full depressed azimuth open fire!"

Evasive action from the Wichita and Chicago made their fire ineffective; the Betty slipped between them, targeting the USS Louisville with a torpedo that just missed before disappearing under cover of darkness. The cacophony of fire ended as abruptly as it had started. All hands stood silently, glaring at Rear Admiral Giffen. Muffled moans were the only sounds.

19:30 Local, 29JAN (08:30 GMT, 29JAN)
Task Force 18 Flagship, USS Wichita, Solomon Sea

Giffen cleared his throat.

"Return to base course, flank speed."

"Admiral, I suggest a zigzag course—"

"I've had enough of your suggestions, Captain Dinella. We are now late for rendezvous. The task force successfully fended off the attack. They will not attack again at night."

"The Brits did," Fournier said.

"As you so eagerly point out, Captain Fournier, this is not the Atlantic, and they are not the Brits. Base course, flank speed."

19:31 Local, 29JAN (08:31 GMT, 29JAN)
10 Nautical Miles East of Task Force 18, Solomon Sea

Lieutenant Commander Higai continued to stalk the task force in the darkness. Clusters of red and green float lights, dropped by scout planes, told him the Americans had inexplicably returned to base course. He radioed the scouts to drop parachute flares, and turned in to attack.

19:36 Local, 29JAN (08:36 GMT, 29JAN)
Overhead Task Force 18 Flagship, USS Wichita, Solomon Sea

A billion candle watts of power lit up the ocean. Eerie, artificial stars cast ominous shadows across the black water as they floated down.

"Parachute flares, all quadrants!"

"Stand by to repel torpedo bomber attack," Captain Dinella ordered as he calmly lit a tobacco pipe.

19:38 Local, 29JAN (08:38 GMT, 29JAN)
Attack Run on Task Force 18, Solomon Sea

Higai's was the first GM 4 to illuminate on an attack run against the Chicago. First dropping his torpedo, he began a strafing run. She fought back furiously; hard turning to avoid his torpedo, the Chicago flamed Higai's Betty, causing it to impact off her port bow. Two of his wingmen saw their leader perish and shifted their attacks to the Chicago.

Approaching from the starboard beam before the Chicago could re-direct her guns, the two Bettys flashed into the incandescent light just above their own reflection on the water. Two deadly fish gracefully dropped from their bellies. In close succession, they struck the Chicago.

19:42 Local, 29JAN (08:42 GMT, 29JAN)
Task Force 18 Flagship, USS Wichita, Solomon Sea

Ripping into the Chicago's exposed side, the first torpedo compromised two compartments, taking out three of the four shafts powering the ship's screws. The second hit fire room number three, flooding the forward engine room, which took out the fourth shaft. The Chicago came to a complete stop, drifting rudderless while Captain Davis and his crew fought to save her.

A signalman leaned into the Wichita's bridge.

"Captain, Chicago signals two hit alphas, potentially fatal to ship. She's dead in the water."

19:43 Local, 29JAN (08:43 GMT, 29JAN)
USS Chicago, Task Force 18, Solomon Sea

Lieutenant Commander Pittman pulled himself off the deck of CIC. Only the battery-powered battle lanterns provided light.

"We've got to get power; I'll be back."

Pittman ran to the bridge. The CHENG, Chief Engineer, was coming out.

"Cheng, I need electricity to the radar."

"Bob, we are just trying to save the ship at this point."

"If they put another fish into us, we're done. The diesels will be up any second to run the pumps. I'll try to get you some power for the radar, but nothing else."

Pittman heard the diesel generators come on line. He could hear the pumps spin up to speed while he ran back to CIC.

"We got power?"

"Doesn't matter, sir. I went out and looked at the dish. It's all shot to hell."

"Okay, pass it to the bridge and signal the Wichita to take over as task force fighter director."

Giffen watched the parachute flares flicker as they landed in the ocean. Still glowing white-hot, the magnesium flares sank deeper into the ocean, taking their unholy light with them to the depths of the Pacific. He directed USS Louisville to take Chicago under tow.

With incredible seamanship, her skipper, Captain Joy, positioned his cruiser 1,000 feet in front of the stricken Chicago. By 24:00 she was underway at four knots, listing eleven degrees to starboard.

01:00 Local, 30JAN (14:00 GMT, 29JAN)
USS Suwannee, Task Force 18, Solomon Sea

Ensign David Brennan sat, disillusioned, in Ready Room 6. Lieutenant Stutzman was passing through and noticed him in the corner.

"Nice join up today, mister. Let's leave the barnstorming in Missouri, shall we?"

He just nodded in reply.

"What's your problem, Sport?"

"Are you kidding? Today was a damn goat rope!"

"Get used to it, Brennan."

"What?"

"Get over it, Ensign. Just because you have rank doesn't mean you are suited for a command in combat. Your job is to carry out your orders the best you can. The warriors will continue to rise to the top. Until then, do your best and improvise."

"Improvise?"

"Have you read your commission?"

"Yes, so what?"

"Have you read the enlisted man's oath? What is the difference?"

"There isn't any."

"Wrong, young Ensign, there is a very big distinction. An enlisted man's oath says, 'I shall carry out the orders of those above me.' An officer's commission says, 'to the best of my ability.' That subtle difference allows an officer discretion, the ability to adjust to the tactical situation or even surrender troops on the field of battle."

"That doesn't explain today."

Stutzman sat next to David and collected his thoughts.

"Look, the rest of the world has been at war for years. We are just getting into the game. We will have days like this until we square it all away. We are the cavalry, the first wave of offense coming to the rescue. It will be up to us to push back and allow the home front to pump out the planes and ships. We will need to drive the Japanese back to Tokyo."

"And then what?"

"Then, young Ensign, we will win the war. And the idiots and paper pushers will move back in during the peace."

"Why do you do it, then?"

"Some things are more important than yourself, or your own self-interest."

Lieutenant Stutzman could see his young protégé was not satisfied with the answers he had received. He patted David on a knee.

"Don't worry. There will be an after-action report. I suspect Admiral Halsey will not be happy. Now hit the rack. This fight is not over."

04:00 Local, 30JAN (17:00 GMT, 29JAN)
USS Enterprise, Admiral Halsey's Flagship, Solomon Sea

Admiral Halsey was indeed unimpressed with Giffen's performance and ordered him to withdraw to the port of Efate. Giffen split Task Force Eighteen, leaving only six destroyers to guard the Chicago from the still non-existent submarine threat. She was a sitting duck as most of the anti-aircraft artillery, and all of the air cover, was withdrawn.

Halsey, upon receiving the movement message, couldn't believe it. After an expletive-filled tirade, he ordered both carriers Chenango and the Suwannee to immediately reverse course and move to cover the Chicago. He also ordered the Enterprise group to steam to her aid.

It was too late. Vice Admiral Jinichi Kusaka had no intention of letting the cruiser Chicago escape. He launched every torpedo bomber he had to destroy her.

15:40 Local, 30JAN (04:30 GMT, 30JAN)
Overhead, USS Chicago, Task Force 18, Solomon Sea

Eight Wildcats circled in the crystal-blue, clear sky. Like their namesake, they were crouched, ready to spring into combat. Below them, the crew of the USS Chicago had worked through the night and day to save her, still dead in the water were it not for the tug, Navajo. Her diesel backup generators were up and running, providing power to the ship and pumps.

A glint of sunlight off a single pane of the Japanese reconnaissance aircraft's canopy jolted the fighters into action. All eight charged toward the lone intruder, led by Lieutenant Commander Jasper. A long chase ensued.

Stutzman, seeing it was a single aircraft, broke his division off from the chase. His section lead, Lieutenant Junior Grade Steed, pressed ahead, hungry for a share of the kill. Stutzman, with David still on his wing, returned overhead the Chicago. He knew she was the target.

Strike control frequency suddenly came alive with the Enterprise's fighter director calling out a bogey position forty miles southeast of the Chicago. Enterprise appeared to be the target; her fighters were vectored to intercept the attackers.

Stutzman turned toward the threat, increasing his airspeed to 220 and signaling David to arm and charge his guns. David's throat was dry and his heart pounded as loudly in his ears as the four .50-caliber rounds that thumped into the chambers of his Brownings. He was surprised when Stutzman began to circle. *What now? The threat is ahead of us!*

After feinting toward the Enterprise, in an attempt to pull all of the Navy's CAP out of position to aid the Chicago, the Japanese had suddenly veered sharply toward the Chicago, descending at full speed on their attack run.

Hearing the confusion over the radio, Stutzman knew exactly what was transpiring and pulled his goggles down over his eyes. David did the same, his stomach empty, his mouth a desert.

Stutzman reefed his Wildcat violently to the right and, with six Gs, pulled the nose forty-five degrees nose low while mashing on full military power. David tried his best to hang on in the power dive as they headed west. Intent on maintaining sight on his lead, he realized they must be diving on something. Scanning past Stutzman's FM-1, he saw three waves of torpedo bombers. Stutzman's guns began to pour smoke.

David was confused, disjointed, with the feeling he was just along for the ride. Then a burning rose from his belly. Acidic, toxic, it spread throughout his body. *Vengeance!* He reacted to it instantly by centering a Betty in his gun sight and squeezing the trigger. His Wildcat shook from speed and the recoil of its guns. Closing in a head-on pass at incredible speed, the Betty's wing exploded and folded, sending it to the ocean.

They slashed at the second wave of bombers as they turned south, dropping one more apiece with high-deflection shots. Stutzman pulled up in a six-G looping maneuver, rolling upright halfway through it, executing a half-Cuban eight. Now headed east, they gave chase to the third wave. Still at full power and running downhill, they traded altitude for airspeed and ran down the slower G4M torpedo bombers.

A few miles ahead, they could see the USS LaVallette had positioned itself to protect the Chicago's beam and was engaging the Bettys in a hailstorm of AAA. One by one, they were dropping into the ocean, on fire. Unlike the magnesium flares from the previous night, they were extinguished on impact.

Stutzman's guns smoked again. David instinctively pulled the trigger and moved the tracers with his rudder pedals to another Betty. Something seemed wrong with his guns; tracers were everywhere, going in every direction. *Holy crap, they're shooting back at me!*

Smoking profusely as it fell toward the ocean, a wing separated and the Betty spiraled into the Pacific. David yanked on the G and began a canopy roll to the right. Tracers and triple-A were all around him. Instead of a graceful maneuver, he manhandled the Wildcat, forcing it nose low and back into the fight.

Ignoring the hot metal flying around him, he used vengeance for his guide as he put the piper of his gun sight on another Betty. Guns blazing, he hit it with a long burst. Smoking and on fire, it was obviously doomed. Not satiated, he continued to follow it toward the water, hammering away with his fifties. His ammunition spent, he pulled off just as the G4M impacted the water with a giant splash. David realized he would have followed it in had he not gone Winchester. He didn't care.

Out of his peripheral vision, he saw Stutzman flame another Betty and pull off, going straight up. David followed, extending vertically out of LaVallette's deadly fire as she brought down the last attacker. Four Type 91 torpedoes sped toward the brave destroyer, which was lying almost on her side to dodge them. The last found its mark.

Navajo had immediately wheeled toward the threat axis, successfully aligning Chicago's bow with it. Pointing west made it a dramatically smaller target to attack waves one and three.

16:24 Local, 30JAN (05:24 GMT, 30JAN)
Overhead, Solomon Sea

Reaching 5,000 feet, David rolled his Wildcat over, pulling its nose to the horizon. He was out of ammunition. All he could do was observe the end of the battle. From three miles away, he watched as Enterprise's Wildcats chased the second wave of G4M Bettys right into Chicago's murderous fire. Attacking from the south, her port side was exposed to the G4Ms. He watched as four Type 91 torpedoes went into the water, along with another Betty. Churning toward the wallowing Chicago, all four struck her vulnerable hull.

Below, her decks were turned into a raging inferno. Captain Davis ordered the lifeline to Navajo cut and commanded his crew to abandon ship. Hearing the 1MC blare out ABANDON SHIP, Pittman glared at his radioman.

"Send a one word message: India, Delta, India, Oscar, Tango."

"Idiot, sir?"

"Send it."

Flames climbed toward the radio room while below the decks, they began to be extinguished by the flooding ocean water as the Chicago sank.

16:44 Local, 30JAN (05:44 GMT, 30JAN)
USS Chicago, Task Force 18, Solomon Sea

With six officers and fifty-six of her sailors still aboard, her surviving crew watched from rafts as the Chicago rolled over and slipped beneath the sea. Her American flag flew defiantly until the end.

10:15 Local, 02FEB (23:15 GMT, 01FEB)
USS Enterprise, Admiral Halsey's Flagship

Admiral Bull Halsey sat slumped in a simple wooden armchair in his quarters. He wore an especially crumpled uniform, open at the collar. Rear Admiral Giffen sat across from him in the coat and tie of dress khakis, freshly starched and impeccable. He had no doubt that Halsey's appearance was a personal rebuff to him.

Halsey sat calmly, reading the after-action report that Giffen had prepared himself. On the desk behind him was the joint report of Captains Fournier and Dinella, as well as the ship's log. He folded the report in half and tossed it onto the top of the stack.

"So, if I'm to understand this, you want Fournier and Dinella relieved for cause?"

"I have already relieved Fournier; he is on my personal staff. No doubt, Dinella will request an Admiral's Mast, legal hearing, with you."

"No doubt!" sneered Halsey. "Tell me, Rear Admiral Giffen, did you see the last message from Chicago?"

Giffen cleared his throat.

"I have been made aware of it, and appropriate action is pending."

"Don't bother. The officer that sent it went down with the ship."

"Nevertheless, Admiral Halsey, a letter should be placed—"

"I agree with that one-word after-action report: succinct, to the point, and accurate. Why don't you go back to DC, Rear Admiral? I'm sure Admiral King has something you can do there. You, sir, are relieved of your command."

CHAPTER 38

19:08 Local, 05FEB (08:08 GMT, 05FEB)
New Georgia Sound, Solomon Island Chain

The Southern Cross began to show itself in the southwestern sky as the sun's radiation weakened. Sunset's colors seemed close enough to touch, while David loitered over one of the most hotly contested waterways in the world. Lost in thought, his subtle, even gentle control inputs guided the aircraft effortlessly.

David thought of what he and his lead, Lieutenant Stutzman, had talked about prior to launch. While the battle of Rennell Island had most definitely been a fuster cluck, the big picture, the landing of reinforcements, had gone off without a hitch. Due to the Japanese command's focus on Giffen's incompetence and the sinking of the Chicago, Halsey was able to land fresh marines on the 'Canal, with supplies. Stutzman was right, even about the sudden departure of Rear Admiral Giffen without fanfare.

His flight would land at Henderson field on Guadalcanal after this combat air patrol and join in its defense. Halsey was pulling the carriers out of range of the Japanese bombers.

Movement, detected by war-trained eyes, drew David's attention. He clicked his microphone once, keeping his gaze on the motion below. The click was to get Lieutenant Stutzman's attention as he dove on his prey.

His control inputs turned aggressive and violent instantly, maneuvering for the attack, his eyes never leaving the disturbance in the air. The movement transformed into an Aichi D3A Val dive bomber in the twilight as he closed. A short burst silenced the tail gunner. Defenseless, the Val's pilot jerked into a break turn to the left with all his might. David chopped his power and matched the maximum performance turn. Yanking his Wildcat behind the slowing dive bomber, he wrestled the buffeting FM-1 into a firing position, pummeling the Val with .50 cal.

Ensign David Brennan was young, aggressive, and now very vulnerable as he slowed with the Val. His instrument panel exploded with the dive bomber. David's first cognition was that he had fragged himself by getting too close to the disintegrating bomber. A second wave of red-hot lead shattered his world. Searing pain ripped at his abdomen.

In a purely reflexive response, his right leg locked fully, throwing the rudder and causing the Wildcat to snap roll right. The incendiary round burned his flesh as he tore at the wound with gloved hands. A guttural cry, strange and foreign, escaped his body. The fragment protruded slightly. He was able to extract it, burning his fingers as he ripped it free.

Struggling to regain his composure and control of the aircraft after a third snap roll, David centered the rudder pedals. An A6M Zero floated out in front of him. Through tears of pain and rage, he grasped the stick with both hands, pulling the trigger. Fifty-caliber rounds spewed uncoordinated across the evening sky. The Zero was so close it did not matter.

The flaming debris came off the Zero in such tight proximity to his dying Wildcat that it impacted all over the airframe. David's Wildcat flamed, the wing and engine torn apart by the fragmenting Zero. Stutzman had not heard his radio click and chased after him too late to cover his six. All he could do was watch helplessly as David's Wildcat spiraled out of control into a layer of cloud.

10:22 Local, 05FEB (10:22 GMT, 05FEB)
Kate's Manor, Bowdown House, Greenham Common, England

She walked through the winter garden, its geometry, like her features, perfect. A large, floppy straw hat flowed in rhythm with the evergreens and her sheer, white linen dress. Unseasonably warm, the fifty-seven degrees felt like a heat wave. With the low sun behind her, the dress became translucent, providing more of an aura than cover.

Unaware, she walked with confidence, moving slowly toward the grey stone edifice. A gardener stood next to the butler at the main entrance, both transfixed by the femininity contrasted against the formal garden. No grander dame had ever presided over the manor in all of its five centuries.

A long, green Chevrolet staff car swerved off the driveway as its driver became momentarily captivated by the scene. Kate watched him leave, wondering what he was doing all the way out here on a Sunday. She called for J.T. upon entering the house. He did not answer.

Finding him in the library, she was shocked at what she saw. He sat in a large, overstuffed brown leather chair, holding a message in his hand. Colonel Dane "J.T." Dobbs, the toughest man she had ever known, was weeping.

Silently, she knelt at his side.

"Dane, what's wrong?"

Ashamed that he could not speak, he simply held out the message.

CONFIDENTIAL

·DTG: 1000Z5FEB43
TO: COMMANDER IX TROOP CARRIER COMMAND
FROM: COMMANDER AIR TRANSPORT COMMAND
SUBJ: ENSIGN D. BRENNAN USNR
TEXT: ENSIGN D BRENNAN SHOT DOWN THIS PM OVER NEW GEORGIA SOUND. LISTED MIA.
CR SENDS

CONFIDENTIAL

~ The End ~
**CONTINUE THE STORY WITH
ENDGAME IN THE PACIFIC**

ENDGAME
IN THE PACIFIC

CHAPTER 1
19:18 Local, 5FEB (08:18 GMT, 4FEB)
New Georgia Sound, Solomon Island Chain

Plunging into a cloud layer, the flaming FM-1 Wildcat quickly began to disintegrate. Ensign David Brennan struggled to escape as fire started to breach the cockpit. He grasped the canopy handle and jettisoned it, releasing his harness and violently kicking the control stick full forward with his right foot. The negative G it produced ejected him out of the cockpit and into the pure white overcast sky. He narrowly missed the tail as he tumbled past it, and the static line ripped the cover off of his parachute. The slipstream activated it with a spine-numbing jerk.

He got a single swing in the chute before slamming into the hard surface of the New Georgia Sound. The impact knocked him semiconscious, but a moment later, the sting of salt water on his open wound and burns revived him. The parachute collapsed behind him and began to fill with ocean water and sink, dragging him below the surface. He flailed at the harness releases with blistered hands.

Ensign Brennan's lungs burned in warning as he was pulled deeper by the silk anchor. Finally, he clawed himself free and ripped at the darkening water until he burst out of the liquid prison. He kicked furiously to keep his head out of the sea, capturing each uncontrolled exhale in the fill tube of his May West life preserver. Once the vest held enough air to keep him afloat, he assessed his situation between exhausted grunts for air.

It was dire: burnt hands and arms, abdomen wound, and while fighting to get free from the grasping claws of Davy Jones, he had released and lost his raft and survival gear. Worst of all, it was getting dark. He knew he had two chances of survival: slim and none.

No doubt his hands would become useless soon, so he prepared himself as best he could to survive the night. He could not dress his wound, but he hoped that by tugging the white-hot bullet fragment out of his side—burning his hands—he had cauterized it. It was now all he had: hope. As the sun slipped below the horizon, dark grew rapidly.

Brennan's flight lead, Lieutenant Bruce Stutzman, had tried to follow him through the overcast but was jumped by two more Japanese Zeros. By the time he could disengage and penetrate the cloud layer, it was dark underneath.

Brennan could hear the Wildcat and knew it was Stutzman, but he could also hear the low murmur of a patrol craft. He couldn't take a chance—if it was Japanese, he knew what his fate would be. He decided to gamble on making it through the night. Ensign David Brennan, the U.S. Navy's newest ace—having shot down his fifth Japanese aircraft as he went down—steeled himself for the toughest test he would ever face.

Overhead, his fuel exhausted, Stutzman headed for Henderson Airfield on the Island of Guadalcanal. VF-27's Air Group had been forward deployed in support of the Marine's Cactus Air Force, while the carrier task force had withdrawn beyond the range of Imperial Japan's bombers. In the darkness, he searched for and found his new home.

Landing on the rough perforated steel plate runway (PSP) was no easy task in the light of day, let alone the dark of night. Stutzman's wings were immediately folded by mechanics after he bounced to a halt and cleared the makeshift runway. Already crowded before the arrival of CAG 27, it was now as tight as a ship's flight deck. Overworked USMC mechanics would be pushed to the limit with the added aircraft. However, the spare parts transported in the bellies of the dive-bombers were a rare and welcome commodity.

Stutzman shut down his Pratt & Whitney R-1830 and jumped from his Wildcat. A young plane captain was chocking his wheels.

"Lance Corporal," he said to the marine, "where is your HQ?"

"We don't really have one, sir. Closest thing is the operations tent."

After getting quick directions, Lieutenant Stutzman jogged to the tent. He found his commanding officer in a crowd and reported to Lieutenant Commander Steve Jasper.

"Skipper," he said, "Brennan is down."

A few men faced him but the busy atmosphere did not abate for the announcement of yet another casualty.

"Any chute?" asked Jasper.

"No, sir. He went into a layer over the slot. I was engaged two against one and could not get under the clouds to look until it was too dark."

"Any flares?"

"No, sir. But that doesn't necessarily mean—"

"Bruce," interrupted Jasper, "he's gone."

"No, sir. I don't believe that."

The lieutenant commander spoke quietly.

"We lost four aircraft today. I know he was your student and you were close—"

"Skipper, I know he's alive—"

"Bruce, he's gone. We have a strike tomorrow. Get some sleep. That's an order."

Stutz hesitated, prepared to argue more, but the skipper ended the discussion with a hard glare.

"Aye aye, sir."

Across the tent, Colonel Sean "Thumper" McDonald, the Marines Air Group Commander, overheard the conversation. Lieutenant Stutzman turned slowly and left the tent, dejected. The colonel followed.

"Lieutenant," he called after him, "hang on a minute."

Stutzman stood fast at attention as the colonel approached him.

"Relax, Bruce. I'm a reservist pressed into position by circumstance."

"Yes, sir."

"Call me Thumper," said McDonald. "This Brennan kid, he wasn't from Texas was he?"

"Yes, sir."

"David?"

"That's him."

"Damn it. DAMN IT!"

Thumper rubbed his temples with his index fingers as if a migraine had instantly gripped him.

"Obviously, you knew him, Colonel."

Pausing to collect himself, Thumper finally spoke.

"Yeah, I was in China with his father and brother on Project 7 Alpha. They didn't make it back."

Stutzman nodded in silence. Both men stood for a moment, and then Thumper turned slowly back for the tent.

"I've got to go send a message."

Stutzman called after him.

"He was an ace when he went down."

Colonel McDonald didn't turn around. Shoulders slumped, he started a slow walk through emotional quicksand toward the message center. *His mother won't care,* he thought.

"Okay, thanks," he called back. "I'll pass that along."

ABOUT THE AUTHOR

Leland "Chip" Shanle Jr., Lieutenant Commander, USN (Ret.), is a contributing editor to *Airways Magazine* and an award-winning writer in both fiction and non-fiction. His first novel, *Project 7 Alpha*, won the Military Writers Society of America's (MWSA) Gold Award for Historical Fiction in 2012. In addition to writing articles on aviation, he has written screenplays and has been an aviation/military technical adviser on five major motion pictures including *Pearl Harbor, Behind Enemy Lines, xXx: State of the Union, The Day After Tomorrow,* and *Stealth*, as well as for a television series pilot which, as of this writing, has not yet been announced. His production company, Broken Wing LLC, is featured in Discovery's Curiosity Series Documentary: *Plane Crash* in the USA, Channel 4 in the UK, and Prosieben in Germany.

He is a member of The Society of Authors in the United Kingdom and the MWSA in the United States and has remained an active member of the Society of Experimental Test Pilots (SETP).

Project 7 Alpha, American Airlines in Burma, 1942 was the first in his World War II Aviator Series, and he now follows it up with *Vengeance at Midway and Guadalcanal.* The third in the series, *End Game in the Pacific*, is scheduled for release in 2013. And he is hard at work finishing his fourth, *A Race With Infamy.*

Chip was born and raised in St. Louis, Missouri, attended Chaminade College Prep Class of 1977. After high school, he joined Naval ROTC at the University of Missouri, Columbia. Upon graduation in December 1981, he was commissioned an Ensign in the United States Navy. A month later he married Laura L. Cantrell, and they set out on their Navy adventure together.

Chip received his Masters from Embry Riddle Aeronautical University and also graduated from the Naval War College CCE. He flew sixteen different naval aircraft in ten squadrons, including the F-4 Phantom II, EA-6B Prowler, and TA-4J Skyhawk. He was attached to CAG (Air Wing) 5, 11 and 1. He cruised on the USS Midway, America, and Lincoln, and flew eighty missions over the war-torn skies of Bosnia, Somalia, and Iraq. An Airline Transport Pilot and Certified Flight Instructor, he has flown numerous civilian types from the Cessna 150 to the Boeing 767-300. Currently he is rated in 767, 757, 727, MD-80, and Sabreliner series aircraft.

Closing out his Naval Aviation career in 1998 with 600 carrier landings (200 night) on eleven different carriers, Chip, Laura, and their four kids moved home to St. Louis. He now flies for American Airlines and concentrates on his writing.